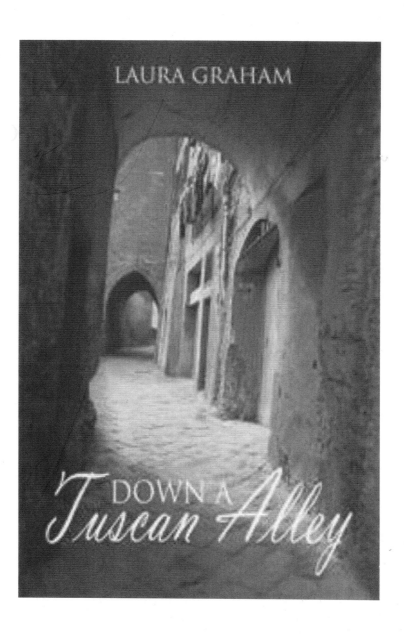

LAURA GRAHAM

DOWN A
Tuscan Alley

DOWN A TUSCAN ALLEY

Laura Graham

realize their own dreams, Lorri's new life is turned on its head. But there is always Lionello, the Roman neighbor and undisputed "wise man" of the village to advise and offer the occasional glass of hallucinogenic wine.

Lorri's narrative voice is both amusing and at times insightful. Eventually, she finds within herself a guiding strength. Coming to Italy was the way to discover it. Definitely the best choice she's ever made. Highly recommended read.
- *'Ex-Pats in Italy' – Alison Kale*

When I began the first chapter of 'Down a Tuscan Alley' I thought, oh, no, yet another long-winded yarn of doing up a house in Tuscany. So I was pleasantly surprised to discover it is about 'doing up a person' in Tuscany without a house or vineyard in sight.

Lorri, an English woman in her late forties, decides to go it alone. Fleeing the UK and a past relationship, she searches for a new life in a minute back alley apartment in Tuscany, which is all she can afford. The strong, often comic, narrative voice, guides the reader through the passion, mishaps and the intrigue. I very much liked the vulnerability of the protagonist and her early struggles with the language, new culture, and the randy plumbers and electricians.

Gradually Lorri finds a new confidence and is able to live out her dream of the good life in Tuscany.

A good read.
- *Emma Harrison, 15 June, 2011*

Publisher's Note:

This is a work of fiction. All names, characters, places, and events
are the work of the author's imagination. Any resemblance to real
persons, places, or events is coincidental.

Solstice Publishing

www.solsticepublishing.com

Laura Graham ©2011

Until one is committed, there is hesitancy, the chance to draw back, always ineffectiveness, concerning all acts of initiative and creation. There is one elementary truth the ignorance of which kills countless ideas and splendid plans: that the moment one definitely commits oneself, then providence moves too. All sorts of things occur to help one that would never otherwise have occurred. A whole stream of events issues from the decision, raising in one's favor all manner of unforeseen incidents and meetings and material assistance which no man could have dreamed would have come his way. Whatever you can do or dream you can, begin it. Boldness has genius, power and magic in it.
  Begin it now.

- Goethe

Dedication: For B without whom there
would be no story

"Christ, you wouldn't get me living down those creepy little alleyways. You never know who might be lying in wait . . . "

Christmas Night
Devon

"What's she like, this woman?" Julian lights up one of the Christmas cheroots I'd given him. It was becoming difficult to breathe. "Have you seen her?"

"Oh, yes, I've seen *Veronica*," I say. "He was *kind* enough to show me a photograph. I could see immediately where she was coming from. A jolly good sort, wide cheery grin, big snappy teeth and little frightened eyes, always paid her bills on time, done everything by the book. You know the type: a sensible, practical, likeable, bloody great bore!"

Maudie pours more wine into her glass. "I'm not sure Devon is right for you, Lorri. You need a complete change. I think that place you've got in Tuscany would be ideal."

"Ideal for what? It's a tiny flat down a dark alley."

"Sounds intriguing. Why not go and live there?"

"On my *own?*" I stare at her, appalled. "I'd have to be some kind of idiot to do something so reckless. No money, a foreign country where I hardly speak a word of the language – I don't know how you can suggest such a thing. I can't even imagine anything so *terrible . . .*"

1

Six months later
Pisa

It's June and sweltering. At the airport, I pick up the hire car, a cherry-red Fiat Uno, and place my two beloved cats, Billy and Gertie, on the back seat in their VIP box. My small case goes in the trunk; my worldly goods are coming later, in the removals van from England.

Important to get the feel of the car, I tell myself, jiggling the gear-stick and flashing the lights. Skirt Firenze, head for Siena, take the A1 for Perugia – Roma. Simple. Now, if I can just find my way out of the airport. I ease the car through the exit gate, on to the main road and enter the great Italian unknown.

Hardly unknown, though; I've done the journey often enough in the past, with Richard. Only then, I'd been the passenger, happy to sit back and enjoy the scenery, thinking of the things I would do when we arrived: add sand to the paint to create my textured finish for the walls, buy acid to clean the ancient floor tiles while he did the skilled work – building the bathroom and the kitchen. We worked well together, pausing every so often with a mug of tea to look round with pleasure at what we were achieving. But that was then. Now I have the present to deal with.

At the toll station, I take my ticket and continue on in the direction of Perugia. I've got this far, I reassure myself; things are going well. After an hour and a half of steady driving, I recognize several landmarks, the group of ochre-colored houses in a field to my left form a triangle and I'm certain I've seen them before. The house with the turret on the hill: that, too, looks familiar. And when, after another half-hour, I see the sign for Valdiciana I know I'm on the right road. I put my foot down and overtake several cars at a stretch, the indicator light flashing until I'm safely past.

This is the way to drive in Italy. Like the Italians, swoop up their bums, overtake, and streak on ahead. I give a hoot of laughter and the cherry-red car flies as if on wings along the *superstrada*. Windows open, warm air whipping hair off my face, I'm free, I've given him the slip and I burst into song. I've done it: survived endless doubts and sleepless nights and come to Italy to start a new life on my own.

I adjust the rear-view mirror. Soon I'll be climbing the street steps to my little apartment. From the bedroom window I'll see the chapel bell across the terracotta roofs, and beyond to the three cypresses, sticking up like dark green paintbrushes. And standing on the roof, if have a mind to, I'll look into the *carabinieris'* bedroom window opposite; pale, defenseless creatures they seem in their Y-fronts. And I'll hear the church bells clanging bing-bang-ding-dang, up in the *piazza;* making enough noise to raise the dead and make them laugh.

And I'm laughing, with relief, as I turn off at the Valdichiana sign. Not long now. Ornelia, in the downstairs flat, will be watering her pots of geraniums; Sergio in the upstairs flat is no doubt playing his tango music, which can be heard all the way down the street to Martino's *alimentari.* "Ahhh!"

he'll shout, sweeping his imaginary partner around the sofa, sliding and bending and stamping his heels, mouth in an oooh of pleasure, and "ahhhh!" again as he collides with the lamp. Nothing will have changed. Happily, nothing seems to in Sinalunga's *Centro Storico* – the historical center.

Keep well to the right side of the road, I remind myself, as ten minutes later, light-headed with heat, excitement and exhaustion, I travel up the familiar hill opposite the station.

But halfway up the hill I hear a bang and the car stops with a shudder. I stare ahead in disbelief. What happened? Everything was fine a minute ago. The cats howl, I swivel round to lift their box back on to the seat. Then I turn the key in the ignition. Dead. Now what? Better not attract attention. The last thing I want is to become a spectacle for everyone to point at. I open the car door and the heat hits me like a furnace. At least the car's not in the middle of the road. And as far as I can see, no real damage has been done; the hood, though, does appear somewhat closer to the ground than before.

Later I am to learn that the whole of the front suspension dropped out. I stare appalled at the white car behind, the door dented and scraped. It's obvious what's happened. In keeping so well to the right, I've veered into a parked car. I feel sick with disappointment. Why does this have to happen when I'm almost home? Shaking, I lift the cat-box and suitcase out of the car and sit on the hot pavement waiting for inspiration.

People are gathering from nowhere. They stare dubiously at the red Fiat, then at me. An old man mumbles something. I smile apprehensively and say, *"Buongiorno,"* the only Italian word that springs to mind at the moment. People move closer. They point at my car, then at the white one behind it. Several people are shaking their heads and tut-tutting. Then to my alarm the *carabinieri* draw up in their dark blue car and park alongside the Fiat, blocking the traffic, causing even more people to stop and stare at the pink-faced English woman melting – with her cat-box and suitcase beside her – on the pavement.

One tall and handsome, and one short and fat *carabiniere* saunter toward me, not so defenseless now with guns stuck in their belts. I stand up and offer my passport.

"Dove abita?"

"Vicolo della Mura."

"But that is *Italia*," the fat one says, loudly, glancing round at the people, making sure they can hear him speaking English.

"I know, I've come to live here."

"But where you live in England?"

"I don't any more."

"Uh?" He turns to his tall companion who is writing in a thick black book. *"Non capisco.* You must."

"What must I?"

"You must to live in some place in your country."

Realizing there is no point in explaining, I give him my English address even though I no longer live there. I hold out my hand for my passport and at this point the cats howl again and all attention turns to the VIP box at my feet.

"*Micio, micio,*" squeals a hefty woman, poking her finger through the mesh door. She draws back hastily at the hissing inside.

The fat *carabiniere* gives me a document that is incomprehensible. The sun beats down on my head. I sway slightly and hold onto the handsome *carabiniere's* arm for support.

Everyone watches avidly. A young woman is looking at me from her car, one of a line moving slowly up the hill with faces turned toward me. I wave and gesture that I need a lift. She nods; I lift the cat-box and suitcase onto the back seat and in less than five minutes, we're crossing the Piazza Garibaldi and turning left down the Via Ciro Pinsuti.

News travels fast here. The first person I see as I emerge from the car is Lionello Torossi, my elderly neighbor from the end of the street, who speaks fluent English, German, French and Spanish. "I have heard of the accident with *la straniera,*" he explains. "And I guessed it was you, and now I have come to help. You have announced your arrival extraordinarily well," he says, chuckling. "Now everyone knows you are here."

"Unfortunately, yes," I say. "I had hoped to arrive quietly and anonymously."

"My dear charming lady, no one arrives anonymously in a place like this. The people are delighted to see you; they want to be entertained. You are their portable theater."

Thanking the woman, whose name I didn't catch, I carry the stricken cats and my suitcase up the street steps, trip over one of Ornelia's pots of geraniums, round into the alleyway, smelling richly of garlic and soap suds, only to find, to my alarm, my front door wide open.

"Tonina!" I call.

"*Madonnasanta!*" Brandishing a key, Tonina, who looks after the place, hurries down the stairs to meet me. "*Signora, signora* Lorri."

"What's happened, Tonina?"

"*Niente acqua, non c'e il tetto -* " Tonina bursts into an excitable flow of Italian, "no water", "no roof", being the only understandable words. Struggling through the narrow front door, I stagger up the long flight of stone stairs to the bedroom, plant the case on the floor and the cat-box on the bed. I stare at the window, and at a man wearing a pork pie hat. "I spik Inlish," he says.

Then a man's voice behind me, from the stairs: "*Signora!*"

Tonina, almost hysterical, throws up a hand. "*Madonnina, Sergio vuole parlare dell'acqua.*"

"Oh no, please . . . not now," I beg. "I can't talk to anyone, about water or anything else. I'm exhausted."

"*Signora!*" Sergio, my upstairs neighbor, hovers outside the bedroom. "*Possiamo parlare?*"

I force a smile. "*Buongiorno.* I am very tired. I have not slept. No sleep? You understand? We talk *domani?*"

Tonina understands, if not all the words, the intentions behind them. She leads Sergio firmly to the stairs with a final "*No, no, no!*"

But the man with the hat, he's still there. "*Sono* Domenico. I make new roof. You Inlish lady? I work in Australia."

Tonina is back at a run. She closes the shutters in his face. *"Non, non, non!* Then she turns to me clasping her hands to her chest. *"Cara Signora* Lorri," she says. *"La situazione é triste."*

I collapse on the bed. In the shadowy light, I watch Tonina pile clean linen from the chest of drawers onto the mattress. It is impossible to explain right now that sometimes one can feel less sad being alone than with someone who makes you unhappy. So, I nod in agreement and say nothing.

"Ah, la vita." Tonina sighs with resignation, patting several strands of gray hair into place. She blows a kiss, and then promises to return later with buckets of water.

An acrid stench fills the bedroom. Closing the door, I ease the long-suffering cats from their box, and taking a pillowcase, the nearest thing to hand, dry their damp fur and offer biscuits from my pocket, which they refuse.

Am I crazy to come here? Hardly any grasp of the language, forty-seven, alone and with virtually no money? Many would think so. But I do at least own the roof above my head, even if it is half off, and that, after all, was the main reason for coming.

The cats reach up to sniff the shutters, where I think I see Domenico peering at me through the slats.

* * * *

"You have an air about you that makes one believe you have reserves."

"Inwardly, perhaps. Certainly not outwardly."

"If you have the one, you'll have the other. It is only a question of time."

I'm having a cup of Sunday afternoon tea with my seventy-two-year-old neighbor, retired film director and undisputed *"wise man"* of the village, Lionello Torossi. I've called round for his advice on how much I'll have to pay for the damaged Fiat, not to mention the other car. "Nothing," he assures me. "The company is covered for such accidents. You do not have to worry about anything."

I gaze at Lionello in wonder. Could things ever be that easy in Italy? "But won't I have to sign something?" I ask.

"There is always something to sign in Italy. But I have spoken to the *carabinieri*. Your car has been collected and now there is nothing more to be done. What will you do for transport in the meantime?"

I lean back in the chintz-covered armchair with no idea what I'm going to do, not really caring at the moment. It's too hot to think; I am happy to have Lionello think for me.

"You will buy a car, of course."

I laugh. "I can't afford one."

Lionello's eyes twinkle. "You know, you English, you are very amusing. One wealthy Englishman I knew was always complaining of not having money. How could he repair his roof? How could he pay for this or that? But the roof was repaired and life continued because when something was important enough he always found the money to do whatever was necessary."

"He probably sold the family silver to pay for it. Unfortunately, I don't have any."

"You English have a talent for pretending to be hard up when really you are comfortably off."

Lionello stretches his elegant linen-clad legs out from the chintz-covered sofa. "Now tell me, I am fascinated; what is a beautiful woman like you intending to do here in this small parochial place?"

Always one for the flattery, Lionello, like most Italians, I was to learn.

"I'm going to do bed and breakfast. I advertised in *The Telegraph* before coming out. The first couple arrive on the twenty-eighth of this month."

"But in what bed will you put them?"

"In my bed."

"You are all sleeping together?"

"No, I sleep in the sitting room."

"In that miniscule *salotto*? How is it possible?"

"All is possible when you have to survive."

"Huh!" Lionello claps his hands. "You English, you never fail to amaze me. Now, of course, you must buy a larger place. Something with a lovely *terrazza* and swimming-pool for the guests, no?"

This is becoming hilarious. "What with?" I ask. "I don't have that kind of money. In fact, I don't have *any* money to speak of."

"But you told me that you sold the house in England. Surely, Richard divided some money with you?"

"There was virtually nothing to divide," I explain. "The bank took everything. Richard had to close his building business and accept a friend's offer of work in Germany where he met another woman with whom he now lives."

I place my porcelain cup on its saucer. I'm finding it difficult to continue. It only feels like yesterday since we sat in this same room discussing, over tea with Lionello, our plans for coming to live in Italy.

"Well, at least, you have your own charming little apartment. And Richard restored it beautifully. I remember how it was in the beginning: a black hole, filthy and with cobwebs."

Richard's Volvo, with the mattress tied to the luggage rack, plus mirrors and pictures. How well I, too, remember; always more items from England on each journey until we had created our ideal holiday home. It was to be our base until we could find our dream house, sell up in England and come and live permanently here.

"And is the wine still there? Or did Tonina's husband drink it all?"

Twelve bottles of *Rosso di Montalcino* were still stacked along the top of the kitchen cupboard, one bottle of which I've already opened. Wine bought to celebrate our arrival in Italy. Little did I think then that I would be celebrating alone.

"And what will you do if Richard returns? Will you accept him back?"

I shake my head. It's too painful to think about.

* * * *

It's Monday afternoon and I'm lying on the bed in my underwear, overcome with the heat. The cats sprawl beside me, their ears twitching at any sound coming from the direction of the shutters, still closed against Domenico. Sweat pours off me. This is only June; what will July and August be like?

I look at the English prints above the Victorian chest of drawers, and spot the small rustic wardrobe next to my mother's hand-carved gilt Italian mirror which had looked exaggerated in her St John's Wood flat, but which now has found its rightful home in Italy.

Lionello said I'm lucky to own such a charming little apartment and it's true, I am. I gaze up at the heavy oak beams. They were covered in whitewash at first; I worked up a ladder for days on end with a carrier bag over my head, scrubbing at the wood, dirty water splashing into my eyes, ears, and down my neck. But the varnishing has made up for all the hard work, worth the aching back to see the color seep into the wood, bringing the light into it. I felt a deep sense of achievement when I'd finished, as though I had passed some kind of inner test. Mixing the paint to exactly the right shade of ochre and spreading it over the dingy bedroom walls had been like bringing the light into myself.

The window had been too high up the wall to see out of at first. Richard raised the floor so we could sit up in bed and look out at the chapel bell and the sky. And through the other small window above the bed, we could see across the village wall to the church steeple shining in the moonlight as if it had been made of silver.

I found his white canvas shoes under the bed earlier and wrapped them in a carrier bag before I had time to think and hid them on top of the wardrobe; out of sight, out of mind.

"No, looki, looki!"

The cats' heads jerk up, and Billy, the tabby, hisses at the sound of Domenico outside the shutters. I hold Gertie, the more timid of the two; she'll spring up on top of the wardrobe, otherwise, and nothing will coax her down for hours.

* * * *

The furniture has finally arrived! The driver tried bringing the lorry down Via Ciro Pinsuti but the street's too narrow. He reversed out into the *piazza*, performed a hazardous three-point turn in front of the astonished priest, knocked an urn off a column, and then headed back down the hill, by which time the whole of Sinalunga had been alerted to *la straniera* once more causing havoc.

I'd almost given up hope of ever seeing my furniture again, when finally, someone provided a pick-up truck and, in slow stages, everything was brought up the hill and into a narrow street beside the village wall. But with so many sheets, dishcloths, stockings and knickers dangling from a line strung across from one side to the other, the alleyway leading to my front door was totally obscured.

Sixty-five packing boxes were unloaded in the narrow street outside Tosca, my other neighbor's front door. Though at least eighty and only as tall as some of the boxes, she was screaming so forcefully that the driver, a weary Englishman from Essex, was doubtful whether to proceed. "*La roba, la roba!*" she cried, waving her thin little arms frantically up into his face. I couldn't help wondering what robes had to do with anything? Something had to be done immediately to sort out the chaos, so throwing myself at the boxes, I pushed and shoved, ducking under Tosca's sheets, stumbling over Ornelia's geraniums.

But several hours later, when the street was clear, Tosca was still at her door shouting about *la roba*, which I have since learnt means 'the things'.

"*Va bene*, Tosca," I tried to reassure her. "*Tutto finito*. No problems."

Tosca squints up at me and cackles, showing two gray tusks. Then breaking into a flow of incomprehensible words, she wraps her arms around me and buries her hairy face in my stomach. Hopefully, that means *la straniera* has been forgiven for creating such *confusione*.

Other curious neighbors gather in the narrow street. Rosalba, known as *la vecchia bionda,* the old blonde, frowns as she watches the activity. She had been the one Richard and I lunched with every first Sunday of our visit: pasta with a tomato or meat sauce, both had to be tasted. This was followed by a horrific row of little roasted birds, a delicacy in the area, better not looked at, let alone eaten. "*Mangia! Mangia!*" Rosalba had yelled above the noise of the television turned up to full blast. "She very funny woman," Giovanni, her husband said, as he'd poured the *Vino Speciale* from Martino's shop.

* * * *

Dave, the removal man, is looking round my small kitchen incredulously. "Where's all this stuff going?"

"I'll find a place."

"Like on the roof?" He laughs.

His mate, Colin, painfully thin and seemingly too weak to lift anything heavier than a box of towels, sinks onto a box marked '*fragile*'. "Oh, no, please be careful." I rush forward. "There are some very delicate things in here."

"Have you come for good?" Colin asks, glancing round at the boxes filling every available space in the kitchen, on the stairs and in the miniscule *salotto*.

"Well, she ain't come for the weekend, has she?" says Dave, cackling.

"What brought you here?"

"I wanted to lose myself."

Neither have an answer to that. Which is just as well as I'm in no mood for conversation. My back is breaking, having heaved most of the heavier stuff up the stairs myself, and all I want is to be left alone with my boxes. Then all I own in the world will be under one sweltering roof. All this effort only to come to another alleyway? But this one is different from the dark and dank one I've left behind in Devon. It's beautiful, with the tawny old bricks, the delicious cooking smells and the general air of colorful dilapidation. And most important of all, it leads to my home. Something no one can take away from me.

Four hours later, it's beginning to look like a home. The chintz armchair, desk, reading lamp, the tall clock and green two-seater sofa have all been squeezed into the *salotto* alongside the coffee table, bookcase and cupboard, which were already there. It's now just possible to take three small steps ahead, two to the right and one to the left without knocking into anything.

Sunlight streams down the kitchen steps, picking out the colors of the old terracotta floortiles. I sit on the top step and gaze round at the boxes surrounding me, one mounted on top of the other almost to the ceiling. How on earth am I ever to get organised before the B&Bs arrive?

I can't help laughing; people come to Italy to live in spacious houses surrounded by vineyards. Whereas, here am I, imprisoned by boxes and furniture and not a vineyard in sight. Only a large pair of bloomers (they surely can't be Tosca's?) can be seen flapping on the line from my *salotto* window; and if I lean further out, the street steps leading down from Via della Mura to Martino's grocer's shop with his fruit going moldy in the sun.

But it's Tuscany! And against impossible odds, I've got myself here. I can honestly say that I have never been so excited in my entire life as I am at this moment.

But contacts are crucial. Who do I know well, apart from Lionello? Vittorio Corrado, a friend from the past – if I can call him that. For I don't entirely trust him; he likes to profit off his friends' vulnerability, if I remember correctly. Nevertheless, right now, I urgently need his support.

I head across the *piazza* to the *Bar Cortese* to use the telephone.

At first no one answers. Then Silka, Vittorio's wife, speaks: "*Ciao,* Lorri! We hear that you arrive, but Vittorio cannot to contact you. You have the telephone?"

"Not yet, no."

"Today is my birthday. You come tonight for dinner with us?"

"I'd love to, Silka. Thank you."

Even dubious contacts are better than none.

I leave the bar and head back across the *piazza,* trying to contain my excitement. My adventure has begun!

2
Fireflies and Magic

I approach the alleyway on my way back from the bar with the same butterfly feelings in my stomach I've always felt at the prospect of going to Vittorio's house. You have to be on the alert, never give too much away; there's no knowing how he might use it against you. And I have always sensed something worrying about his house. It's on the wrong side of the hill and in the shade. "I swear I'll never go near that shit's house again," Richard said, the last time we went. Perhaps it's disloyal to be going myself. Except, what choice is there? I have to contact Vittorio, he knows everybody. It's crucial for my survival in Italy.

It's hard to recall exactly what triggered the row that led to Vittorio thumping Richard in the diaphragm. "You give nothing, my friend," he'd said. Poor Richard had been outraged, especially as he'd just paid for an expensive dinner. Then Silka hadn't helped by saying that Vittorio wasn't speaking of material things, only of Richard's true self that he must try to give more of. "That's not the way to encourage anyone to give of his true self," Richard had said in the car, going home. "I feel I've been hit deep down in my psyche. And can you imagine what he'd do with my true self if he ever got hold of it?" I can't help feeling he had a point, even though he did tend to take things too much to heart sometimes.

I spot the roses before I reach my front door. I stare at them with a sinking feeling. Then quickly I carry them upstairs and place them on the kitchen table. The card reads:

Please don't be angry that I've come to Sinalunga, I've so much to tell you. I long to be reunited and will wait for you in La Torretta at 8 this evening. I do hope you will come.

Love,
Richard

Oh, my God! I don't believe it. What do I do? Sinking onto a chair, I look wildly round at the boxes surrounding me, only three of which I've managed to unpack. What the hell is he doing, turning up now? I'm getting my new life in order. He's trying to invade it. I want to scream. Try and release the pain and anger inside me. But I've shed so many tears over Richard that there's nothing left to squeeze out, only something that feels like blood and little stones.

How can I face him? It's taken seven months to build my strength. If I see him again, it will crack like the shell of an egg.

Six-fifteen. Enough time to take a letter to *La Torretta,* our favorite restaurant in the *Centro Storico* and which holds more memories than I dare to remember.

* * * *

It'll be something of a miracle if I arrive at Vittorio's house tonight. I set off in Lionello's battered Alfa Romeo, lent to me for the evening, and in my rear-view mirror notice what I thought to be a white VW Transporter van following me. Richard had bought one in Germany. I spurt on ahead, but it's still there, menacingly in the background, so I turn off the main road to escape it, tear up the hillside, snake round the houses, past gigantic rocks and vineyards I'd never been to before and it was getting later all the time.

I stop outside the gates of a villa and wait to see if the van follows, wondering what on earth I'll do if it does. I look at my watch. Eight ten. He'll still be in the restaurant, reading the letter I'd left with the waiter, saying that I'd made other arrangements with my life. I wonder now if I should have phrased it better.

Swinging the car round, I make a three-point turn too fast and the Alfa's back wheel spins precariously over the edge of a fifty-foot drop to the rocks below. Thrusting the gear into first, I shoot forward onto the narrow road and ease the car cautiously down the hill to the main road. At this rate, I'll never make it to anybody's house for dinner again. What's the matter with me? Other people went out to dinner without these problems. Except other people don't have their ex on their tails. Except he wasn't on my tail, but in the restaurant reading the letter. Fortunately, when I came out in the spring I changed the lock on the door of the flat: three strong bolts through the wall; it makes me feel a lot more secure.

I turn right onto the main road and continue calmly along past a tractor, two cars and a cyclist until I spot the sign for Rapolano Terme, the thermal baths, *Antica Querciolaia*, somewhere I intend visiting at a later date. I swing left onto a dirt track, my headlights illuminating the familiar row of dark green cypresses with the small wooden arrow on the trunk pointing the way to Vittorio's house.

Two white *Pastori Maremmani* bound toward the Alfa Romeo barking as I drive through the gates.

"*Finalmente!*" Vittorio, his dark hair streaked with gray, deeply tanned and wearing a Hawaiian shirt, is waiting in the driveway. He opens the car door, pulls me out and swings me round in his strong arms. "*Buonasera cara.* You arrive at last in Toscana."

"*Finalmente, si!*" I cry, relieved at having arrived at the house, never mind Toscana.

Silka, tall and blonde, in jeans and a slinky top, kisses me. "I never thought it possible that you come without Richard."

"Neither did I." I reach into the car for the pot of pink geraniums tied up with ribbon and white crepe paper. "Happy birthday."

Four pairs of eyes scrutinize me as I follow Silka across the terrace to the candlelit table under the vines. One man I recognize instantly, Ronaldo, naked to the waist, tanned and sinewy. I catch my breath as I look at him. In April, when I'd come out to change the locks, he'd met me at Sinalunga Station and taken me in his van to Vittorio's house where he was building a dance floor in the garden. A dusty gray man he'd been then, his clothes and hair covered in a powdery film of cement. He'd put his foot down when we'd reached the main road and the van had zipped along. It had been exhilarating, if somewhat alarming, for he'd kept looking at me instead of the road.

I'm introduced to Filippo, the butcher; to Hans and Hilda who are renting Vittorio's apartment in the house further up in the wood.

"You remember me?"

"Yes, I do remember," I say, and move round to the vacant chair beside Ronaldo. Had he kept it especially for me? Dream on. He hadn't known I was coming. Or perhaps he had, there's no means of knowing. Hopefully, things will become clearer when I speak the language.

"Do you stay for long here?" Hilda, the German woman, asks.

"Forever!" Vittorio cries, appearing with three bottles of his special wine, which he passes to Ronaldo to open. "Now she arrive," he sets his chair close to mine, forcing Hilda's aside, "she stay always close with us."

Ronaldo, drawing the cork from the bottle, chats in Italian to Filippo, on his left, who also seems to be scrutinizing me.

I feel elated; I can't help it, it doesn't matter that I can't understand the language. I belong; it's enough simply *being* here, sipping the *Rosa di Montalcino*, looking at the fireflies, little glowing embers flashing so close I can almost catch them in my hands.

Everyone's jabbing forks into singed chunks of barbecued steak that Ronaldo's handing round on a large flat dish. I chew on a bit of salami, too excited to eat; I've been too excited to eat anything other than muesli since arriving in Italy and the weight's pouring off.

"Valli!"

Oh, God, the dreaded daughter. Valentina in nothing but knickers and her mother's high-heeled silver sandals three sizes too large, she comes clip-clopping round the back of the house dragging a damp towel. She has lipstick smudged on her mouth and instead of looking funny she looks precocious. Anna, four years younger than her eleven-year old sister, is different. With her dark hair and eyes, she's the physical image of her Neapolitan father. But she has her mother's timid nature. She follows Valentina, naked, holding a sopping wet teddy bear by the leg. Silka speaks to Valentina in German. Valentina, hands on hips, shouts back in Italian. But when Vittorio rises from his chair she kicks off the sandals and runs to him. "*Babbo!*" she cries, covering his face in kisses. Now she has everyone's attention, which is what she'd intended. Anna stands forlornly by, clutching the teddy. Silka lifts her onto her lap and the bear is dropped in the dust.

Then a pretty girl with a shock of black hair walks round the back of the house carrying a bundle of towels. "Giuseppina!" She steps sulkily forward when her name's called and scowls at the ground as Silka addresses her in rapid Italian. She dumps the towels at Silka's feet and carries Anna into the house. Valentina runs whooping after them. Defeated, Silka sighs and gathers up the damp towels. I watch her walk away on long slim legs; poor Silka, she always seems to be carrying a burden. Is this what comes of marrying an Italian, or is it only Vittorio, a certain kind of Italian, one who, like his daughter Valentina, needs constant attention?

The atmosphere feels different. Difficult to know in what way, exactly, but certainly different; as though the temperature has dropped slightly. I glance at the guests, wondering if they too feel it. Apparently not: Vittorio is holding court and everyone is listening, gazing at him, laughing in all the right places.

I straighten my shoulders. I must try to relax, enter into it all, in spite of the language problem. I look into my wine for inspiration, allowing the incomprehensible chatter to pass over me.

"You think much." I glance up to see Ronaldo watching me.

I give a little laugh, annoyed at how easily the heat rises to my face.

He throws a lighter up and catches it with one hand, his arm rippling with muscles. He's so sure of himself in this place. But then perhaps he'd be sure of himself wherever he went. He reaches across me to light Vittorio's cigarette, resting his arm lightly on my bosom. The heat rushes to my face. But I make a point of looking down at his arm with amusement. I notice Filippo watching, he seems amused too. I want to laugh out loud. I'm thrilled; ready for anything that life offers me tonight.

Vittorio's in the middle of telling a story, or joke, it's not easy to know which. He keeps laughing at what's presumably the punch line. The trouble is there appears to be more than one. I've often wondered in the past if his row of dazzling white teeth came out at night to grin at Silka from the bedside table. I laugh at the thought, a fraction of a second before anyone else laughs. Ronaldo looks at me, impressed, as if I'd been the first to understand the joke. "*Capito?*"

"Not really," I say. "But I'm learning."

"In 'alf an 'our you are learnin' to speak Italian?"

That time in his van in April when I'd tried to speak Italian and told him I'd be fluent in half an hour, "*Parlerò in mezz' ora.*"

"Oh? What will 'appen in 'alf an 'our?"

"No, I mean, *un mese,* in one month I'll speak your language."

We'd laughed together, he'd seemed so full of energy and life; being with him had brought *me* to life. He'd given me a little kiss that evening and told me he liked my perfume and when I returned to England in the rain I had thought of him.

Fireflies, crickets, the scent of rosemary, jasmine and salvia, it's heady stuff. Headier still is Ronaldo's spicy cologne and clean male sweat of his skin. I can't remember ever having smelled anything so arousing and I lean closer to him while scratching the mosquito bites around my ankles.

Somehow, I have to make this new life work. There can be no going back; I haven't any money. And besides, I have nowhere to go back to.

* * * *

This would all read like a novel, I'm thinking, lying exhausted in bed several nights later. Who would believe so much could happen so quickly? It's like being caught up in a tornado that's rushing me headlong into whatever lies ahead. And I intend to do nothing whatsoever to resist it!

"Now you come in Toscana you are flying in the mind with a new energy," Vittorio had said. "But not too high, the flying, otherwise, you fall." He'd thumped the table to make a point and my plastic cup had fallen to the ground. "Ah, you see," he'd said, "because is empty, your cup fall. We must to keep the feet on the earth, the logic in the head and the fantasy in the heart. Only then do we have the balance. And, of course, the good wine in the stomach, eh? *Questa è la cosa importante nella vita, cara mia.*"

We had laughed and I'd thought perhaps he wasn't so bad after all and I'd been too hasty in my judgment. He'd re-filled my cup with his special red wine made from grapes, he never tired of telling enthralled tourists, grown from his grandmother's ancient vines. Although, where these ancient vines are I've never been able to discover in the three years I've known him. He then launched into his favorite tale (heard several times in the past) of his teaching Italian to foreign students at the *Università di Straniere* in Siena and how he'd met the timid young German Silka, married her and brought her to live in an abandoned farmhouse which he'd restored single-handed. "And when you see what I stay doing..." He'd waved bunched fingers in the air. "I create the Bar Silka."

"Bar Silka?"

"Up in the forest, in the *cantina* of my two apartments, where live Ronaldo and now stay Hans and Hilda, I make the best bar in the hillside."

"Really?"

"*Si, cara.* The people will come from far to drink my wine and eat the food what Silka cook. He looked closely at me. "I see you worry. Your face, it have much tension. Why? I know why. It is bad what happened between you and Ricardo, eh?"

Ricardo, as he always called him or *veccio lupo,* old wolf. Richard had loved that, until he heard him call everyone else *veccio lupo.* "Well, yes," I began, "it was very painful." I checked my impulse to open up. I wasn't sure how he would use the information. Yet I badly needed his support. And then, before I knew it, out of my own weakness, the whole story of how I'd found the roses and taken the letter to the restaurant came pouring out like wine from the bottle. And immediately I regretted it. My instinct not to trust him was right. He would somehow use the information against me – or Richard, even worse!

Vittorio inhaled on the last of his cigarette and ground the butt into the remains of the steak. "What does Ricardo look for here?"

"I think he wants to be reunited."

"And you want also this?"

"No, no," I said, hastily, "I don't."

"Because if you want this, I know you are crazy and I don't invite you more in my house."

"No, no, I've come here to start a new life without him," I said, panicking at the thought of not being welcome, even though I didn't trust his motives. Where else would I go?

Vittorio was staring at me. I've never been sure what those meaningful stares meant. I was even less sure that night.

"And he follow like the dog, eh?"

"Er – no . . . " I began, feeling that I'd betrayed Richard in some way. "It's not quite like that. I think he's finding it hard to let go."

"Why he cannot let go with elegance, this man?"

"Well . . . I think he is *trying* to let go. "

"If he come in my house I make him let go."

"I don't think he will . . . come here, I mean."

"You know where he stay?"

I shook my head. "I've no idea."

Vittorio lit another cigarette. He made a comic face. "I know where he stay."

"You do?"

He stood up suddenly and whistled for the dogs; they ran from the driveway and trotted after him round the back of the house into the garden. My eyes followed, picturing him, as I'd often seen him in the past, standing by the swimming pool, legs apart, inhaling on his cigarette, then tossing the lighted butt into the water. You never quite knew where you were with Vittorio, apart from a few dodgy deals I'd heard about from the German tourists, the wine in the bottles they'd bought not being the wine they'd drunk in his house, even though the label was the same; it was the fact that he appeared to be your friend one minute, your enemy the next that was so bewildering.

Billie Holiday began singing the Blues in the *cantina*. Vittorio had cut through the garden, down to where the wine was stored, where his treasured collection of 78 jazz records was kept, and where the walls were covered with photos of himself, all bearing a remarkable resemblance to an ageing Al Pacino. Even his mother resembled Al, staring menacingly down from the wall in an elaborate gilt frame. Then poor Silka, minus a frame, propped against a jug of dried flowers on the piano with baby Anna in her arms and Valentina, hand on hip, lolling provocatively against her knee.

Holiday sings about a man coming along, a man to love, the lyrics almost too painful to bear.

People got up to dance on the terrace, Hans with Hilda, the linen of his white jacket stretching across his broad back.

Another white-jacketed figure came to mind. I had chosen the jacket for Richard. We'd spent hours in the shop trying to decide which was the perfect fit.

Now Holiday sings that the man who came along would be strong. I hope he will, dear Billie, for both our sakes.

I glanced round at Ronaldo. He was in animated conversation with Filippo. Berlusconi's name was being banded about, no thought of dancing; that kind of talk could take all night.

No one seemed to notice me get to my feet, make my way past the dancers, down to the wall where the yellow flowers grew. Silka had left her pot of geraniums on the wall, the ribbons fluttered in the breeze like the wings of a bird. I breathed in the scent of jasmine and listened to the only sound apart from Billie, the cri-cri- cri-cri beating of cricket's legs. What would he do when he had read the letter and realized I wasn't coming?

I crossed the driveway and stood in the shadow of the pines looking up at the old farmhouse, light spilling from every window. It had been our dream once to buy such a house. But that had been the trouble; we'd lived too much in a dream. The night was brilliant with stars, as if someone had flung a fistful of diamonds into the sky; something precious tossed away, lost forever.

"You like to stay alone?"

I started; I hadn't heard Ronaldo approach. "Why you stay alone in the dark?"

"It's not dark. There's light from the windows. I can see everything."

"But I no see you." He took my hand. "You are sad?"

"No, I'm fine. Very happy to be here."

"You speak much with Vittorio."

"You noticed?"

"I see all."

"Oh."

"You are now free from Ricardo?"

"As a bird."

"A bird no always can fly."

"This one can, it's found its wings."

"You are sure?"

"Yes."

"I 'ave waited for your return."

"You have?"

"Now I want to dance with you. You come with me?"

I would have gone anywhere in the world with him at that moment.

I watched him sprint across to the *cantina*. I felt my heart racing. Was this really happening? I lingered uncertainly by the Alfa Romeo, listening to the dogs barking up in the hills. Someone passed silently in the shadow of the trees, someone watching, showing only the tip of a burning cigarette. Then relieved, I saw Ronaldo buttoning his creased silk shirt as he came toward me. "We go." He jumped into the Alfa as though it was his, turned on the ignition and swung the car round, wheels crunching along the dirt track.

He held my hand. "You 'ave a strong woman's 'and. Ow old are you?"

I told him the truth. "Forty-seven."

"I am forty-one."

"Six years younger."

"It is a problem?"

"Not for me."

"Also not for me. You are beautiful no matter your age."

Beautiful? I couldn't remember when Richard had last said that to me.

Ronaldo drove fast, the Alfa flew through the silver-edged night while I sat breathless, wondering if we would ever arrive, part of me not caring if we arrived or not, we could drive on for ever through eternity. And when we swung into a crowded car park, eased our way through the door of a disco and passed bodies even sweatier than ours, I was like someone standing outside myself and looking at the English woman with the soulful-eyed Italian leading her into the dance.

In the early hours of that morning we walked up through the forest to his apartment and, concealed beneath the trees, held each other. "Not the bed tonight," he whispered. "I no want to 'urry."

"I'm not ready either."

"You are too important to me," he said, and covered my face with hot little kisses until I felt my legs would give way beneath me.

On the way home I glanced in the rear-view mirror for the white Transport van. Arriving in Ciro Pinsuti, I parked alongside Martino's shop. Then looked furtively up and down the street for the van.

But saw only the usual row of parked cars and a lone cat sitting on a Peugeot washing itself.

I stumbled on the street steps, leading up to Vicolo della Mura and leaned against the crumbling wall for support. Was I in danger of losing my head? Perhaps I had already lost it in coming to Italy.

I climbed to the top step; accidentally kicked over another of Ornelia's geranium pots, ducked under the bloomers and passed along the shadowy alleyway to my front door.

3
Gossip and Intrigue

The tools are all here, hidden in a box under the bed where Richard left them: a power drill, screwdrivers; various boxes of screws, nails, rawlplugs, three hammers and a saw. "You must be very careful how you handle these things," he'd said. "Don't mix the screws with the nails and the nails with the screws. They must be kept in their separate boxes. And never use the drill; it's far too dangerous. In fact, it's better if you don't touch these things at all. Just leave it to me."

What would he say now, I wonder, if he could see me balanced precariously on top of the sideboard, clutching a large mantel mirror, mouth full of screws, screwdriver behind my ear and brandishing a power drill? I position the heavy mirror against the wall and mark with a biro where I have to make the holes. Remarkable how many skilled jobs you can learn in twenty-four hours when you have to.

And I do have to, for the odd-job man doesn't appear to exist here. "*Oooh, no!*" Tonina had looked incredulously at me when asked if Alberto, her husband might lend a hand with the mirror. "*Suo cuore non sta bene,*" she'd said, patting her heart. "*Deve riposare.*" Ah, yes, of course, poor thing, he must rest. Sit with his other retired cronies in the *Bar Cortese* playing cards, while Tonina, according to Lionello, works herself into an early urn already reserved for her in the crematorium.

After drilling two holes in the wall and filling them with wine bottle cork, I ease the mirror into place, take two long screws from my mouth, twist them into the cork, then frantically screw and – hooray! The mirror is up, and holding, and reasonably straight.

Kneeling to place glasses in the cupboard underneath, I hear women's voices out in the street shouting guttural, foreign words. I sit back on my heels in a beam of sunlight and a million stars dance in the dust. Can this place ever really be my home? The English seascapes on the walls, the treasured old books on the shelves: Bucham, Hardy, Wells, Bronte; they're as out of place as I am in this Italian village.

I get up and stand at the window; the women have gone inside now. Tosca's peeling green shutters are closed against the sun. Ornelia's pots of scarlet geraniums crowd on the doorstep and a hefty pair of pink bloomers dangle on the line today.

In time I'll learn the language and the culture. And in time I might work out the mentality. I might also find it's not all that different from my own.

* * * *

"Lei-deve-guardare-la-pompa," Tonina's explaining slowly and loudly to me this morning. It's important to keep an eye on the pump, make sure the reserve tank is full, the boiler not furred up with calcium. Which was why, apparently, there's been no water.

"But how will I know?" I ask. *"Come saprò* - if it's furred up, if you see what I mean?"

Tonina bursts out laughing. *"Perche, Signora* Lorri, *l'aqua non viene."* Because no water comes. That makes sense. But how can it be prevented? Ah, I need a water softener. Where do I go for that? No answer. I sigh. Without the language I'm handicapped and nothing makes sense. Sergio's making no sense either. Water's been dripping into his fireplace. He blames Ornelia; she must replace her down-pipe and poor Ornelia has cried all morning, she told me. There's nothing wrong with *her* pipe. He should get *his* pipe seen to as there had been water leaking down her bedroom wall, which was directly under his kitchen, for years.

This heated discussion had taken place at seven-thirty this morning directly beneath my bedroom window. When Tonina had thumped on the front door I had stuck my head under the pillow. But when the thumping had become pounding, the cats flying to the top of the wardrobe and Tonina screeching up at me, I'd had to respond before the entire street gathered beneath my window wondering if *la signora Inglese* had died in the night. I've since learned what the discussion had been about from Lionello who was back from visiting his daughter in Rome and had heard the story of Sergio's pipes from Martino when buying his bread this morning.

It's now midday and they're still up on the roof: Domenico, the builder, a bandy-legged plumber, Domenico, Tonina, and Sergio, who, bored with tangoing, is now trying to find gaps between the tiles where the rain has got in. But the problem is, there's been no rain for months. Domenico's on his knees – I can see him - on the roof tiles, clasping his hands at the sky and praying for the rain. *"Prego per la pioggia!"* he cries.

By twelve-thirty they all clamber down the kitchen stairs, still arguing, but Sergio seems to have something else apart from his pipes on his mind. "I learn English with you?" he says, yellow snappers advancing and a strange look in his eyes.

"I don't teach English," I state, backing against the sink.

Whatever other problems there may be, hot water now gushes from the kitchen tap, and with gentle persuasion, once the rust cleared, also from the bathroom, which means the B&Bs can at least have a decent shower when they arrive. It's as they're all trooping out through the front door that the bandy-legged plumber suddenly sprints back up the stairs and ducks past me into the bedroom. I stare in amazement at a pair of dirty trainers sticking out from under my bed, wondering what's going on.

The leak is coming from under the bed? I can't decide whether to laugh or not. Someone's forgotten to close the pipe that affected the overflow? It's beyond comprehension. The plumber emerges from under the bed, perspiring copiously and talking rapidly. *"Piano, piano,"* I say. "No understand. Too quick."

"Slow, slow." He grins and introduces himself as Massimo. Then carries on about how he'd known all along where the leak was coming from but said nothing because he didn't want to get me into trouble with Sergio who is crazy – at least, I think that's the gist of it. "I make good, no problem," he adds.

I move quickly from the bedroom to the kitchen. Judging by the way he's looking at me, there could well be a problem, which has nothing to do with water!

"I don't have the money to pay you, at this moment," I explain. "But would you accept a bottle of wine for your kindness?" I reach up to the cupboard for a bottle. He plants his hands on my waist. I hold the bottle between us. He tries to kiss me. I step back and the bottle slips from my hand, wine and shards of glass at our feet.

He laughs, seeming to think it all very funny and normal. I'm a woman alone, therefore I must need a man and I had offered him wine, which was obviously an invitation. He insists on cleaning the floor with bundles of kitchen towel, saying something about his uncle having a vineyard and how he would return, tomorrow being Saturday, with his own bottle of wine. Again, I *think* that's what he said. Whatever, I will make a point of being out.

The heated discussion is still underway outside Ornelia's door as I close mine against Massimo; the voices travel back along the alley to my door. I flee upstairs, praying not for rain, but to be left in peace with my cats and my boxes.

* * * *

Still another fifty-two boxes to unpack and fifteen days before the first B&Bs arrive. I heave the Welsh dresser against the kitchen wall. Cups on hooks, plates on shelves, pots and pans in the cupboard; things are finding places. I'll hang strings of onions and garlic and herbs from the beams. It will look like a welcoming home when I've finished.

The copper pans hang from the beams; the copper warming pan Richard gave me, I've hung on the wall next to the dresser. What to put in the corner of the room? Richard wanted to build a fireplace, but there'd never been time, we were only ever here for two weeks at the most. Then we always had to get back to England and try to earn a living: Richard with his building business, *'Creative Renovations'*, and me, caring for an elderly lady in the day, attempting to write my first novel at night.

Perhaps Ronaldo might build me a fireplace. Then we could snuggle up together on cold winter evenings, if there are such things in Italy. But better not fantasize too much, it may never happen and then where will all the fantasizing get me? But I can't stop thinking of how he said I was important to him. I'm glad we never went further; I don't want to hurry things either. I'm definitely not ready. But I think of his kisses under the trees, his face against mine; I'd felt all the heat of the day inside his skin. It was while opening the box marked *fragile* that I heard the ominous rattling within. From under the bubble-wrap I tentatively lift out a teapot minus a spout, every cup but one of my grandmother's Victorian tea set smashed to pieces!

I sit on the floor and look at the devastation around me. A heavy frying pan has been packed on top of the delicate items. So much for *'Removals on the Cheap'* advertised in a Devon newspaper. "You've got enough china for two Pakistani families," the removal man had said. Was placing the frying pan on the china his way of saying no one should have more than they need?

I arrange the fragments of china on the table and photograph them, a spout here, a handle there. I could claim on the insurance; that at least will give me some much-needed money. Sweeping the devastation into a plastic bag, I try not to think too much about the loss. It's gone to make space for something better, I tell myself, and carry the clanking bundle downstairs.

There's a note under the front door. My stomach lurches. He's written. I'll see him tonight, tomorrow, or the next night? Eagerly I pick it up.

'*Tu sei una cattiva donna perche hai abbandonato tuo marito . . .*'

I stand for several minutes very still. I can feel the beating of my heart as I re-read the words. You are a wicked woman because you have abandoned your husband; that much I understand. It's the rest that's totally incomprehensible.

"'*You are a wicked woman because you have abandoned your husband who was a good husband . . .*'" Lionello, reading the note from his chintz sofa, can't stop laughing. "You must write a book," he says. "Scenes from Tuscan life, you can call it. It will make a fortune then you can buy the house with the *terazza* that you dream of."

"But is it a joke, or what?"

"A wonderfully funny joke. This woman is an artist in her own way."

"You think it's a woman?"

"Of course it is a woman – '. . . *you will be punished like all the wicked women before you.*' Only a woman can write such things. A man would never write something so colorful and dramatic, he hasn't the imagination."

"But who is she? And why is she doing this?"

"Because you are stirring the passions."

"Not intentionally."

"In less then two days of your arrival here your ex-husband arrives with roses."

"I never asked him to come. And now he's gone back to Germany, as far as I know."

"But you do not know and that is why it is so exciting. From one moment to the next you cannot imagine what is going to happen. There is Domenico on the roof looking at you through the shutters, you have the over-sexed plumber in the bed."

"*Under* the bed, not *in* it."

". . . and now you have the anonymous letters."

"Only one so far, which I could do without."

"But more will follow."

"Oh no, I hope not."

"This is only the beginning. It is your presence here that is creating the drama. The curtain has risen, as you say in England. You are creating the wonderful theater and someone is bound to be murdered in their bed before long."

"Not me, I hope."

"You are disturbing the blood pressures, you are making the women jealous, the temperature is rising and it is already insufferably hot."

"I came here to live quietly, not to disturb everyone."

"But, my dear beautiful lady, you are disturbing the whole village with your blue eyes."

"Oh, come on."

"The women have fear of losing their husbands, and however useless they are it is better to have someone than no one to cook the pasta for."

"But I don't *want* their husbands."

"And you don't want your own, it seems. Therefore, you must be looking for another in their imagination. You are an English woman with blue eyes and red hairs. You are alone, you are a mysterious *straniera* and available."

"Not for their husbands I'm not."

"Ah, but they don't know that. And you must understand, every Italian man, even one as old and as ugly as me, believes he is Casanova. The mother tells us in the cradle how handsome and clever we are even if we turn out to be ugly and stupid. But you mustn't worry. I am sure there is no problem. The people will like you. They already do."

"Do they? How do you know?"

"You salute everyone, they say. Always you are smiling. They are curious. They want to know why you are here alone. Where is her husband, they ask me. And I try to explain that you are – "Lionello circles his hand in the air, "divided for now – "

"Divided forever."

"I tell them you are searching for a new life. But that they must keep their husbands safely inside the house when you are about."

"You didn't say that?"

"Of course not." Lionello begins laughing, his laughter developing into a fit of dry coughing. He reaches for the decanter of white wine on the glass-topped table beside him. "I am getting too old for all this stimulation," he gasps. "And I am too old to live here alone, Tonina tells me. I am not sure what she has in mind, do you?"

"I hate to think."

"Perhaps she is planning to move in with me. Ha! What would her useless husband say about that?" He pours a generous measure of white wine into two goblets. "But these people, you know, they are not bad. They have their own beliefs and superstitions; it takes time for a stranger to be accepted, even one as charming as yourself. I have been here for twelve years but they still think of me as *il Romano.*" He hands me a glass. "You know, I think there is something in this wine – " He swallows a mouthful. "I have an idea there is in this wine a substance that is making me hallucinate. I see things."

"What things?"

"Faces in the stones. There is one in my garden wall, you must look, he is wearing a three-cornered hat and I swear it is Napoleon. He salutes me when I approach the house, and I always return the salute. I think he must have taken a round trip from Elba to Sinalunga and back to Elba. What do you think?"

I sip my wine. It tastes like chilled peaches and honey. "I think everything is possible here," I say, and swallow more of the magical wine. He could be right; perhaps I've been hallucinating ever since I arrived.

"We are surrounded by the past and I feel sometimes the past and the present merge and become one all-consuming present." Lionello swallows more wine. "And the light here, you know, it is like a drug, the extraordinary luminosity plays tricks with the mind. Yet the people do not see anything. They were born here and see nothing exceptional. And now, here you are, giving some theater to the people and making Italy your home."

"There was nowhere else to go."

"Huh! There is always somewhere else to go. You wanted to come here, and so you came. And now you are making the best of things. But what will you do here alone in the winter with no tourists?"

"I'm not sure. I've not really thought about that. Look for work of some kind, perhaps?"

"You must learn to speak good Italian. Then doors will open for you. You will meet interesting people. A fine man, a count perhaps, who would carry you away to his *castello*. And this is what the people here are waiting for, to see whom you will choose to be with. And then the women will be happy, so long as it is not one of their husbands, of course. Ha-ha! I love this theater. I hope it is going to continue."

What would Lionello say, I wonder, if I told him that I had already met a fine man whom I couldn't stop thinking of, younger than me, with no *castello* and nothing to carry me away with; even the clothes he wears are Vittorio's cast-offs, he told me.

"The best thing for you to do now," Lionello is saying, "is to go to Siena, to the *Università degli Stranieri*. They do inexpensive summer courses. Make the people here wait for the next scene of the drama until you are ready to play it."

* * * *

When I leave Lionello's house I look at the rockery at the end of his garden, trying not to think of another, smaller, English rockery where I buried my ring before setting off down the motorway in search of a new life in Devon. I would prefer to forget that, but the past has a way of springing out on me from round every corner.

I lean against the jasmine-covered wall, scrutinizing the rocks from various angles. I can see no sign of a stone resembling Napoleon with or without his three-cornered hat. Perhaps I haven't had quite enough of the hallucinogenic wine.

4
Wine, food and Michelangelo.

20th June.
Today is my birthday. I'm 48.
Imagine me in the Piazzo del Campo in Siena sitting
in a bar under a yellow umbrella, jotting in my
notebook between bites of brioche and sips of
cappuccino sprinkled with chocolate. I have enrolled in
the *Università degli Stranieri* for a month's course in
Italian. Someone canceled so I stepped in. The price is
affordable and – I'm going to wake up any minute
and find myself back in Devon staring out of a
window at the rain. But no, I'm here. The sun is
shining – it's real.

There was an early morning mist when I got off
the bus at San Domenico. It wrapped itself around
people's legs, making them invisible so that only their
upper torsos floated silently across the *piazza.* I must
definitely be on some kind of hallucinogenic drug.
Siena, the city of dreams and I'm part of it all. What a
wonderful thing to be happening!

A sudden burst of happiness swept through me
this morning, carrying me along, feet hardly touching
the ground, up the meandering streets, all the way to
the *Questura* for permission to stay in this magical
country.

An hour of waiting in the stuffy office with six
other impatient *stranieri* before a dark, aggressive
woman called me to the desk in a deep and throaty

voice. "You must to return next week," she growls, and pushes my passport across the counter at me.

"But I have to have my *Permesso di Soggiorno* now," I plead. "This minute, to take to the *Università degli Stranieri.*"

"*No, signora.*"

"But I want to learn Italian and they won't allow me to enrol without it." The woman frowns, the air seems to get hotter; everyone is listening. "Please, I beg you - "

A young man behind the desk whispers something to the woman. "Wait," she says to me, and storms off through a far door. I look at my watch, nine forty-five; I've got to be at the school in fifteen minutes and I'm uncertain how to get there. I don't want to be late on my first morning. The woman returns waving a sheet of paper. "Sign." She jabs the dotted line with a dirty fingernail. "*Un documento provvisorio.*"

Having thanked the angry woman and the kind young man, I escape out into the warm air, along the street, clutching the precious *documento,* through a crowd of slick Italian businessmen; running now, downhill, uphill, out of breath, to the Via Banchi di Sopra. People crowd in the doorway of *Bar Nannini,* coming and going, adding to the melée of Japanese tourists massing in the middle of the street. Flags flutter from windows, yellow and purple, red and green. An air of expectancy for the coming event, *il Palio,* August third, but no time to think of that now, I must arrive on time. Down a narrow street, second right under the arch, running on sandaled feet to the bottom, to a small *piazza,* at the end of which, I can hardly catch my breath, stands the school building with impressive Doric columns on either side of the entrance.

In the high-ceilinged reception hall a group of German students with blond hairy legs gather round a diminutive *professore* who is pointing something out to them in a book. "I've come to enrol in a month's course in Italian," I pant at him.

"*Signora,*" he wags his finger at me. "*Siamo in Italia. Parliamo Italiano.*"

"But first I have to learn Italian. Otherwise, how can I speak it?"

One of the German boys laughs. "I think also like this," he says. The *professore* slides papers out of his briefcase and shuffles through them.

"I'm a beginner," I explain. "And I'm already twenty minutes late."

He hands me a sheet of paper with my name on it and points to the stairs at the end of the hall. "*Classe uno. Secondo piano.*"

Class one turns out to be on the fifth floor. With my blouse sticking to me, I creep into a long room full of students seated at desks with sheets of paper in front of them. A girl passes me a questionnaire; where was I born, why had I come to live in Italy, what kind of food did I like and all to be answered in Italian. I do the best I can, writing the language is easier than speaking, and half an hour later, hand in my paper. The test is over; I'm free to go. The beginner's class starts on Monday, July 1st, at nine o'clock and finishes at midday.

' . . . and now Lionello's gone to the mountains for the whole of July and August, my safety-net's been withdrawn, I'll have no one to talk to. . .'

But what does it matter? I drop the pen. Here I am sitting in the middle of a medieval, walled city munching a second brioche. I don't have to go home next week, or the week after, or ever again, come to that. *This* is my home; I'm actually *living* here, watching Japanese, Americans, Germans, Italians and the English - you can spot the difference a mile off – they're wearing silly straw hats. The whole of the world, it seems, is strolling by.

What would I do if I suddenly saw Richard? Duck under the table. Except the cloths aren't long enough to hide me. He'd spot me and I'd look ridiculous. I'm certain I saw his van outside Martino's on Tuesday morning. I ducked back up the alleyway. But when I looked again, it had gone. Thank heaven for Domenico, still mending the roof, on special look-out for a bearded man climbing the drainpipe.

A group of slim dark-haired girls sashay past. I pick up the pen: *'Each one has perfect legs, shapely, tanned and oiled. Unlike mine, which resemble pale sticks of celery, best hidden under a long cool skirt . . .'*

"You write dangerous secrets that when published will expose us all?" Vittorio, immaculate in a white linen suit and open-necked black shirt, leans over me.

I flush as I close my notebook. "Oh, no," I laugh nervously. "I don't know any."

"You will if you live here long enough. We drink champagne?"

"Er, well . . . "

"*Bene.*" Vittorio calls a waiter, who appears as if by magic, bearing a tray with two flute glasses of champagne and a dish of olives. I drop my notebook and pen into my basket as Vittorio sits next to me. This is all happening a little too unexpectedly.

"We drink to you, for having the courage to come here alone. *Salute.*" He drinks and sets his glass down. Then lights a cigarette and sucks the smoke in between his teeth with a hissing sound. "You know why I come to Siena today?" Smoke trickles out of the corner of his mouth as he speaks. "I look for a house for you."

"A house?" I set my glass down.

"A house with frescoed ceilings. I know of such a house."

"But, I-I don't want a house with or without frescoed ceilings."

"What, you prefer to stay in that dog kennel down a back street in Sinalunga?"

I'm speechless.

"Now you come in Toscana you must to have some style please."

"But I love living there and I can't afford anything more."

"And the old Alfa Romeo that you arrive in my house. Where you find such a car?"

"It belongs to a friend. I don't have a car."

"What a kind of friend give you an old broken car like that, eh?" Vittorio gives a knowing laugh. "A friend like that don't do nothing for you, *cara.* You say you don't have a car? I find you a car."

"But I don't want a car."

"I say I give you a car and you say you don't want a car? I don't understand."

"I'd prefer a bicycle."

Vittorio is looking at me as though I've said something indecent. "A bicycle?" he echoes. "You are a little crazy, I think, no?"

"Well, maybe. But that's how I am."

He makes a face. "And what you do in the winter on this bicycle?"

"Well, I . . . "

He drains his glass. "How much you want to pay for a car?"

"Nothing."

"Okay, I find already. A Lancia, five year old, *tremila euro.*"

"That's about two thousand pounds, isn't it?"

"Where you buy a car for less?"

"But I don't have it."

"If you don't have that you don't come to live in Toscana, *cara mia.* But no problem, *il macellaio*, Filippo, he is like my brother, he want to sell his Auto-Bianchi. We do for only six hundred *euro.*"

"The butcher selling a car?" I giggle; the champagne must be going to my head.

"It belong to his mother, she die last year."

"What color is it?"

"What difference makes the color? It is the car what is important."

The waiter refills our glasses then plonks the bottle in an ice bucket. Five hundred pounds, approximately; I could pay that out of the insurance cheque for the broken china, which would be around two and a half thousand pounds, they'd told me on the telephone. I sip champagne; I'm beginning to enjoy myself. "Today's my birthday," I announce, and pop an olive into my mouth.

Vittorio taps the rim of his glass against mine. "Now we go and eat the fish. I take you to a special restaurant where the *padrone* is my very good friend and we drink the very good wine *per pochi soldi.*"

This is all turning out better than I could ever have imagined. "I'm going to the *Università degli Stranieri* for a month to learn Italian," I say.

Vittorio's mouth turns down. "In one month, you think you learn the language? Six months, one year, at least. In one month you do nothing."

"I could learn the ground work, couldn't I?"

Vittorio waves his long-fingered hand in the air. "What is ground works? First you learn the *mentalita, la cultura*, and then you learn the language. You think you learn all this in one month? You must to go around and look at what there is to see."

"Couldn't I do that in the afternoons?"

He looks at me quizzically. "You do what you want in the afternoons, *cara*. What I say is, you must to meet the people who can show you the life here." He puts on his wrap-around sunglasses. "*Questa è la vita*, something Ricardo no understand nothing. It was a good thing that you leave him."

"He left *me*."

"But he come back, eh?"

"Yes. But now he's gone away again."

"If Ricardo come back, I know."

"How?"

"You think I don't know what is going on? Do I look stupid to you?" He whips off his wrap-arounds and stares at me.

Whatever else he looks, I think, gazing back into his dark, deep-set eyes, he doesn't look stupid. "No," I say. "You don't."

"I am relieved, *cara*. I don't want that you think I am stupid. Then *you* would be stupid, and I believe that you are not so. Now - " He gets to his feet. "We put the fish in the stomach, then the good wine to follow." He laughs, showing off his dazzling white teeth. A blonde in shorts is watching him from a nearby table. I can see why, he is undoubtedly attractive if you happen to like that kind of thing. And judging by the look on several other women's faces, they obviously do. Then it dawns on me, maybe they think he's Al Pacino. Stifling laughter, I get to my feet; he's my height, tall for a woman, short for a man. They'll be asking for his autograph soon, mine too, for being with him.

I step unsteadily out, his arm holding mine rather too tightly as he guides me across the sun-baked *piazza* to the restaurant where his good friend will put fish in our stomachs with a good wine to follow for very little money.

* * * *

The *trattoria* is full. But because Vittorio is known here we are ushered across to a corner table next to a large fig tree in a terracotta pot. Accordion music plays from a speaker behind the leaves. It reminds me of a night, two years ago, when I tried to dance the tango with Vittorio in his house and he told me that I was like a piece of wood. He had pressed his thumb hard into the small of my back and ran his long bony fingers up and down my spine as if playing an instrument. It had the most extraordinary effect on me. My body seemed to melt and move entirely with his. I'd been embarrassed at how aroused I'd felt, in front of Richard, and especially Vittorio's wife. "You obviously fancy Vittorio, don't you?" Richard said on the way home in the car. It had been difficult to explain that it wasn't the man himself so much as being physically controlled that excited me.

The waitress offers a menu that is waved impatiently aside. Then a discussion starts about some special dish that has to be tasted on a birthday. Food is not that important to me any more, my main diet still being muesli, yoghourt and brioche since arriving in Italy. I'm too keyed-up to think of food. What I'm really hoping to do is talk about Ronaldo without making it seem too obvious that I'm interested in him. What has he been doing? Has he mentioned me at all? I shake the white linen napkin onto my lap, feeling unexpectedly hungry.

Vittorio twirls the empty wine glass in his fingers. "What Ricardo stay doing in Germania?"

"He's working for a friend who has a swimming pool business."

"*Incredibile.*"

Incredible or not, now's the time to get him off that particular subject. But it's difficult to move onto the subject of Ronaldo, because Vittorio launches into a lengthy tale of how he and his elder brother had tried to survive as waiters in Napoli pinching food to take home to mother, *una donna fortissima*, who, when his father died, took control of the family, and her sister's family too for some reason, not entirely clear, as he keeps breaking into rapid Italian. Something about his father having too much *anima* but not enough *palle,* the one meaning soul, the other, balls, he explains. I'm lost. Now it's the story of his brother and how he'd fallen on a piece of glass and cut his throat, the brutal details of which are being described throughout the first course of *panzanella,* a tasty bread salad with fresh tomatoes and onions.

"And how is your house?" I ask, forcefully, determined to change the subject, having made several previous attempts and failed.

Vittorio looks blankly at me. "My house is still there, as far as I know."

"No, I mean - " I give a little laugh. "Ronaldo tells me he's redesigning everything, building extensions in the garden."

"Ah, Ronaldo." Vittorio wipes the perspiration from his face with his napkin. "One day he make the Roman arch, the next day he break everything to make the *colonna Dorica.* He want to be like Michelangelo, he believe he *is* Michelangelo come back from the dead." He fills his glass from the bottle of *Bianco Vergine* that *il padrone* had sent to the table. "You have seen the swimming pool?"

"Not recently, no." I think it wiser not to mention that the last time in March when I'd seen the pool it had been full of stagnant green water and discarded wine bottles, and surely anything Ronaldo had done since must be an improvement.

"He make a mosaic on the floor like - " Vittorio waves his hand in a gesture that could mean anything, "*una tappezzeria nel museo.*"

"A tapestry in a museum? But that's beautiful, isn't it?"

"Not if it take more monies and time. He want to do *his* way and I want to do *my* way what cost *meno soldi, capito?*" He pours a splash of wine into my glass then tops his own up to the brim. "Last night we make many discussions and I throw him in the swimming pool. Then I remember he no swim. He panic much, I am laughin', he cry out and then I jump in still laughin' with all my clothes and I drag him out."

I stare at Vittorio, appalled. "He could have drowned."

"No, no, he is like the cat, he know always how to survive. But he stay good with me. He is my protégé, I don't let him drown, I give him work, I give him my family. I give more than all. Before he come to me, he have nothing."

"How terrible."

"*Terribile, si.*" Vittorio drains his glass. "I have much thirst in this heat." He pours himself more wine. "One day he tell me he finish with his woman and want to change his life."

I feel my eyes widening. "What woman was that, then?"

"I give my house, my food, my clothes, I give all to him. Now he give me his beautiful friend-a-ship. I look for him, stay always with him close, like he is the brother I no have more. *Ecco, spaghettini con salmone.*"

The waitress sets the food on the table. But when she tries to serve it onto Vittorio's plate, he waves it away. "*No, no,* I stay good with the *Vergine.*" He winks at the waitress and she giggles. He pours the last drop of wine into his glass. *"Buon appertito, cara,"* he says, raising his glass to me.

I force down the spaghetti and salmon. I seem to have lost my appetite suddenly and it's becoming increasingly difficult to swallow. I drink a little wine, another bottle of which is already on its way to the table. "So, what happened to – er - Ronaldo's woman, then?"

"Ronaldo have many women. But he have no family. He was abandoned when he is a boy."

"Abandoned?"

"He has the hard life. But Ronaldo is moving like the eels, with me he stay very good."

The more Vittorio drinks the *Vergine* the worse his English is becoming and although usually he speaks his own language clearly and well and is easier to understand than most, he's becoming progressively more difficult to follow. Also, the noise level in the restaurant has risen considerably. A group of Germans at a nearby table are fighting a losing battle at out-shouting Italians at a neighboring table. I watch Vittorio's lips, straining with all my attention to make sense of his words. ". . . then he go in the *istituzione.*"

"Institution? Who, Ronaldo?" But there's no answer, only a long passage in Italian about priests in Pienza who are somehow involved in the story. It's riveting stuff. If only I could understand it. But the few words that I have managed to grasp are worrying. What chance can there possibly be of getting together with Ronaldo if Vittorio is always watching, sharing his clothes and staying close?

I gulp down a glass of water, hoping it might help clear my befuddled brain. Vittorio shakes his head in disgust when offered water. "I use only to make the shave, *cara.*" He pours himself more wine as yet more food appears. *"Vitello alla Milanese con limone e salvia.* You eat good in Toscana, eh?"

Feeling uncomfortably full with more food inside me than I've eaten for a month, I help myself to one small sliver of meat. I then try to continue the conversation where we'd left off. But Vittorio has lost interest in Ronaldo, and is now on to the subject of Rocco, his wealthy cousin living alone in the house with the frescoed ceilings. *"Un musicista bravissimo,* he play the flute for the guests in his house. You come also to hear him play."

Not remotely interested in hearing about Rocco and his flute, I try steering the conversation back to Ronaldo. "You say he was living with the priests in Pienza?"

"*No, no,* his mother die and leave him the fortune."

"Ronaldo's mother had money?"

"Rocco, *non* Ronaldo. He marry soon. I speak of Rocco. He is a good man, he take much care of his mother when she is ill. Now he help me with the bar which I open when Ronaldo has finished the work - if he ever finish." The waitress hovers with a dish of *pecorino* and *la Torta della Nonna.*

I stare vacantly at the cheese, uncertain of what I've just heard. I turn to Vittorio. "Did you say that Ronaldo will marry soon?" Vittorio shrugs and tops up his glass. "Is that what you said?" I persist. "Ronaldo's going to get married?"

"Ronaldo is Ronaldo. He need a young wife to give him children. Why you eat nothing, *cara?* You must to taste the *pecorino di Pienza.*" He cuts a slice of cheese for himself and bites into it. "It is best to marry a young girl and shape her for the wife you want. You marry Ricardo when you are a young girl, he shape you good, eh?" He laughs and pinches my cheek.

I fumble with the cheese on my plate, feeling faint. Vittorio throws back a strong black coffee, then gets to his feet. "I must to have a cigarette," he says, and snakes past the crowded tables to embrace a formidable Mussolini look-alike emerging from the kitchen. The waitress sets the bill on the table in front of me. Seventy-five *euros.* Surely, I'm not supposed to pay it? Grabbing my bag, I get up, collide with the fig tree, and move unevenly past the tables to the door.

Vittorio, with a final slap on *il padrone's* meaty shoulder, steps out after me into the blazing heat. "But you pay or no?" I look at him, alarmed.

"*Cara mia,*" he places his arm reassuringly around my shoulders. "*La cultura* in *Italia* is for invitin' a friend on your birthday. I am this good friend, or no?"

"Oh, of course." I laugh, rather too loudly, and turn back to hand my credit card to Mussolini.

I feel dazed as I walk across the crowded *piazza,* heat rising off the ground in waves. I'm not used to the heat and so much food and wine in the middle of the day; my legs feel like cotton. It's as well Vittorio is holding my arm, even though I long to escape; without him, I might collapse.

"Rocco, my cousin, we go to see his house with the frescoes, eh?"

"No. I have to go, Vittorio."

"Where you go now?"

"Back on the bus."

"I take you in the car." He pinches my arm playfully. It hurts and I pull away. "You lose much weight, *cara*, your arm is like a stick. What is the matter with you?"

"I have to go. It's very important. I have to go at once."

"What is so important in Sinalunga?"

I could say two beloved cats waiting to be fed. "I have important things to do," I say instead.

"You meet with your friend with the old Alfa Romeo?"

"No, not at all. I must get home."

"First you come with me to meet Rocco. Then we stay together with Silka and *mie figlie*. Silka make the English tea for you."

I stumble determinedly across the rest of the *piazza* refusing to listen.

"You are a little crazy, or no?"

"Yes." I wave. "I'm sure I am."

"We make the celebration for your birthday on Saturday," he calls after me. "Rocco come for you at eight. He has the green Mercedes."

I can feel him watching me as I climb the steps to Banca di Sopra, long skirt flapping round my ankles. This crazy woman is flying out of her head, he'll be thinking.

Well, let him! I push on through the jostling tourists down the hot, dusty street to San Domenico. I have a thumping headache and cannot, for another second, tolerate Vittorio's company. And the fact that

I've spent seventy-five *euros* on a lunch I can't afford, makes me feel even worse.

But I'll go to his wretched party on Saturday night; I might even wait for Rocco his cousin in his green Mercedes, if that's what it takes to see Ronaldo again. But right now I have to get back to my cats and books. My sanity depends on escaping Vittorio and the confusion and the blistering heat of Siena.

5
Party at Vittorio's

The *Piazza* Garibaldi in Sinalunga's *Centro Storico* is
set out rather like a theater. The magnificent ochre-
colored church, *la Collegiata di san Martino,* the steeple
of which I can see from my bedroom window,
dominates center stage. To my right, facing the
church, is the *Bar Cortese,* a friendly, intimate
atmosphere presided over by Paula, the owner.
Behind, runs the Via Ciro Pinsuti leading down past
the recently restored aquamarine-colored church, the
S. Maria Della Neve.

Across the *piazza* there is the Corner Bar with
tables and chairs set out under red umbrellas
encircled by plain trees. This is where I'm sitting,
watching the old men of the village playing cards.
Small groups of men (it's nearly always men, the
women are at home cooking the pasta, Lionello tells
me) cross the *piazza*, stop, gesticulate, slap each other
on the shoulder and move lethargically toward the
bar. The young priest, *Don* Giuliano, crosses the
piazza, waves to someone sitting on the church steps,
then disappears into Armando's jewelry shop.

It's partly because of the elegant Armando that
I'm here. He had a handbag shop in London many
years ago, close to where I lived. One day I heard he
wanted to sell his grandmother's flat in Tuscany and
went to see him. "It's in Sinalunga, which you may
never have heard of. It's small and needs work. But it
has potential and not far from Siena." As Richard and

I were going on holiday in that area, we took the key and decided to drive down and see for ourselves. The place was filthy and draped in spiders' webs. "You'll either love it or hate it," Armando had said. We loved it and I bought it with my savings for seven thousand pounds.

I amble down the Ciro Pinsuti to Martino's shop and pick out a lettuce from the box of overripe fruit and vegetables outside. There's always a great waving of arms in greeting from Martino when I enter the dark interior. "*Cara signora, come va? Brava, brava, lei.*" Antonio, the brother, joins in with several more *brava, bravas.* Then an ancient little lady in an apron, the mother, appears from the back room with: "*Si, si, lei é molto brava, Signora.*" Dear lady, how are things? How clever you are, yes, yes, very clever. Beats anything I've ever had said to me in England when I bought a lettuce.

I pay for a bottle of water but am not allowed to pay for the lettuce. I notice a slug on the leaf as Martino wraps it in newspaper. "*Speciale,*" he says, which means, I believe, that Martino has picked the lettuce this morning from his allotment over the village wall.

I climb the old stone steps to Vicolo della Mura, feeling privileged. Moving from a Devonshire alley to a Tuscan alley was definitely the right thing to do. How it's all going to work out, I'm not sure. But somehow it *will* work - I'll find a way to *make* it work. Then the first thing I see on the floor as I open my front door is a dark blue envelope with the familiar slanted writing and my heart drops.

. . . I've wasted nearly a week here waiting for you to contact me. You knew where I was staying . . .

I take the card that had been attached to the roses down from the top of the wardrobe next to the out-of-sight out-of-mind shoes I'd hidden up there the week before. It has an address on the back. *Albergo Gino,* in Croce. How come I never saw it?

I had hoped you might wish to contact me on your birthday, we could have spent it together as we've always done . . .

I can't read on. Through the open *salotto* door I catch sight of the roses in their vase on the cupboard, their heads drooping lower each day. I can hardly bear to look at them, yet haven't the heart to throw them out.

I imagine that not understanding the meaning of the word loyalty you spent the evening with Vittorio. Well, much happiness may it bring you. He'll use you as he does everyone else.

I push the letter back into its envelope. But it's no use; it will have to be answered immediately, got out of my mind once and for all.

Dear Richard,

I never asked you to come here . . .

I tear it up. I'll answer when in a calmer state of mind.

* * * *

Today is Friday and another letter has arrived from Germany.

Dear Lorri,

I wrote that last letter out of anger and pain and I think perhaps it should not have been sent. But I have to be practical about things and think positively. My skilled work on the apartment gives me certain rights. I feel it fair to warn you that I have been to the Land Registry in Germany and should you decide to sell the property I've been told I have the authority to block the sale.

I look up for air.

However, you may continue to live there, but no decisions can be made without first consulting me. I am sorry if this is a shock. I can only add that had you made it possible to accept me back in your life none of this unpleasantness would have been necessary. But I have to think of myself now and my future happiness, something you never gave the slightest thought to.

This one has to be answered immediately. But I can hardly hold the pen for trembling. *Thank you for allowing me to live in my own home, it's very generous of you. But let me tell you right away, I have no intentions of selling it for I'm now a permanent fixture in Vicolo della Mura.*

I seal the envelope of the third and shortest version of my reply. Land Registry? He's trying to frighten me. He'd succeeded for a minute, until I'd thought it through and realized it was *my* name on the deeds, not his. I address the envelope. *Grogenbaum 85.* Still with the darling Veronica then: poor dear, what a sad time it must be for her.

I head along the alleyway with the letter. Rosalba is closing her shutters and waves as I hurry past. I walk to the end of Via della Mura, up the few steps toward the postbox. As in Devon, when I'd replied to Richard's letters, I'd always felt better. It was like unloading everything into the postbox. Now I'm feeling the same satisfying finality about it, as I had then. The only difference is that here I'm crossing a sunny *piazza* to unload; there, I'd walked down to the postbox in the rain, the sea veiled in a damp gray mist and seagulls screeching, swooping and diving over my head.

* * * *

By Saturday all the boxes are out and folded up against the street dustbin. And almost everything is arranged in the apartment: blue towels in the bathroom, a jug of fresh flowers on the kitchen table, English prints on one wall leading down to the front door, Italian on the other and a tub of scarlet geraniums on the front step. The ceramic *La Casetta* sign, which I'd had made in Devon, is stuck on the outside wall with superglue. So far, it's holding. Hopefully, the Coopers will approve when they arrive for their two nights' stay and won't think fifty pounds a night too much to pay for such a tiny place. But the advertisement clearly states bed and breakfast in a Tuscan hilltop village, double bedroom, wonderful panorama across rooftops to the Umbrian hills, fruit, bread and local wine included. And that's precisely what they'll be getting.

My bed under the desk in the *salotto* is made up from the sofa cushions, my clothes from the bedroom wardrobe draped over the sofa back, contents from the chest of drawers on the sofa seat, the cats' litter tray behind the sofa. The door *must* be kept locked at all times. I can't have unsuspecting bed and breakfasters walking in and falling headlong over the sofa into the litter tray. Whatever happens, they must never discover I'm sleeping under the desk; that would be deeply humiliating. I live downstairs in my other apartment, as explained in my letter. It will mean going to bed early when they've gone out to dinner, locking myself into the *salotto* and then appearing early the next morning with a smile to provide breakfast in the kitchen-diner. And when they've left to explore Tuscany, I'll shower, have my own breakfast and clean up in preparation for their return. Simple enough, and with luck they'll be none the wiser.

"*Permesso?*"

I start: a voice on the hall stairs. The cats fly through the kitchen window.

"I have *permesso?*"

"Silka! What a nice surprise."

"The street door was open so I come in."

"Yes, of course. Please do." I feel suddenly flustered; it's the first time Vittorio's wife has ever visited. What could she want?

"You must put in the telephone. No one can contact you."

"I know, I keep meaning to."

"But this is beautiful." Silka is gazing in wonder at the Welsh dresser, plates on shelves, cups on hooks and dried lavender hanging from the beams. "It is so beautiful."

"It's a bit of a muddle – I still haven't quite finished - "

"Oh no, I . . . " Her voice trails off as she looks at the row of gleaming copper pots hanging from the beams. "I've never seen anything I like so much. You have put everything so well together. And I like the old stairs to the window."

"Richard made those. He did most of the work here." Billy, the tabby, has reappeared. From the top step he regards Silka through narrowed eyes.

"The tiger cat, he look fierce at me."

"He looks like that at all strange people. Not that I'm suggesting you're strange, of course." I give a laugh. She blinks uncomprehendingly. "Never mind," I say. "Come and see the rest of my mansion."

"I am astonished," Silka says, following me into the bedroom. "Vittorio say only how small it is, but you live in so beautiful a house."

"Hardly a house, there's only three small rooms."

Silka touches the white linen bed cover, the mosquito netting draped from a wooden pole above. "Where do you find so nice things? England?"

"No, from the market here in the *piazza*. It costs very little."

"I never find so nice things here. I go always shopping in Germany with my mother. Ah. She gazes out across Domenico's new roof. "Look, you can see so far. I would sit in bed all day and dream if I lived here. You are lucky. I would like to change my life like you have done it."

"But why would you want to? You have a beautiful house with a swimming pool and a whole forest outside your door."

"Yes, but I cannot see the sky like I can here. I look only at the dark trees from my window and I never have the time." She turns back in to the room, her ice-blue eyes absorbing every detail: the brass bedside lamps, the Victorian chest of drawers, the Italian mirror with photos of the cats, Billy and Gertie, wedged around the hand-carved frame.

"I haven't had much time for cleaning," I say, apologetically, eyeing a spider's web stretched across the beams.

"It's not important, I clean all the time but my house does not look like this. You have created your world around you. Did you have all these things in your family?"

"With Richard. He was my family. My parents are dead."

"I am sorry."

"No, it's . . . " I shrug. I'm not sure what to say.

"Sometimes it is good to escape the family?"

"Yes. Definitely."

Silka smiles. She has one of those long bony faces that could look plain. But her smile transforms her face making her seem beautiful. She's dressed in the style of a long-forgotten film star. Draped skirt caught with a purple belt slung low on her narrow hips, a matching ribbon around her high forehead. "My house will be more beautiful when Ronaldo has finished the work."

"There's still a lot for him to do, is there?"

"Vittorio find always more work for him because he don't want him to finish. He don't want that he will go away."

My pulse quickens. "Go away? Where?"

"Who know? He is free, like you. Only I am not free. I am a prisoner."

"Surely not."

"I have always to do something for somebody else, Vittorio, the children, never for myself. When my mother is coming, she do everything and Vittorio is angry. He is generous, but only when he want something from me. But," Silka sighs, "I have much and Ronaldo create many special things for me, like Richard do for you."

"That's true."

"You have seen the swimming pool?"

"Not yet."

"He make with little pieces of marble, like an old Roman mosaic. Everybody say it is so beautiful. Ronaldo is an artist, he always create something special, every touch he make his own."

"I can imagine."

We move back into the kitchen. Billy hisses from the window.

"I think your tiger cat does not like me."

"He's suspicious of people at first."

"Like I think I am. But I have no choice, I must welcome always the friends of Vittorio also if I don't like them."

"I hope I'm not one of those."

"No." She turns to me. "You have kind blue eyes." Silka lifts her fine blonde hair off her neck. "It is very hot, you are light-skinned like me. How can you take the sun?"

"I don't sit in it for long. Would you like some tea? Or coffee?"

"No, I must go." She glances at her Rolex. "Giuseppina, my maid, she wait with the girls and Ronaldo and I have to prepare for tonight. You remember we have the *festa*? You come?"

"Yes, of course."

"This is the reason why I come to see you. Vittorio think you don't understand when he speak to you in Siena. He say you are strange that day."

"It was a strange day."

"I say, she is English, and I am German and we have different ways. It is important she come, he say, because he want to present his cousin, Rocco to you."

"Yes. He told me."

"He is a lawyer, but he prefer to be a musician. He play the flute and sometime he give concerts in his house. He live with his mother and wait always to meet someone English like you. He will come here for you at eight. You will wait for him, please? Now I go."

"And Ronaldo?" I follow Silka's tall figure down the stairs. "He'll be there tonight, will he?"

"He cook the *bistecca*."

That means another inedible dinner with half-raw meat being passed round on plastic plates. But then seeing that Ronaldo is the only thing that really matters, all interest in food, regardless of the plates it's served on, is immaterial. I will eat before I leave; a little tuna, or *mozzarella*, followed by the usual muesli and fruit, maybe.

But who needs food with so many turbulent emotions churning in the stomach?

* * * *

If you go down the hill to the station, turn right, then left under the underpass, you'll come to the Co-op, a wonderful find, for it's air-conditioned and sells most things anyone could need to make a feast. It even has a bar selling coffee, brioche, salads, and freshly squeezed orange juice. I've managed to hire a cheap second-hand bicycle from them. It looks sturdy enough, with gears and space in the front to tie a shopping basket. Sinalunga is not the most ideal spot for cycling because of the hills. But it will at least get me about independently of the buses and trains and, most important, give me the chance to give Rocco and his green Mercedes the slip.

* * * *

I'm pedalling along the Siena road in my white off-the-shoulder blouse and long blue skirt. I keep well in to the side, no parked cars to crash into this time. It's still light at seven thirty; even so, I have turned on the front and back lamps. Cars are racing past, some unnervingly close. I wobble slightly in panic, hoping the Rocco character won't come swooping up in his green Mercedes and offer me a lift.

I reach the Rapolano Terme, turn off and pedal slowly along the dirt road to Vittorio's house, dust rising under the wheels. There's no hurry, I remind myself. I don't want to arrive with sweat stains under my arms.

It's further than I'd realized to Rapolano. Cycling back in the dark will be daunting. Unless, of course, Ronaldo drives me home in Vittorio's Lancia. We could put the bike on the luggage rack. Failing that, I'll get a taxi, if such things exist in the neighborhood. I can afford it now that the insurance cheque for the broken china is in the post. Two thousand, three hundred pounds, the company manager assured me on the telephone this morning; I left the bar elated.

Loud Latin American music greets me from the garden as I cycle through the gates. A mass of cars is parked haphazardly in the driveway. I had no idea so many people were invited. I'd thought it was going to be a simple evening like the last time with only a few friends around a table on the terrace. Now the whole garden is ablaze under the lights. I glance uneasily round for a place to park the bike. Then prop it against the garden stairs. I can make a quick getaway if necessary.

The dogs come barking and gamboling toward me, their paws kicking up dust from the dry earth. Tentatively, I stroke the two white heads. They jump up, almost as tall as me, and touch my white blouse with their dirty paws. "Down, down," I cry, then realize they can't understand English and scramble up the stairs out of their way. Arriving in the garden, I brush the dirt off my sleeve, feeling slightly overwhelmed and wishing more than anything that I could speak Italian.

The garden, on three levels, is floodlit and bedecked with geraniums tumbling from terracotta vases. It resembles a Hollywood film set with expensively dressed extras placed in animated groups under the cypresses while others drape themselves exotically in deckchairs around the swimming pool.

I spot Ronaldo immediately, on the top garden level in front of a smoky fire, barbecuing steak, his green silk shirt open to the waist. He's laughing with Filippo and a woman with long silken hair like a cape about her shoulders. His eyes hold mine for the slightest moment, and then look back at Filippo. I glance nervously away, wondering why he didn't acknowledge me. Perhaps he hasn't seen me. Yet, I know he has.

Stepping up to the top level, I turn deliberately from the fire and make for the drinks table where I pour a cup of red wine. So much for romantic words;

it must have been the sultry heat of the night bringing out passions all too easily forgotten the next day. I gaze round without taking much in; everything seems a blur of trembling lights.

Sipping my wine, I casually wander along the cobbled passageway around the back of the house. It looks like a little Parisian street now with a lamppost and yet more geraniums spilling from pots. Two years ago it had been full of dead ivy and dog shit.

At the front door of the house I collide with Giuseppina and spill the wine down my skirt. "*Scusi,*" she says, and brushes past. I swear she did it deliberately. Or am I being paranoid?

The kitchen's full of young women shouting orders at each other over copious plates of food laid out over the worktops. New blue fitments and a spiral staircase lead up to a jungle of plants extending over the banister. Ronaldo's been busy.

I find the bathroom and lock myself in. New fitments here too, an apricot-colored basin with gilt taps under a gilt-framed mirror. I stare at my reflection; white cotton blouse with a dirty sleeve and now a skirt with a wine stain down the front, not the best way to start an evening. I hold my skirt up under the cold tap and then rub it dry with one of the apricot hand towels.

Why am I ignoring the one person I've come to see? These things are supposed to get better when you got older, not worse. Someone turns the door handle. I take a last anxious look in the mirror, and then open the door. An anorexic, dark-haired woman in black lace slides into the bathroom leaving a wave of exotic perfume in her wake.

The dogs are barking, greeting new arrivals, as I head back along the cobbled passageway. Several couples are dancing to the music playing from speakers in the trees. A little wisp of a woman in a frilly pink dress teeters on high heels, her partner elegantly swinging her in circles. Silka, draped in purple like a great moth, languishes by a stone vase. She has a headband with a black ostrich feather stuck in the side, and is talking to a man the size of a barrel in a light gray suit. I know, without having to be told, that it's Rocco, the cousin with the frescoed ceilings. He looks exactly as I had imagined him.

I pass Ronaldo and his smoking barbecue without a glance, and step down to the dance floor with a racing heart. A part of me wants to get on my bike and flee into the night. But that would be giving in too soon. Now that I've got myself here, I'm determined to enjoy the evening. No matter how it turns out.

6
Dangerous Passions

It's the Grim Reaper himself sitting at the table beside me. Pallid face, dark hair sticking up in short tufts and dressed from head to toe in black. "I am depressed here," he's telling me.

"Where?" I ask. "At this party or Tuscany?"

He raises his eyebrows at me, as though I should know better than to ask such a foolish question. "All is for show here," he says. Then looks scathingly at Vittorio holding court at the top of the table; dressed in the white linen suit and black shirt he wore in Siena. He's talking to the skeletal dark-haired woman I'd passed in the bathroom. On his other side sits a plump elderly blonde fanning herself with a plastic plate. "It is important to know what is going on here."

I look at him. "What is going on? I wish you'd tell me."

"He wants to make always the show with the women. He uses them to help his business. This is what is going on. I feel sorry for the wife."

Silka, down the end of the table, ostrich feather wafting as she nods in response to something her daughter Valentina is telling her, seems unconcerned with whatever Vittorio is doing. The girls are dressed like miniature adults in white sequined tops and long black shirts. Giuseppina spoons yoghurt into Anna's unresisting mouth.

"In what way do they help his business?" I ask. But the Reaper isn't one for listening. From what I can gather, he seems to think Vittorio is involved in shady business. "He want to be like the Mafia boss," he now tells me.

I laugh for the first time this evening. "But Vittorio hates the Mafia and everything they stand for. He's told me so often enough."

"He hate them, but he think like them."

"That doesn't make him one of them."

"If you think like them, you become like them. There is always the price to pay here."

"Price? What price?"

"You pay always the price to come to his house. You pay another price to eat his dinner and you pay again the price to drink his wine. And every time the price become more high. I do not support someone who like to profit off his friends. Has he asked you for the money?"

"What money?"

"Ah-ha. There will be the money to pay for tonight."

"There wouldn't be much point," I say. "I don't have any." Then I remember the expensive lunch in Siena. Surely tonight isn't to be a repetition of that, is it? Coming to his house and paying for my dinner? If I'd known, I would have brought it with me.

"Soon we sell our house then we are escaping."

"Why do you come here if you dislike it so much?"

But the Reaper turns to the hunched, gray-haired woman in black sequins beside him and begins speaking in German.

Rocco is sitting opposite, gazing at me with eyes like two currants pressed into soggy dough. The

Mafioso henchman? I've a sudden urge to giggle. He's removed his jacket. A gold crucifix glints through the forest of chest hair bushing up under his open-necked shirt. He smiles, showing a neat little row of uneven teeth. "How are you?" he asks.

"I'm very well, thanks. How are you?"

"I am searching in many streets for your house tonight." He'd already said that earlier when Silka spotted me lingering on the edge of the dance floor and dragged me over to meet him. "I could find no person to ask where is Vicolo della Mura." He'd said that too. Is everything he's said now to be repeated? He shrugs his massive shoulders. "So, I am happy to be arriving alone tonight, like you. No - I am not."

"I'm sorry?"

"I am – er - disappointed to arrive not with you - excuse me, my English is no good."

"I wish I could speak Italian as well as you speak English."

He smiles, pleased with the compliment. "I am teaching German students to play the flute and we are speaking some English together."

The last thing Rocco looks like is a flautist but then how is a Mafioso flautist supposed to look?

"And so, I am pleased to meet with you. I think it is going to be very, how you say - pleas-a-rubel?"

"Pleasurable." I smile lamely and turn to the attractive German woman on my left; something to do with the theater, she'd said. Quite what, had been impossible to find out, because most of the time, when not in animated conversation with Silka, she's been talking on her mobile phone.

I eye the English woman in the Indian dress further along the table. "What are you on?" she'd asked me, as we'd gathered to eat.

"On?" I'd said. But there'd been no chance to pursue that question for people began scrabbling for chairs as Ronaldo appeared bearing a dish of singed steak and sausages. He served everyone in turn. There'd been no special little look or touch when he'd served my meat. Nothing to indicate there'd been anything special between us; I could have been any other guest.

I catch Giuseppina watching me. I smile but she looks abruptly away. It's all very confusing.

I push my blackened sausage round the plate. Is Ronaldo eating his burnt offering in the kitchen? Or perhaps, like me, he's lost his appetite. I reach for the bottle of red wine, but Rocco reaches it first, spilling it over my cup in his haste to fill it.

* * * *

It's eleven o'clock and everyone has finished eating. The musicians - three elderly men, one wearing a Stetson - arrive as the plastic plates are being thrown into the bins, the bones to the dogs. They've assembled themselves and their instruments, accordion, saxophone and drums, at the end of the dance floor beneath a canopy decorated with fairy lights. And from the moment the band strikes up, everyone sweeps onto the floor and begins gyrating. Prodigious bottoms and monumental hips sashay past. Sequins and tight satin trousers, shapely legs in fishnet stockings, high-heels turning together with their partner's shiny black pumps. Everyone is tangoing. The children together, Valentina with Anna, even the elderly are twisting themselves about as though they are young and supple again. Vittorio grabs the microphone and begins singing in a powerful baritone. I'd love to dance. I glance around, but Ronaldo is nowhere to be seen.

"Why you don't dance, Lorri?" Silka flutters toward me. "Rocco want to dance with you. But he is too timid to ask. He think you don't like him."

I opened my mouth to speak, but Filippo, smelling strongly of hair tonic, intervenes before I can answer. He leads me onto the dance floor and spins me round with quick bouncing steps. Then it's a white-haired man, the top of whose head hardly reaches my chin. Am I German, he asks. And when I say English, he clicks his tongue and holds me closer for some reason. Now it's one, two, three and slide with a man in a green jacket, spinning and catching me in his sweaty hands. And then Rocco, having recovered from his timidity, taking my arm before I have chance to recover, twirling and tripping me over his feet. "I am sorry, I am sorry, you are excusing me?"

"Yes, yes," I gasp.

Encouraged, he places his meaty hand on the small of my back and off we jig again, almost crashing into another couple that dodge out of our way. Eyes, noses and teeth flashing past, it's like being on a merry-go-round, spinning dangerously out of control. The music stops; I step giddily onto the safety of the grass and clutch a stone vase as if it is my last link with stability.

But Rocco looms like a monolith. "We are dancing good together, you think?"

"Yes, but no more for now, please." I move unevenly over the grass to the swimming pool. Two elderly women are sitting together with their feet in the water. I kick off my sandals and sit splashing my feet. A thousand mosaic eyes stare up at me through the floodlit green pool, flashing and blinking in the light. I glance round in the vain hope of seeing Ronaldo. But Rocco hovers. "You like to dance more?"

"No thank you. I need to rest."

"But we are only to begin."

"No, I'm tired."

Rocco laughs, as though I can't be serious, and taking my arm, tries to pull me to my feet.

I jerk my arm away. "I don't want to dance!" The women at the pool observe me curiously. I grab my sandals and get up. My head aches; it must be the wine. I clutch a deckchair for support.

"You are ill?" Rocco is frowning. He must think I'm drunk. "I accompany you to home?"

"No, no, please – I'm perfectly all right. All I want is water. Just a glass of water?"

"I take for you."

Suddenly everyone is clapping and whooping; the musician in the Stetson is leading a horse up the garden stairs and onto the dance floor. Vittorio grabs the Stetson and, placing it on his own head, mounts the horse to everyone's shouts of approval.

"You want to ride the horse?" Rocco hands me a cup of water.

"No, no," I say, and drink thirstily.

"You don't like the horses?"

"I didn't say that." I move further away.

Vittorio is handing down cards in red envelopes. "Luciana," he calls. The woman with the long silken hair steps forward to collect her card, and then sings a song at the microphone and everyone applauds while someone takes her photograph, the flashlight glinting on her teeth. Then comes Bruna, a little fat woman who tells a joke and makes everyone laugh.

"Lorri! Lorri!"

I look wildly round. Ronaldo is waving at me from the barbecue. "Lorri, *avanti! Tocca a te.*"

"My turn?" I ask, horrified that I'm being asked to sing or something equally disastrous.

"*Avanti! Avanti, Lorri!*"

I stumble forward with a smile and the camera flashes in my face. "*Per tuo compleano, cara,*" Vittorio says, as I reach up to him for my envelope. "I do not forget my good friends, eh?"

I keep smiling and stroke the horse's nose. Whether it is the stroking or not, is uncertain, but the horse chooses this moment to lift its tail and drop a pile of shit on the dance floor.

"*Allora!*" Vittorio jumps from the saddle to thunderous applause, plants the Stetson on the horse's head and begins singing a rumbustious Neapolitan song, with everyone joining in, clapping their hands in time to the music. The horse is led away by a man in a black suit as Ronaldo, holding a bucket, begins cleaning up.

"You see what is going on." The Reaper materialises. He indicates the man in the black suit. "The Albanian is the bodyguard of Vittorio."

"What does he want a bodyguard for?"

"There are those who do not support him."

"Then why do they come to his house?"

But without answering he drifts away like a shadow into the night.

* * * *

From the red envelope I draw out a card with a hand-painted rose. *'Auguri Lorri, Vittorio, Silka, Valli, Anna, Ronaldo.'* I can feel something else in the envelope. Car keys. I hold them up, looking questioningly across at Vittorio who is singing 'I Did it My Way' in English. He winks knowingly at me. I blink nervously. I know the price, 600 *euros,* he'd said, and that's what I'll pay him for the Auto-Bianchi. Not one *euro* more!

Ronaldo is discussing something in earnest at the bottom of the garden stairs with the black-suited bodyguard who waves his cigarette about in response. He doesn't seem to be doing much guarding of Vittorio's body; if anything, he seems to be avoiding it, preferring to walk under the trees, studying the ground, as if searching for some precious jewel he's lost.

"Rocco is leaving!" Silka calls to me.

Thank goodness, I think, and wave to her as I turn down the stairs. I have to speak to Ronaldo, if only to thank him for the card. Then I'll leave. But he speaks before I have a chance. "Later," he says, touching my hand as he passes. "I leave the best for last." I watch him walk away, at a loss for words.

"Rocco want to call you but I explain that you have no telephone," Silka is saying at the top of the stairs.

I climb back toward her.

"Rocco think you do not like him."

The skeletal woman has her arms round Ronaldo's neck. He's holding her in a close embrace, bending her slim body back and sideways in time to the music, while she anticipates his every step and turn.

". . . so I tell Rocco that he must call me to make an arrangement with you."

The woman's eyes are closed, her head resting on his shoulder. I feel a stab of jealousy; I can't help it. All night I've waited to be with him and here he is flaunting himself with another.

"Do you have the telephone line outside?"

Valentina is separating them now, smiling coquettishly up at Ronaldo, silly child. Then Anna is lifted up in his arms and swirled about like a doll. And then it's the woman with the long silken hair, spinning and caught in his arms while people stand back to watch.

"He is a good dancer, don't you think?" I stare blankly at Silka. "Everyone want to dance with Ronaldo." Then whooping like a teenager, she races across the floor and grabs him.

That's it! I head down the garden stairs with a lump in my throat. I seem to have forgotten how to behave normally. I'm not fit to be out in public. The sooner I leave, the better.

The bicycle is where I left it. Wobbling across the driveway and out through the gates, I pedal into the semi-darkness, trying to distinguish which shadow is what. Then the worst thing possible happens. I swerve against a tree and fly over the handlebars into a ditch.

For several minutes, I lie in shock. I hardly dare move lest I've broken something. Silence. Only the sound of the crickets. I raise myself up on my elbow. Miraculously, nothing seems to be broken. I get to my feet and lift the bicycle out of the ditch. The front wheel is slightly buckled and the lamp has fallen off, but apart from that, it's rideable. I begin pushing it along the track when I hear the sound of feet running across the earth behind me.

"Lorri! Lorri!" Ronaldo catches me in his arms. "What you do? Sherif see you go. You go always alone in the dark. I have waited all the night to speak with only you."

My heart leaps. "So have I, so have I."

"But when I look at you, you no look at me."

"But when I looked at you, you looked away. I thought you didn't want to see me."

He holds me close. "We are like the children. No I am the stupid boy, *insicuro*. You are the very true woman."

"I'm just as insecure, believe me. You can't imagine how."

He wheels the bicycle with one hand, the other, holding me against him. My legs are shaking so much I can hardly walk the distance back to the house. And the black-suited man called Sherif watches Ronaldo drop the bicycle and dance with me in the driveway. Sees my body sway with his in time to the music, sees how we cling ever closer, his hands on my hips, my back, fondling my hair; how I seem to lose control of my senses and he might understand that there is nothing in the world I can do about it, for I have never wanted anyone so much.

* * * *

Later, much later, I look at the man lying beside
me. His lean, tanned body is even more beautiful than
I had imagined. And I keep on looking until the stars
disappear into the dawn sky.

I dress quietly so as not to wake him and let
myself out of the house. It is still warm at six a.m. The
birdsong is so loud I can hardly hear the sound my
feet make stepping over mounds of earth and dry
sticks. I walk down through the trees to where
Ronaldo has left the bike on the edge of the driveway.

At this hour, no one will see me; no awkward
questions to answer as to where I've spent the night. I
need time to reflect, to hold myself together. But
when I arrive at the place where the bike should be, it
isn't there. I look about in dismay. Then spot it.
Someone has propped it against the gates.

As I run across the driveway, I'm convinced
there's someone watching from the edge of the forest.
Later I am to learn that Giuseppina, the maid, who is
infatuated with Ronaldo, followed me at a safe
distance and sat all night grieving outside his front
door.

7
First Day of School

Saturday afternoon. Expect us around four, the B&Bs had said in their letter. It's now five-thirty. They're probably lost, wandering about the back streets somewhere, unable to find '*La Casetta*' down the alleyway. In which case, they've probably given up and gone to the *Santarota* Hotel. But I do at least have their fifty pounds deposited safely in my bank in England.

A phone is now crucial. I went to the bar on Thursday to ring Vittorio and ask for his help. Silka answered. "My neighbors tell me it could take months to get a phone installed," I'd said. "Is that true?" And then my main motive for ringing: how is Ronaldo? Which I didn't ask.

Vittorio would send Patrizio to install the telephone, Silka assured me. How to pay him is another matter - the insurance cheque still hasn't arrived. There's the B&B money, only that's to live on. And then there's the Auto Bianchi to pay for. I thought of ringing back to explain that as I can't pay for the car until the cheque arrives, perhaps I should call round to return the keys. But the last thing I want to give is the impression that I can't wait to go to the house, even though it's true.

I can imagine what Vittorio would say if he knew I'd slept with his protégé. I was messing up the wedding plans with Giuseppina. I should have had more intelligence. But he should know, if anyone, intelligence plays no part when the blood is on fire. "I say to Vittorio only the things I want what he know," Ronaldo had said. Nevertheless, doubts linger. What with Silka trying to pair me off with the grisly Rocco, and Ornelia, my downstairs neighbor, suggesting Domenico the builder as a suitable companion, I'm beginning to feel like a pawn on a chessboard, uncertain of where I'll be moved next.

That Saturday night, a week ago, it's been on my mind ever since. His flat where the bed had taken up most of the space in the bedroom, which served also as a sitting-room with a wardrobe, a fake leather sofa, the shower and toilet screened off from the kitchen with a flowered curtain and a small dirty window overlooking the courtyard. Every detail is stamped indelibly on my memory.

I'd lain on the bed, half covered with a sheet, and he had stepped across the room still wet from the shower and stretched himself on top of me. I'd gasped at the hardness of his body.

After, I'd sat at the window, looking out at the stars. The insistent thrumming of the crickets, the distant humming of the generator in the vineyards, the vibration sounds had closed us off, created our own separate reality. "Don't think too much," he'd said, turning over in bed.

I closed the shutters. When it rose, the sun would toast his body. It was not so much thinking as adjusting, I'd liked to have said, but couldn't find the words in Italian. It would have to wait until I'd studied the dictionary . . .

"*Signora Inglese . . .* "

I'm jolted back into the present at the sound of Martino's voice in the street below. I look out of the *salotto* window. He's leading a flushed-face English couple round into the alleyway. "Hello, you poor hot sweaty Brits," I call. They look up, relief on their faces. Martino waves. "*Signora!*"

"I suggest you call it the Hideaway instead of the *Casetta*," the man says, waving a brochure at me as I open the door. "We'd never have found it, if it hadn't been for this man." He indicates Martino. Martino beams. "I'm Bob Cooper, by the way. And this is Sharon."

I say hi to Sharon and *grazie* to Martino who, with his foot in the doorway, shows no sign of leaving.

"You're fluent in the lingo, then?" Bob says, following me up the hall stairs.

"I've only said one word, so far." I laugh, trying to hide the anxiety I feel at welcoming my first guests, praying they will like it, not think the place too small and demand their deposit back. Floor tiles polished, flowers in vases, jug of wine in the bedroom on a tray set with two glasses. They *have* to like it!

Billy hisses from the window as we walk into the kitchen. Martino waves at him, which makes the cat even angrier. "He's not as fierce as he seems," I apologize. Not true. Billy, if he doesn't like someone, has a nasty habit of sinking his teeth into their Achilles tendon. But Sharon is up the kitchen stairs before I can stop her. "I wouldn't do that - " Billy, with tail thrashing, darts out onto the roof. Sharon, dauntless, climbs on. And Bob joins her to gaze out at the chapel bell and the three cypresses. "Oh, look. Isn't it lovely?"

"*Complimenti,*" says Martino. "*Sinceramente, è la prima volta mi capita di vedere una casetta cosi carina.*"

"What's he on about?" Bob asks from the stairs.

"He says it's the first time he's seen such a pretty place. Now, what can I offer you?" I open the fridge; my hand shakes as I pull out the ice-tray. "Wine, fruit juice, water?"

"I'd kill for a gin and tonic with plenty of ice and lemon," Sharon says, descending the wooden stairs in perilously high-heels.

Fortunately, I'd bought lemons and tonics that morning from Martino. The bottle of Gordon's Gin had been a present from Lionello and had stood unopened in the cupboard for two years.

Bob wants water with ice and lemon. And Martino, hopefully, will say no and return to his shop. But not at all, it's *vino bianco,* and *grazie, signora, grazie tanto.*

"So, where do you live then?" asks Bob.

"Me?" I drop ice into the glass and pour wine into another at the same time. "I er . . . I live downstairs, actually." How fortunate Martino doesn't understand English.

"You own the whole house, do you?"

"Ye-es. Now, that room . . . " I indicate the closed *salotto* door, eager to take Bob's mind off who owns what and where, ". . . is my study, which I keep permanently locked. I, er - do an awful lot of writing in there."

"I thought you might be something artistic," Sharon says and giggles. "I couldn't have another G&T, could I?"

"Of course." I splash gin into her empty glass.

"I'll bring the cases up," calls Bob from the stairs. "I take it the car's all right outside the grocer's shop, is it?"

"*La macchina sta bene,* Martino?"

"*Si, si, si, si, signora. Non c'e un problema.*"

Martino, who's been sipping his wine in the kitchen doorway, refusing to venture further into the room, and nodding in agreement with everything said, hands me his empty glass with a little bow and escorts Bob down the stairs and along the alleyway, talking loudly, hoping, no doubt, to attract the attention of curious neighbors, like Rosalba, who, certainly by now, would be fixed to her window.

"I'm dying to ask," more giggling from Sharon, "what made you come and live here?"

"That's a long story."

"Are you writing a book about it?"

"Sort of." I direct Sharon up to the bathroom.

"Surely nobody eats that fly-blown fruit outside Martino's shop, do they?" Bob was saying, carrying two suitcases up the stairs and into the bedroom.

"Sometimes, yes. He does have fresh fruit but you've got to dig under the rotten stuff to find it."

Bob chortles. "Where do you suggest we eat tonight? Is there somewhere near here?"

"*La Torretta.* It's reasonably priced and the food is delicious. It's within walking distance. You go up to the *piazza*, then start to go down the hill, past the park area, on the left, set off the road - "

"Why not join us for dinner? Then you can show us the way."

* * * *

The white-jacketed figure sitting at the table with the roses and champagne watches the door with anticipation. I see him clearly in my imagination as we enter. I try to shut the painful image out. But there Richard is, all the time, watching, watching.

Mauro passes with heaped dishes of pasta and thin slices of meat, mushrooms, fresh tomatoes and *basilico*.

"I take it you know what to order."

"The menu of the house, Bill, which means you eat what's put in front of you. You're not obliged to eat it all. But you can if you wish."

"Sounds good to me."

Except no one seems to want to take our order. Mauro, the waiter, is avoiding eye contact. He vanishes into the kitchen when not serving the people at the three occupied tables. Perhaps he knows Richard and I have separated and feels embarrassed.

"I'm starving," says Sharon, eyeing a bald young man stuffing himself with the *antipasto,* pieces of toast dripping with mushrooms in olive oil and garlic.

"Could we order some wine, at least?" Bob is on the point of getting to his feet.

"I'll go and get someone." I'm about to stand when Margherita, the owner, comes to the table. *"Buonosera,"* she says. She's as glamorous as ever in a white sequined T-shirt, her hair the color of polished copper. She looks quizzically at me. *"Come stai?"*

"Bene. Grazie." I want to say more – explain the situation to her, but I don't yet know how.

"Che desiderate?"

"The menu *della casa.*"

"Rimarrai per molto tempo in Italia?"

"Si. I'm here for ever." I'm forgetting my Italian. *"Questa è la mia casa adesso."* I want to say Italy is my home now. I hope I've said it correctly.

Eduardo, elegant as ever in his crumpled linen slacks and silk shirt, brings red wine to the table. He seems friendly enough. But I feel a distance. As a couple, Richard and I were part of things here. Now I'm here alone, they're puzzled: I can see it in their eyes.

"He's a bit of all right, isn't he?" Sharon whispers to me as Eduardo heads for the kitchen. I smile vaguely. Yes, they're keeping their distance. Richard must have said something. I glance across at the table near the door. He's still there, the white-jacketed figure, shaking his head at me now.

"Ma, sempre da sola?" Margherita is back with the food.

"Sola, si –" Alone, yes, but who knows what tomorrow may bring? I wanted to add, but again, I'm not sure how to.

There's something else I'm not sure about, either, as we work our way through the *pasta con pomodoro:* how long am I going to have to wait out in the street before the Coopers go to bed? And what will I say if they catch me creeping up to my bed in the *salotto?* I'll have to say I've forgotten something and then go out again. All night could pass going in and out of the house with memory problems. It's bordering on insanity!

Later:

It's worked! I'm under the desk in the salotto writing this and Billy and Gertie are looking at me from the sofa wondering what we're doing locked up in this stifling little room. The Coopers are going to Florence tomorrow morning. They'll return around 6, they said, which means I can clean up, shower and have a rest. And when they go out for dinner, I'll grab a meal and crawl back under the desk before they return.

* * * *

It's Monday, 1st July. The first morning of the *Università* school term has finished and I'm having lunch with Gerry Croft, the only other English woman in the class, who lives with her estate agent brother in Umbria.

We're seated at a crowded table in the *Grattacielo* (skyscraper), the oldest *trattoria* in Siena and with the lowest ceiling. The fresh tuna, green tomatoes, potato salad made with garlic and olive oil and half a carafe of house red costs hardly anything. I shall eat here every day.

The insurance cheque still hasn't arrived, but the hundred pounds the Coopers gave me for two nights will be eked out until the Barkers arrive on Saturday for their two nights' stay, and then Elizabeth Barnet from Plymouth on Tuesday for a whole week. As for the sleeping downstairs story, it's unlikely that I can keep that going. I'll have to come clean and admit to sleeping in my "study" as it is now to be called. The important thing is to keep the door securely locked at all times so no one can see the confusion of clothes, bedding, furniture and a cat-litter tray.

"Do you think you can forget how to make love?" Gerry is asking.

We're getting on well – just what I need, someone to share a laugh with. "No, not really," I say. "It's like riding a bicycle, it always comes back."

The people at the table beside me get up to leave and two others jostle into their place

"I haven't made love for four years."

"*What?* That's terrible." Who am I kidding? Neither had I for a year until that Saturday night, and now that's beginning to feel like a year. I can't understand why he hasn't contacted me. I suppose it was just one of those things – bewildering.

An elderly man in a beret is telling a story and making everyone laugh at the food counter.

"I don't know what it is about me - " Gerry tops her wine up with water. "I get so far with a man and then no further. They just don't seem interested when it comes to going to bed."

I could have told her why: she has a set of jacket crowns that sit *on* the gums instead of *in* them. We have become rather too close too quickly, due to loneliness and the fact that no one else speaks English. There were ten students in the class this morning, two strapping Hungarian girls, a Japanese couple and four German youths who seemed to think they could speak Italian already. *Professore* Rudolfo, who looks around forty, has piercing blue eyes and a ginger mustache and doesn't look in the least Italian.

He began by asking each student his or her name in Italian. For some reason, he seemed to enjoy making us fumble for the words. "*Questo è il miglior modo per imparare la lingua,*" he said. It might be the best way to learn the language, but baffling if you only understand a little Italian.

He asked each student in turn to explain why he or she had come to Italy to learn Italian, to be answered, of course, in Italian. When I'd struggled to say, with the help of a pocket dictionary, "*vorrei perdere me stessa in Inghilterra a trovarmi in Italia,*" Rudolfo had moved me to the front of the class next to Gerry. "I want to lose myself in England and find myself in Italy? That's pretty good for a beginner," she'd said. "I think you've impressed him."

"I only wish I knew what it is about me that puts men off," she's still saying, between bites of tomato roll.

The teeth are definitely something to do with it, I'm thinking. It was the first thing I'd noticed about her when she smiled. Apart from that, she's attractive, tall, athletic, long legs, and looks good in shorts.

"But from what you tell me, you seem to be having a whale of a time dancing and canoodling the night away with this Ronaldo. Have you been to bed with him yet?"

I swallow wine; that part of the story is not for sharing. "I'm not sure if I'm going to see him again," I say, riding over the question. "He hasn't contacted me for a week."

"Well, without a phone, how can he? You must ring him."

"No, I can't do that."

"Why not?"

"Fear of rejection, I suppose." I lean forward as someone passes behind me. "Although, I did ring the other day and spoke to Vittorio's wife, and reminded her that I was in school every morning. Maybe she'll tell him."

"Tell him yourself."

"I can't."

"Why?"

"He never answers the phone. And whoever does answer will think there's something going on between us."

"Well, there is."

"I know, but – "

"Does it matter?"

"Yes, it does at the moment. It's been so long since I played the courting game, I feel out of my depth in it all."

"You're in Italy, aren't you? Jump in! I would, given half a chance."

"It's what happened this morning that bothers me. Sherif, the gardener, and who is laughingly known as Vittorio's bodyguard, was on the bus."

"Bodyguard! I don't believe it. It's priceless."

"He came in to Siena."

"So?" Gerry forked potato salad into her mouth some of which fell onto her bare thigh.

"I wonder why he took the bus from Sinalunga when he could have taken it from Rapolano which is on the way to Siena."

"Perhaps he's following you."

"Why should he want to do that?"

"Don't ask me. You're the one in the plot."

"He sat three seats behind me and held his newspaper up as though he hadn't seen me, which is ridiculous when he obviously had. And when I got off the bus in San Domenico, he was there. When I stopped, so did he, pretending to look in a shop window."

"Oh, he's definitely shadowing you. How thrilling! You should have asked him what he wanted. There's nothing like a direct question, it floors them. What's he look like, this bodyguard-cum-gardener?"

"Good looking in a sallow kind of way. But he gives me the creeps, I'd rather have nothing to do with him."

"This Vittorio guy, you say he's given you a car?"

"Only the keys so far."

"Be careful."

"What of?"

"If he is something to do with the Mafia, from what I've read, you may have to pay a high price for it."

"I know exactly the price I'm paying, we discussed it over lunch. And anyway, he's nothing to do with the Mafia."

"You said he was."

"I said a guest at the party said he was. But he's mistaken."

"You can't always be sure in Italy. I bet he's dark, tanned and wears shades."

"Well, yes, he does, actually."

Gerry hoots with laughter. "I can just imagine it. And I bet his wife's tall, blonde and bony."

"Yes, she is."

"Typical."

"What's Vittorio's hold on Ronaldo?"

"Work, I imagine. And gratitude for being given a home."

"Like a stray dog, you mean?"

I laugh - I can't help it. I've been bottling my feelings up for a week. It's a relief to share it all with someone else – English especially.

"Intrigue as well as romance. How lucky can you get?"

8
The Concert at Rocco's

Gerry has gone off to meet a friend after school today and the thought of going to eat tuna salad alone at the *Grattacielo,* sharing a table with others who are part of a happy couple, doesn't appeal.

The students come streaming down the wide marble staircase from all the classrooms, in pairs, in groups, boys and girls laughing, calling to each other, swinging along on long bronzed legs, secure in their youth and boundless energy. I follow wearily along behind, and though I'm loath to admit it, I feel old in the midst of all this surrounding exuberance.

Vittorio was right. I pause in the *piazza* outside the school wondering what to do. It's impossible to learn a language in a month. But if I make enough money with letting my bedroom and bathroom, I might be able to enrol for six months.

I don't want to go back to Sinalunga immediately, to sleep or to walk around the narrow streets as I've done nearly every afternoon. Memories are stuck to the walls there, seeped into the very bricks, springing out of the buildings at me. There isn't an alleyway or turning that doesn't have Richard's phantom. Yesterday, I imagined him accompanying me up the hill from the station wearing the funny straw hat he used to wear and carrying two terracotta pots he'd bought in the market. It's as if he's died and left his ghost behind to haunt me.

The midday sun beats down on my head. The small church across the *piazza* seems the best option; it would offer a refuge against the heat and blinding light. I push open the heavy oak door and step into the incense-laden gloom.

The church is empty. I slip into the back pew. I can't remember when I've last been inside a church. I never like attending services, people kneeling and praying and trying to out sing their neighbor. Clusters of white candles flicker on tall wrought iron stands along the aisle. A painting of Santa Caterina, the patron saint of Siena, gazes down at me from the near wall. San Domenico, San Martino, La Madonna delle Grazie and further along, a painting of the Christ being taken down from the cross: then two formidable marble statues of angels with drawn swords on either side of it. White lilies decorate the altar, above which hangs an immense golden crown against a backcloth of cobalt blue.

I breathe in the musky air and listen to the sound of my breathing, deeply in – deeply out. If my mother had been alive, she might have said that everything will work out for me in the end.

There again, she might have said how can I sleep with a man whose name I don't know. I smother a laugh. I know his first name – Ronaldo. That will have to do for now.

I stare up at the high window with the blue and red stained glass. And then, as I've nearly always done on the few occasions I've been to church, I close my eyes and still my thoughts. "Hold me," I whisper, to whom I'm not sure.

I open my eyes and look at the altar. To the far right of it, I gradually become aware of - a shape. I'm hallucinating! Lionello said I would if I drank too much of Martino's special Tuscan wine. As my eyes focus I can make out a woman's head, bowed, draped in a veil. But of course it's a statue of the Madonna. Such statues are everywhere. I saw one in the university this morning in a niche above the stairs. "Let everything come right," I say. I don't need to be a Catholic to need a mother. I light a candle on the way out; it feels like the right thing to do.

"Hi! Are you Lorri?"

I look round, startled. "Yes. Why?"

A girl comes striding across the *piazza* toward me, wearing shorts and tossing a blonde ponytail. "I've been trying to find you. I'm a student in the advanced class. A man gave me this; he said it was very important that I give it to you." She hands me a paper Japanese fan. On the back is written:

'Lorri, I wait but you do not arrive. Ronaldo.'

My heart skipped. "How did you –?"

"Know it was you? He described you – English with blue eyes, *occhi azzuri* he kept repeating. "

"Where is he?"

"Outside the main entrance to the university. But I don't know if he's still there . . ."

"You can't imagine what this means to me."

I tear round the block to the main entrance and look into the reception hall: plenty of people milling about, but he's not one of them. I hurry back along the streets, searching the faces that pass in front of me. But there's no sign of him.

On the way home on the bus, I open the paper fan. It has a picture of a Geisha girl offering a cup of tea. *'Lorri, I wait but you do not arrive. Ronaldo.'* I touch the letters: it's almost like touching him.

* * * *

Friday morning. Journal Update:

The Insurance cheque's arrived! £2,500 and £50 from the Coopers, a £50 deposit from the Barkers paid into my English bank, and another £50 cheque from Mrs E Barnet who's driving all the way from Plymouth. In spite of a water shortage and not being able to shower, things are definitely on the up.

I rang Vittorio this afternoon and he asked me if I'd gone to Africa as he hadn't seen me for so long. Then he said he's got my car and I must sign the insurance papers. When I said I could pay him immediately he changed the subject to my telephone saying how he's sending Patrizi to install the phone on Monday and could I make a point of being in. He's forgotten I'm in Siena every morning. I reminded him that I had the money for the car, but he pretended not to hear. Is it that he doesn't want to take the money because then I'll owe him a favor? A good old Mafia trick, I can hear Gerry Croft, my English friend from Siena saying.

Tomorrow, I'm going to a flute recital at Rocco's house and Vittorio's going to sing 'Nessun Dorma.' Can't miss that! I nearly asked him to thank Ronaldo for the fan, but thought better of it. I can thank him myself. Knowing he wants to see me is all that matters. I'm counting the hours and minutes.

I'm in the right place. The architecture, the warmth and light, the russet and ochre-colored bricks that absorb and give out the light. How different from the depressing gray and white boxes I've left behind in Devon. Those frightening, windswept days seem a long way behind me now, standing on the deserted beach watching the gray, turbulent sea, wondering if I walked into it, would it matter? Then trudging back up the beach, realizing I had two cats to feed, that it was them that kept me going. It's like looking through a glass at a dark and watery nightmare that shatters into a million fragments with the light.

* * * *

Rocco's house is in Asciano, a small town on the outskirts of Siena. Threatening rolls of thunder accompanied me on the bus, and now at six o'clock the sky is covered with a lid of cloud. After ten minutes of waiting at the bus stop I'm beginning to think Silka has forgotten me. Then I see the silver Fiat Punto coming and wave. I climb into the back beside Giuseppina with Anna, Silka's youngest daughter, asleep on her lap.

"*Che profumo.*" Valentina, in a red mini skirt, swivels round in the front seat to look at me. "*Come si chiama?*"

"*Niente di speciale,*" I reply, determined not to tell her the name in case her mother buys it for her then we'll both be wearing the same perfume. I slew my eyes sideways at Giuseppina who is fussing with Anna; half awake now, and dressed up like a pink doll. "*Guarda,* Anna," she says, pointing at the streaks of rain on the window. Silka, puffing nervously at a cigarette as she drives, seems edgy and uncommunicative.

"There's going to be storm, by the looks of it," I say, as a way of making conversation.

"Yes, there will be a storm," Silka says grimly, as though speaking to herself. Her fine blonde hair is swept off her face in a black chiffon bow. She would look beautiful except her ears stick out.

"Ronaldo's coming, is he?" I try to disguise the concern I feel at the prospect of him not coming. Especially as I'm wearing my turquoise silk suit, brushed and ironed especially for the occasion.

Silka clicks her tongue irritably. "Of course he come. He will drive the car because Vittorio want to drink much. He is going to sing *Nessun Dorma*. You think something will stop him to sing? He will kill who try to stop him." She slams her foot on the brake at the lights and we all jerk forward. "He come in the Lancia, it is not possible to stop him. It is so stupid that we bring two cars. And your car has been at the house for a week. Why you don't telephone us? You must come to take the car. And you must bring a copy of your *Permesso di Soggiorno* and your English driving licence."

I give a nervous cough. "Well - yes, I'd like to collect the car. I've got the money now to pay for it."

Silka pulls sharply away at the green light, just missing a pedestrian. I'm not sure whether she heard me. "I'm ready to sign the papers and pick up the car whenever it's convenient."

I'm uncertain this time if Silka has understood. Anna, now fully awake, is howling, her dark lashes wet with tears. Giuseppina, in a short pleated skirt, jigs her up and down. She has long dark hairs on her legs. The sight makes me shudder. Is she like that all over?

Rocco lives in a villa much like others in the street, painted antique-rose with heavy oak doors and ring-shaped brass handles. His door is ajar. The name

Miullo is engraved on a brass plaque to the right of the wall, plaster flaking off in places. I follow Silka and Valentina across the black and white tiled floor to where a group of people gather at the foot of an impressive marble staircase. To my surprise, Silka flings her arms round a woman in a purple sari and begins weeping. Then she rushes up the stairs with Valentina, followed by Giuseppina carrying a still wailing Anna.

"*Ciao*, I'm Lisa," the woman in the sari says. "We met briefly at Vittorio's party. You're Lorri who's looking for a new life, aren't you?" She gives a disconcerting snort of laughter. "In Sinalunga's Centro Storico, isn't it? Christ, you wouldn't get me living down those creepy little alleyways. You never know who might be lying in wait. I couldn't handle it."

"I'm just about handling it. Where do you live?"

"In the Rapolano woods and that's creepy enough, you can't see anything for trees. We'd like to be nearer Siena but can't afford it. You're lucky to own your place."

"Yes, I suppose I am."

"How's it going, the new life?"

"All right, so far."

"You look better than you did the night of the party. I thought you were on something. You looked wild-eyed."

I give a laugh. "I don't know about wild. Perplexed, more like. What's the matter with Silka?"

"Don't you know? You must be the only one who doesn't. Vittorio raped her last night, poor love."

"*Raped* her?"

"She's not giving him his oats, poor thing. She's rung everyone to get their support, bless her. But it'll blow over, it usually does."

"You mean, he often rapes her?"

"Wouldn't be surprised, knowing him." Lisa's mauve eyelids match her sari and her silver hoop earrings are large enough to swing a budgerigar. She begins furtively rolling a cigarette. "I've got to have a quick ciggy before it starts," she says in a rasping voice. "We can't smoke up there."

"Up there" is the *salone* where the concert is due to start in ten minutes, and where chattering groups of Italians are now heading.

Someone is playing a Chopin prelude at the grand piano as I enter the spacious cream-colored room. A dusty chandelier hangs from the center of a high frescoed and plaster-medallion ceiling. Antique mirrors in heavy gilt frames hang on the walls along with various portraits of a stern looking woman in evening dress: Rocco's mother?

At the far end of the room is a stone fireplace resembling a sepulchre in front of which people are standing, talking and half-listening to the pianist, an elderly man with a drooping mustache, his half-empty glass of red wine on top of the piano. He seems a little drunk; Chopin slurring, the notes running into one another. Giuseppina stands awkwardly by the piano, watching him. Then she looks up suddenly, sees me and scowls. A sudden draft stirs the lace curtains at the open window behind her, sending a row of greeting cards on the sideboard fluttering like dead birds to the floor.

"You are arriving at last." Rocco, in a cream crumpled suit that appears a size too large for him, presses my hand to his moist pink mouth. "I will play for you tonight with much emotions."

"Oh. Thank you," I say, and withdraw my hand.

"*Il Gambero Rosso*, you know him?"

"Er – no. Is he the composer?"

"No, he is the restaurant for the fish." Rocco gives a shout of laughter. "He bring the fish for tonight. You are very funny."

"Oh, I see," I say, and turn to the door to hide my embarrassment. I must have known Vittorio would be entering the room at this precise moment: he's followed by Ronaldo with the bodyguard in his formidable black suit.

"Tonight we will have the storm, no? How you say *il tuono* in English?"

"Tuna?"

"No, that is the tuna fish. This is going bang in the sky." Rocco claps his hands in my ear and makes me jump.

I catch Ronaldo's eye as the three men approach. Vittorio, a white leather coat draped casually over his jacket, greets people en route, then comes swaggering across to Rocco and clasps his hands. Ronaldo in a light blue suit, probably Vittorio's, touches my hand with his fingers, sending a shockwave of pleasure surging through me.

A decrepit old woman in a striped overall is lining up the chairs around the piano with the help of Valentina, while Anna drags them off to the other side of the room where people are sitting on moth-eaten looking sofas. Valentina tugs a chair from the hands of her sister, who screams so piercingly that the Grim Reaper, standing nearby, jumps round in alarm, probably thinking he's trodden on her. Vittorio intervenes and leads Anna over to where Giuseppina is in furtive conversation with an elderly priest.

"How you stay?"

"I stay well." I can smell Ronaldo's cologne. I inch closer. "And you?"

"I stay always good."

"Oh."

"And now?" He looks at me expectantly.

"The fan – of course. Thank you for the fan."

"*Cosa?*"

"The paper fan you left for me in Siena."

"*Il ventaglio.* I buy in the *Cinese* shop. It is nothing."

"Not for me it wasn't – nothing I mean."

He frowns. "I wait for you."

"I know. But you went to the wrong entrance."

"I not know this." He looks into my eyes. I look back, heat rising at my throat; the room and everything in it could collapse around us, I'll still be looking at him.

"It is 'ot 'ere." He loosens his tie. "I go."

"Where?"

"For to smoke."

"Will you come back?"

"Of course."

I watch him walk to the door. Mustn't pin my hopes on him. I know. But I can't help doing so right now.

Silka sits in the front row of chairs with the children, the priest, Giuseppina and Lisa, the sari-clad lady, with the Reaper. The exotic dark-haired woman, I recognize from Vittorio's party, and her elderly blonde friend in dark glasses, are helping to fill up the second row. People are arriving all the time; soon there will be no chairs available. I sit in the third row and place my hand on the adjacent chair, turning anxiously to the door. Should I go and look for him? Then he returns, rounding the door, accompanied by a roll of thunder. Vittorio makes a joke about the drummer arriving and everyone laughs.

The noise level is rising as Ronaldo takes his seat beside me. To my irritation, so does the bodyguard, on his other side. "You know Sherif?" Ronaldo says. "He want to learn the English."

I smile distantly at Sherif. Why couldn't he sit in the front row where there's still a vacant chair and where he could make sure no one bumps Vittorio off? Which, by the way Silka is glaring at him, she may do herself before he's managed to sing one note of *Nessun Dorma*.

"*Signori e Signore.*"

The chattering dies down as Vittorio takes the microphone and introduces Carlo the pianist and Rocco the flautist. The mustached pianist bows low, Rocco inclines his head, huge legs apart, flute in hand, frowning at the music sheet on the stand before him. Vittorio clears his throat in preparation and then instead of singing begins a lively discussion with the pianist.

"What's going on?" I mumble to Ronaldo, although, as far as I'm concerned, the only thing going on which matters is I'm sitting close to him, feeling his knee pressed against mine, which is enough in itself, with or without a concert.

"Vittorio want to sing, but Carlo say Rocco must to begin."

Everyone is talking at once and a woman further along the third row in a black sombrero stands up. "*Allora!*" she shouts. "*Allora!*"

Then the thunder claps and the rain starts. The old woman lurches forward on sparrow legs to close the windows as the pianist begins stumbling through the opening bars of something familiar. People are still chattering when Vittorio booms *silenzio* through the microphone and now Silka stands up and flaps her hands and says, "Sshhhh!"

Only when Rocco begins to play a passage from the Magic Flute does the room become still, the people listening with delight to the trilling sounds soaring like a flock of birds up and around the frescoed ceiling. "*Sente,*" says someone; "*Che meraviglia,*" says another. And I listen too, in awe, amazed by Rocco's sudden authority, his fat fingers moving like agile sausages along the delicate instrument.

Music almost too painfully familiar: I am back in the blue Volvo, a tape of *The Magic Flute* playing as Richard drove us over the Somerset hills in the spring sunshine. It's those fleeting moments of intense happiness I yearn for that have been somehow lost along the way.

Ronaldo is staring ahead, hair curling onto his jacket collar, nose slightly crooked, a frown line etched between his eyebrows. Would there be any magical moments with him? He must know I'm looking at him, for he presses his leg closer to mine sending another thrill rushing through me.

These are the magical moments, if perhaps, somewhat unnerving ones. For when I am with him I no longer feel myself. Who I am is uncertain: someone with no will of her own, it seems. Someone who might say yes to almost anything he asks.

The music stops. Then comes thunderous applause and shouts of *bravo* and *bis, bis,* to which the pianist gives another low bow and Rocco wipes his sweating face with a voluminous handkerchief. Music sheets are shuffled about and another heated discussion is taking place between the pianist and Vittorio, which results in Vittorio announcing that due to the lateness of the hour he will sing *Nessun Dorma* after dinner. This sets off a chorus of more *bravos* as everyone scrambles to their feet.

The dining room is painted yellow with another dusty chandelier hanging from a frescoed ceiling of vine leaves twining around a sculptured-stuccoed framework. A long banquet table draped in white linen, laden with plates and glasses, candelabra and jugs of wine leads down the center of the room. Vittorio is seated at the head of the table, Rocco to his right, the priest to his left, Silka, Giuseppina and the children next to him.

People are shuffling chairs about, shouting, laughing, and deciding whom they wish to sit next to. "You remember me? My name is Heinrich Von – "

"Yes, I do . . . " I move hastily away; I don't want to be stuck with the Reaper again. A man with a bald head brown as a walnut pulls out a chair for me. I thank him and sit. Rocco at the top of the table smiles at me. Silka waves. I wave back: I would like to congratulate Rocco on his playing, but that will have to wait. I put my bag on the vacant chair beside me and glance over my shoulder. Ronaldo is talking to Sherif at the door. I take a bite of the slice of toast dripping in olive oil that the old woman in the overall placed before me on a large white plate. I finger the tablecloth, wondering if she washes and starches the linen every day. The baldheaded man says something to me in rapid Italian: I don't understand a word, but nod as though I have. The oil drips down my chin. He hands me a starched linen napkin.

"I need the bathroom," I mouth, getting to my feet, and then hurrying over to Ronaldo, who is approaching the table now with Sherif, and several other people who have entered the room.

The old priest, I notice, observes me through heavy-lidded eyes. This *straniera* is trouble, I expect he's thinking. And when later, after the *noci con sugo* was served, and the lights had gone out after another clap of thunder and the candles lit, I'm certain he noted with a sardonic smile, that we were no longer in the room.

9
An Unwelcome Guest

We are in Vittorio's Lancia heading for Sinalunga. It's still raining and thunder is rumbling on the horizon. Ronaldo has told Sherif to tell Vittorio that I'm not feeling well and he's escorting me home. It's partly true, for with the excitement of being with Ronaldo I sipped nervously at my wine, ate nothing and now have indigestion. I understood little of the animated conversation around me at the dining table and even when Lisa in the sari called out something to me in English I'd been unable to understand much of that either.

Ronaldo lights a cigarette. The windshield wipers click-swoosh back and forth, the rain pattering on the car roof like dancing feet. White lights coming at us, red lights vanishing into the night: I snuggle to his shoulder as we rush on into the raining dark.

He presses his hand on my thigh. I say nothing. And when he pulls into a lay-by and looks intently at me, I still say nothing. Better not to speak, to break the spell of whatever extraordinary thing it is that's happening between us. He kisses me. I sit in the car trembling as he pulls out of the lay-by. I never imagined desire could be so overwhelming.

The rain has stopped as we we reach Sinalunga. But the air feels hot and clammy. We drive down Ciro Pinsuti and he parks the Lancia next to Martino's shop. I climb out and run ahead up the street stairs to make sure no one is watching. Then round Ornelia's geraniums we go, and into the alleyway. When I open my front door and step inside, he presses me against the wall and holds me close.

"I look at no other woman now. I see only you."

"And I see only you."

"You are sure?"

"Yes, I am sure."

By three a.m. we lie exhausted on the bed, shutters open to the night. I know that if I move, even a fraction, we will start all over again and I will still want him as much as he seems to want me.

* * * *

Looking back, I'm not sure what it was that woke me. The rain perhaps, it had started again, tapping softly against the windows. The luminous dial of my watch showed five a.m. He lay on his side with his eyes closed - twin dark hollows. I smoothed his hair off his face, long and tangled, so different from Richard's, short and neatly brushed. How many times had he caressed me in the night, touched me in his own special way? I traced the line between his eyebrows; he seemed to be frowning even in his sleep. "Vittorio will know we are together," he'd said and sat up in bed and lit a cigarette.

"How will he know?"

"I 'ave the Lancia. But if 'e no like, I come to live with you. What you say?"

I'd gasped at the thought. But knew it was impossible. How could I run my business with him here? The Barkers were arriving that very afternoon, the Plymouth woman on Monday. How could I hope for such a possibility?

"My place is too small," I said. "I have to run a bed and breakfast business here. We couldn't both sleep under the desk."

"Your 'ouse is leetle, I know, but in Toscana there is many big 'ouses. We find another."

"Where?"

He shrugged. "For now I no know. But one day I find the 'ouse. Vittorio want that I marry with Giuseppina and 'e give me the 'ouse. But I no marry with no woman for the 'ouse."

"Do you want to marry Giuseppina?"

"No. I prefer no 'ouse. My father is dead, 'is 'ouse go to my sister. I no cry when I go in the *funerale*, I turn back with the priests to live and to study with them."

He'd gone on to speak of his mother, but in Italian, infuriatingly, all the things I longed to know, to try and understand about this strange new man in my life.

He stirred in his sleep and turned around. I lay close to his back; the soft tapping of the rain on the window was disturbing; it reminded me of the painful things I was trying to forget. The tearful goodbye, Richard's words, I'll always love you, we'll find each other again. But when I drove away I'd known it was for good. I'd felt a sense of relief as I sped along the motorway. In spite of the loss, a part of me had wanted to be free, wanted to find a new life.

A small sound caught my attention. I tensed and listened. Where had it come from? The cats, trying to get out on the roof? I'd closed the shutters before coming to bed. I got up, wrapped my dressing gown around me, and quietly let myself out of the bedroom. Both cats looked at me from their kitchen stairs. They began purring. I embraced them. Then, opening the shutters, I watched them slope across the roof and look tentatively in at the bedroom window, curious to see more of the new man sleeping there.

I too climbed out onto the roof. The rain felt soft against my skin. Slashes of pink light opened up a corner of the dawn sky. A shuttered bedroom light from the *carabinieri:* Rosalba's window darkly shuttered.

The sound came again, like someone trying not to make a sound. I listened intently. My pulse quickened as I stepped across the wet roof tiles to look below. Tosca, in her dressing gown, was placing bottles of water outside her front door. Strange customs these people had. She gave a rasping cough then, muttering something, went inside her house and closed the door.

At first, I didn't notice the figure. Then as it emerged from the alleyway, I stepped hastily back so as not to be seen. I heard the halting footsteps tread heavily along Via della Mura. But when I inched forward to look, no one was there. The narrow street was dark and deserted.

* * * *

I'm putting the final touches to the bedroom: a jug of roses on the chest of drawers and a carafe of chilled white wine with a pretty hand-painted glass beside it.

After all, Mrs Elizabeth Barnet from Plymouth is also a lady on her own; she must be made to feel even more welcome. I straighten the *'no smoking'* sign above the bed. It hadn't occurred to me to ask Ronaldo not to smoke, lying beside him in bed, watching the smoke spiral between his fingers; it had been the last thing on my mind.

I glance at my watch; the one Richard bought for my birthday, an oblong face with a black leather strap. If I could afford to, I'd buy another and put his on top of the wardrobe out of sight, along with the other disturbing items of the past.

Five o'clock. Where has she got to, my Mrs Barnet from Plymouth? This time a carefully sketched map of the *piazza* and the Via Ciro Pinsuti with the street steps leading up to the alleyway, Vicolo della Mura, was enclosed with the deposit receipt. Hopefully Mrs Barnet will like cats, I think, brushing cats' hairs off the bedspread. So far, I've been lucky. The previous guests, the Barkers, left a note saying how honored they'd felt that Billy and Gertie had rattled the shutters to come in to the bedroom and then slept all night on the end of their bed.

I'm almost dead on my feet with exhaustion: what with cleaning the apartment after Ronaldo left, then preparing the place for the Barkers, and then cleaning up after they left and now preparing for Mrs Barnet.

Tosca's cough, rasping under the *salotto* window, makes me start. I've become somewhat nervy since seeing the figure in the alleyway and the front door has remained permanently closed. Even when Tonina called round earlier with grapes from her vines, I'd asked who it was before opening it.

Tosca is pegging dusters on the line. There were bloomers hanging there earlier, large enough to cast the alleyway in shadow. They can't be hers, surely? My no longer virginal cream sheets kept them company: those mail order sheets I'd ordered to start my new life in Devon and then vomited over on that terrible Christmas night I'd spent with Maudie and her companion, Julian, in Devon: stuffing myself with turkey, sprouts, roast potatoes, Yorkshire pudding and Christmas pudding, trying to fill the void inside me.

"Boo!"

I stare down at the woman smiling inanely up at me from the street. She's carrying a suitcase.

"Maudie!"

"Bet you didn't expect to see me, did you?"

"I don't believe it. I've just been thinking of you. What on earth are you doing here?"

"Had you forgotten I was coming?"

"What do you mean?"

"Shall I go away?"

"N-no, no. Come in - for a moment, anyway."

I run down the stairs to open the front door, feeling confused and profoundly startled. The sight of Maudie is alarming, it's as though thinking of her materialized her. But she'll have to go; I can't run my new life with Maudie on the scene.

Maudie walks up the stairs ahead of me, into the kitchen and puts her case down. "Oh, I like this," she says, looking round. "It's a minimalist's idea of hell, but I can see the point of it. What spooky little streets, though. The old man in the shop brought me, otherwise I'd never have found it. How do you manage to run a B&B business here?"

"Maudie, what -?"

"I had no idea it was going to be this hot." She lifts the skirt of her black linen dress and flaps it round her thighs. "Do you have something cold to drink? Iced water, for instance? And do stop staring at me as though I'm an apparition."

"You can't possibly stay."

"Well, you certainly know how to make a guest feel welcome. Is this how you treat all your paying guests?"

"W-what?"

"I've driven all the way from Devon with one night's stop in Switzerland. I'm exhausted, hot and sweaty. Can I look in the fridge?"

"Yes, but - " I sink to a chair.

"Oh, I know, I'm sorry. I shouldn't have played such a joke on you. I wasn't sure if you'd fall for it or not." Maudie begins giggling. I look anxiously up at her. "I'm Mrs Elizabeth Barnet from Plymouth, your paying guest."

"You can't be."

"I can be, and I am. Are you all right? You don't look too well."

"I don't understand, I'm sorry," I say, shaking my head. "I just don't understand any of this."

"I pre-ten-ded to be Mrs Eliza-beth Bar-net." Maudie speaks the words slowly as though I'm an idiot. "And do stop shaking your head in that daft way."

"But why?"

"I thought you wouldn't let me come if I said it was me."

"Oh, for God's sake, Maudie."

"Well, I didn't behave myself last Christmas, did I? But I only drink water now. Can I have a glass? Or do I have to get on my knees and beg?"

"Of course. Take whatever you want."

"I don't have to stay, you know," Maudie says, taking a bottle of water from the fridge. "I passed a hotel on the way. I could go there, if you wish."

"No, no, of course you can stay. I'm just - " I take a breath, "totally amazed – and yet, pleased to see you now you're here. But why Plymouth? And how come I got a cheque from a Mrs E Barnet?"

"Elizabeth, she's a friend who lives in Plymouth. She wrote the cheque and I paid her. If I'd written the cheque you'd have known it was me, wouldn't you, darling?"

I stare at her. "Yes, I suppose I would. There's even wine prepared for Mrs Barnet on a tray in the bedroom."

"I've given it up, Lorri, like I said. I've changed. I just want to read and reflect quietly on my life now."

I try not to laugh. How many times have I heard that? I lose count.

"And I want to change my life like you have."

That's new. I haven't heard that before. "Since when?"

"Since three weeks ago. I know it's *me* that's got to change before my life changes. Well, I'm a teetotaller. That's the first change. I've not touched even a wee drop. Where do you keep the glasses?"

I point at the cupboard. "What brought this on?"

"Julian. He said he was tired of seeing me lurching. Do you remember me lurching, Lorri?"

I remember all right. Lurching from one man to another at that awful pre New Year party in Devon, telling them all what beautiful spirits they had. "No, I don't remember," I say. "But I'm glad for your sake you've given it up."

"Will you drink wine, Lorri? Or are you still into your tea and scones?"

I chuckle. Maudie had made scones for tea that first afternoon I'd arrived in Devon, none of which she'd eaten. She had pushed the plate to me and I'd eaten every one. I ate a good many scones at that time; in various hotels overlooking various gray seascapes. The action of pouring tea and buttering scones had made me feel that a certain balance was being restored to my life.

Perhaps it won't be so bad after all having Maudie to stay for a week. "I'll have water, like you," I say. "And you look stunning in that black dress, slimmer than ever, and I like the copper tint."

"You're not looking bad yourself. Better than I've ever seen you, actually. You've got a glow about you."

"It's the sun."

"Yes, but *whose* son, is what I'm thinking."

I hesitate. "I don't want to talk about that right now."

"Which means there *is* someone. One only has to look at you to know." Maudie lights a cigarette. "No, don't give me that old- fashioned look; I need some vices." She inhales and blows smoke out through her nostrils. She looks around. "Where are the precious puddy cats?"

"On the roof, sunning themselves."

"Do you believe any of this is happening, Lorri, darling?"

"Not really, no. You seem to have materialized out of my thoughts."

We laugh. Maudie tips her glass against mine. "To our friendship, which is real and which I hope we can repair."

"It's repaired. And Julian?" I look at the door, half expecting to see her tall good-looking young man walk in.

"He's flat sharing in London. As you may remember, he's sick of hairdressing and wants to be an actor. But he failed his entrance exam for LAMDA."

"I'm sorry."

"He had hoped because you used to be a student there yourself, you'd put a word in for him."

"It's all too long ago. And besides, it doesn't work like that. They've got to think he has talent. It's no use my recommending him."

"Well, he thinks he has, even if no one else does. But he'll have to win a scholarship because I can't pay the fees. Which reminds me." She reaches for her bag on the table. "A hundred and forty pounds for the week, less fifty for the deposit, leaves ninety. That's correct, isn't it?"

I push the money away. "You're here as my friend, you don't pay."

"I'm also here as Mrs Elizabeth Barnet, remember, darling."

"How can I forget?"

* * * *

I made a light supper of Mozzarella cheese, tomatoes, olives and *basilico*. Maudie showered and went to bed early after she'd eaten, tired after her journey.

"And don't think of sleeping under your desk while I'm here," she said, sitting up in bed and creaming her face. "There's plenty of room in this bed for all of us, you me and the cats. And would there be any chance of an ice-cream, maybe?"

* * * *

Several elderly men eye me curiously as I enter the *Bar Cortese*. Some I recognize from when Richard and I drank *digestivos* after dinner. I greet them and they nod in friendly response. But I feel they are wondering what I'm doing out at night in the bar on my own buying ice creams for two.

"He's blown it," Maudie had said, when she'd learned of Richard's visit. "He should have waited, allowed you space to make up your mind. How could he imagine you'd have him back just like that? I'll send him a book on how to heal his life, like the ones I gave you in Devon, you remember? You said they helped you."

They had, along with the scones, the tea and the cats: they'd been about the only things that had helped. And the affirmation cards Maudie gave me. I'd drawn one out of the box the day I'd arrived in Italy: *The only adult I need take responsibility for is myself.*

A ghost follows me home from the bar. It flitters on ahead under the Gothic arches along Via della Mura, pausing to look up at the *salotto* window. I too, pause to look. The window box is full of geraniums now. Once it was full of dead ivy, all those years ago when we found the place; there'd been nothing then, apart from cobwebs and dreams and a happiness greater than anything I'd ever known.

I turn cautiously into the alleyway, no ghost now, I'm alone peering into the shadows; noting how the alley becomes narrower still as it leads along beside a high wall to the end of the cul-de-sac.

I let myself quickly into the house and bolt the door. It's a relief to have Maudie to return to, even if she is bringing the past insidiously into the present. She knows Richard, understands the situation, and is clearly on my side – at least, I think she is. You can never be too sure with Maudie. Fears, doubts and hopes for the future can now be shared. For she is someone also alone and, above all, who speaks my language!

10
Of Telephone Lines and Legal Matters

"Am I in this journal you're writing?"

"No. It's only a few jottings about Italy."

"I bet it's a secret journal all about this new man in your life. Are you going to tell me about him, or what?"

It's the following morning. I'm tucking into toast thickly spread with the Dundee Marmalade Maudie brought from England.

"Enough to whet your appetite, perhaps."

"Go on then, I'm waiting."

"There's not a lot to tell."

"Oh, go on, you always say that when I want to know something tantalizing."

"I hardly know him. And right now I'm finding it difficult shaking off Richard's ghost. I see him everywhere, down every street. I wish I could have gone somewhere with no past associations."

"And couldn't you have done that?"

"Of course not. I came here because there's no rent or mortgage to pay."

"Surely, that's not the main reason for coming here. You wanted to change your life, you said." Maudie tops up my tea. "Shall I make a fresh pot?"

"Would you? You're the guest; I should be looking after you."

"I don't need looking after. But you do, in spite of being extremely strong and courageous to come and live here all on your own." She gets up to fill the kettle. "So, what's his name, this new man? At least you can tell me his name, can't you? Where's the harm in that?"

There's no harm in telling his name, I think. No harm at all. "Ronaldo. His name's Ronaldo."

"What a beautiful name. And what does he look like, this Ronaldo? Have you a photograph?"

"Oh no, nothing like that."

"What do you mean, nothing like that? It's quite normal to have a photo of one's loved one."

"He's not my loved one, it's not like that. And...well, we're not clicking cameras at each other the whole time."

"Too busy doing other things, no doubt?"

I shake my head. Maudie is too intrusive by far. "No, it's not like that."

"There you go shaking your head again. What *is* it like, then? Every time I ask for details, you shake your head at me."

"It's difficult to explain . . . " I'm regretting having mentioned Ronaldo's name. "I don't see him that much and he hardly speaks about himself and when he does I don't understand."

"Can't be easy communicating. Verbally, anyway." Maudie giggles. "I hope he's not got a wee wifie hidden away somewhere in the hills."

"Oh, no, he's not that type."

"What type is he then?"

"Not the type you imagine."

"He's not the type to deceive you, you mean?"

"No, I don't mean that."

" Is he in love with you?"

"No."

"Are you in love with him?"

"Absolutely not!"

"So, it's only a mad sexy fling?"

"No . . . I . . . I don't know . . . I'm not sure - quite what it is."

And it's at this point when all the pent-up feelings of the past, the doubts and fears I've been holding close for so long rush to the surface and I cry like an idiot with my head on the table and Maudie stroking my arm and repeating in her soft Scottish accent: "There, there, pet, now come along, pet, you're going to be all right," and other such reassuring things.

But it's a relief to talk, to unload; to share with Maudie all the things that have happened since my arrival; the car accident, Lionello, the only English speaking person in Sinalunga who has befriended me and who has now deserted me for the mountains. The anonymous letter; how I met Ronaldo at Vittorio's dinner party and returned home with the last star in the dawn sky.

Maudie is fascinated, and becoming more so with every word I utter. I'm encouraged to continue, even embroider a little, and tell her how after making love all night I'd seen a terrible hunched figure like Quasimodo in the alleyway. Maudie's eyes are widening as though she's never heard anything like it in her entire life.

* * * *

It's Thursday afternoon and we're drinking tea in the *Poliziana* bar in Montepulciano. A long room comfortably furnished with red velvet chairs around glass-topped tables. Mouth-watering cakes and biscuits, English teas and coffee, decorate the counter.

"So, when am I going to meet this fascinating Ronaldo?"

She won't give the subject a rest. "I've no idea. I never know when I'm going to see him myself."

"Can't you ring him?"

"No, I couldn't do that."

"Oh, for heavens sake, Lorri, why ever not?" Maudie is speaking in such a loud voice that several people in the bar look over at our table. "He stayed the night with you, didn't he? He's probably desperately waiting to hear from you."

"Shhh." How I wish she'd shut up.

"It's all right, no one can understand."

"You don't know that."

We sip our tea. "I don't think so," I whisper.

"What do you mean, you don't think so? And why are you whispering?"

I roll my eyes.

"Why shouldn't he be waiting to hear from you? Invite him for dinner tonight, why don't you?"

"I don't want to hurry things, Maudie. Anyway, I can't, you're staying with me and I'm glad you are."

"Oh, I can take myself off, don't worry about that. I think you don't want me to meet him, is that it?"

"No, of course it's not." Yes, it certainly is, I think. "And I wouldn't dream of letting you take yourself off. This is your holiday, Maudie, which you've generously paid for."

"Invite him tomorrow then. I'm glad that's settled.

* * * *

It's Friday morning: I'm not inviting Ronaldo round tonight, or any other night while Maudie is here. I'm not prepared to subject her half-naked body to his scrutiny.

Yesterday, when we got back from Montepulciano, she'd laid out her clothes on the bed for my inspection. I eyed the shorts and skimpy tops dubiously. "It'll be a simple dinner at home, Maudie, not a swimming pool gala. Why not wear the black linen dress you arrived in? It's more elegant."

"It's too hot. I can't bear the feeling of clothes next to my skin in this heat."

That had decided it.

"Tosca dropped her washing earlier when you walked past in that short skirt and transparent blouse you're wearing. We're in a parochial little village, remember."

"A goldfish bowl, I'd call it. I don't know how you can stand it. Everybody watches your every move here. There's that tango man leaning out of his window making amorous suggestions whenever he sees me, and not only that, the priest followed me home the other morning."

"That's what I mean, Maudie. You need to cover yourself up a bit. You're asking for trouble otherwise."

* * * *

It's useless trying to point out the unsuitability of her clothes and how it's a mistake to upset the locals in a small Italian village. Maudie only listens to what she wants to hear. And sharing the bed with her is another mistake. Her proximity makes the bed hotter and it brings back dreams of being in the rented cottage in Devon she found for me when I'd left London. The smoothing of the mail-order sheets on the king-size bed, hoping for a better future. And that nightmare day outside the house in London, watching my home being taken apart, the green two-seater sofa, the last item to be lifted into the removal van, my eyes following it to the end of the street, wondering where and if I'd ever sit on it again.

* * * *

"What statue, where? "

"To the right of the altar. It's in shadow; I can see it clearly. You will too in a minute, the Madonna's head will begin to appear."

"How terrifying!"

"There's nothing terrifying about it. It gives me strength."

"But you're not even religious."

"I know. But I don't have to be. It's a comfort, that's all."

It's Friday afternoon: fortunately, I've managed to put the idea of Ronaldo coming for dinner on hold. Now we're sitting in the back pew of the small candlelit church in Siena next to the university. As before, it is empty.

I've taken time off from my classes. I'll miss out on my course, but I want to share with Maudie as much as possible in the short time we have together.

"I've been coming here every day," I say. "I love it."

"I don't understand why. You've always said how you hated churches."

"It's not the church itself I'm against, only the dogma surrounding it. But this is different somehow. It's simple."

"Hardly that with all this gold and gilt everywhere. It has little to do with what I understand of the teachings of Jesus. He was, after all, a humble man."

It had been her Jesus talk in Devon, when I'd arrived trying to rebuild my fractured life that now made me want to share my experience in the church with her. "I want to be able to breathe . . ." I remember her saying, inhaling a lungful of cigarette smoke on that unforgettably awful Christmas night. She'd read passages of the Bible to me and I'd asked her if she'd become a Born Again. She'd looked scathingly at me and said how she'd been born again every day since Jesus had come into her life.

"How long has this been going on?" I asked.

She gave a splutter of laughter. "You make it sound as if I'm having an affair. I've opened myself up to His influence." She's swallowed wine. "And I've changed because of it. I don't need certain things in my life right now – sex for one."

"That can't be much fun for Julian."

Maudie had flushed. "Julian's not looking for fun, Lorri. He understands how I feel. That I need to be with myself since Mum died, to find out who I am and that sex gets in the way of my spiritual journey."

I had lain in bed that night in Maudie's spare room, contemplating my physical journey. That long drive from London down the motorway to Devon in the black Citroen, needing to be close to a friend:

cases, boxes, blankets, pots and pans crowding on the back seat; I could hardly see out of the rear window.

"I'll light a candle for Mum," Maudie is now saying, as she steps out of the pew. "That will give me strength. She was a holy mother if ever there was one."

I walk softly down the center aisle to take a closer look at the statue. I gaze into shadowy emptiness.

"You probably imagined you saw the Virgin Mary because you had an emotional need," Maudie says on the way out of the church.

I turn in the doorway and look back toward the altar. There is no statue. Never was. Even though I'd seen it clearly on entering. There never will be again; I realize that, no matter how many times I revisit the church. Yet, something had been given to me because I'd had a need. "Maybe it was only imagination. But for that I'm grateful. And for what I heard."

"Heard?"

"Conversations."

"With the Virgin Mary?"

"Who knows? I only know I felt better afterwards."

"What things did she say to you?"

"Wise things."

* * * *

There is an unreality to it all, I thought later. Something tapping in my head, trying to make me see things as though for the first time and not in the limited way I have usually perceived them. Perhaps it is as Lionello says, the hallucinogenic effect of the light (and the wine, of course) that is making a shift in my consciousness. How could one hope to live a normal life in such a place? Yet people are living perfectly normal lives in Tuscany. It's *me* who is on the high, seeing images tinged with theatricality, wondering, almost fearfully at times, if the curtain lifts will there be anything substantial behind it? Or merely psychedelic images crumbling like old frescoes into the dust?

* * * *

"*Signora* Lorri . . . "

It's Saturday morning. I wake to the sound of someone banging on the front door. Eight forty-five. What on earth is going on now? Maudie is lying on her back, making little snorting noises. How can she sleep through such a noise? The banging becomes more insistent. "*Signora* Lorriii!"

I scramble out of bed, into my dressing gown, and stumble downstairs to the front door.

Tonina thrusts a carrier bag of spinach into my arms. "*Scusi il disturbo. Ho incontrato Patrizio, l'operaio del telefoni.*" She blows a kiss and hurries away.

I stare at the handsome young man on the doorstep. He carries a tool bag and a red rose wrapped in cellophane and tied with blue ribbon. "Have you've come to install the telephone?" I ask.

"*Si, si, mi chiamo* Patrizio."

"Vittorio sent you, right?"

"*Si, si, si* - I come to make *il telefono.*"

"*Viene.*"

I lead Patrizio up the stairs to the kitchen and dump the spinach in the sink. "*Per me?*" I say, eyeing the rose.

"No – yes - I like to give, but - "

"Grazie." I place the rose in a glass of water: the telephone man bringing a rose, what next? But this is Tuscany where all things are possible.

"I spik Inglish, so much." Patrizio holds his thumb and forefinger an inch apart.

"Bene."

I glance quickly about, wondering where the telephone could go, praying that Maudie will remain comatose until her usual hour of eleven-thirty.

"Stile Inglesi?" Patrizio asks, looking round the kitchen.

"A little of both, English and Italian."

He smiles, his crooked white teeth showing a contrast to his tanned face. Then he withdraws a beige telephone from his bag like a conjurer producing a rabbit. Billy, the tabby, tired of being ignored, advances down the steps toward him. *"Viene tigra."*

"I wouldn't touch him. He bites."

"I 'ave much gats." Patrizio rubs Billy's head. Then begins counting on his fingers. *"Uno, due, tre, quattro* gats." Billy's head butts his hand for another caress, purring audibly.

"He doesn't usually do that with strangers."

Patrizio makes clucking noises with his tongue. "What is name?"

"Billy."

"Billii. *Bello,* Billiiiii . . . "

"But where's the best place for the telephone?" I ask, anxious to get on, for Patrizio could well remain hugging the phone and stroking the cat all morning. "I think the phone line's outside this room." I hurry in to the *salotto,* squeeze round the back of the sofa and fling open the shutters. Billy springs up on the sill and looks down as if he too is searching for the phone line. Tosca, pegging pillow-cases on the washing line, waves up at me.

Patrizio squeezes his way round the sofa next to me. "I can?" he asks, removing his sweat-damp shirt and revealing a tanned tattooed torso. He leans out of the window.

Tosca gapes.

"*Ecco, la linea!*" he shouts. "Okay, all right, we do in *salotto?*"

I duck from the window. Ornelia is outside now; Tosca cackling to her. Something has to be said before they get the wrong idea. "*Buongiorno,*" I call down to the two amazed women and anyone else who may happen to be listening. "Patrizio *fa il telefono per me.*"

Tosca says, "Aaah," and Ornelia says, "*Brava.*"

Then I hear the sound of Maudie flushing the lavatory. I shoot across the kitchen and shut the door. I would have locked it had there been a key; instead I hold onto the handle. "We can put the phone on the windowsill," I whisper.

Patrizio looks at me, curiously, clearly not having heard. I repeat what I said a fraction louder.

"*Troppa confusione,*" he says, stepping back into the kitchen, Billy at his heels. "We must to - " he holds his arms wide, "make more long *la ligna. Facciamo sul tetto.* We do on the roof?"

"On the roof? Is that necessary? Why not in the *salotto,* it's quicker."

"*Poco spazio.*"

"We could make space if - "

The door handle jiggles.

"Patrizio's fixing the telephone," I shout through the door, gripping the handle even tighter. "Can you wait in the bedroom, Maudie, there's enough confusion here as it is."

"I won't add to the confusion. What are you talking about in there? It sounds interesting."

"Nothing – it's nothing."

"I just want my coffee."

The handle suddenly comes away in my hand as I grip it; the door opens and in bounces Maudie in her shorti-nightie.

"Oh, excuse me . . . " Her eyes dilate at the sight of Patrizio's naked torso. "I didn't realize you had such gorgeous company."

"This is Patrizio, he's installing the phone."

"Is he, now? How kind of him. Would you like a coffee, Patrizio?" Patrizio shakes his head, clearly mesmerized by the sight of Maudie's naked white legs. "What's all this stuff in the sink?" She hovers over the spinach with the percolator. "And who brought the rose? Did you bring it, Patrizio?" He nods dumbly. "Well, isn't that the most beautiful thing to do? You wouldn't find an English telephone engineer bringing a rose. How romantic you Italians are."

I climb the bathroom stairs two at a time, my face burning. It's suddenly become suffocatingly hot. I splash cold water on my face, clean my teeth and brush my hair. Back in the bedroom, I throw on jeans and a T-shirt. The whole operation couldn't have taken more than ten minutes. But when I walk back into the kitchen and see Maudie on the roof kissing Patrizio, I realize plenty has happened in those ten minutes.

"You'll have to take down the mirror," she calls to me from the window, one arm hooked around his neck.

"Maudie! Will you please put Patrizio down."

"I'm talking about the mirror."

"So am I, and I'm not moving it. It's an antique."

"All the more reason to move it then. Otherwise Patrizio will drill a hole through it, won't you, Patrizio?" Maudie gives him another little kiss on his cheek. Patrizio grins foolishly.

"He'll do no such thing. It's far too heavy."

"I expect Patrizio will move it for you if you ask him nicely, won't you, Patrizio, pet?" Patrizio is obviously finding it hard to concentrate. He's looking at Maudie as though he's never seen anyone like her in the whole of his life. I'm sure he hasn't!

"Maudie, we're not moving anything and will you please stop molesting Patrizio. The *carabinieri* are opposite, have some respect." I sound like a school marm. But I can't help myself – I feel invaded.

She's not doing anything I wouldn't want them to see, she's saying. "And haven't you been doing far more outrageous things on the roof yourself with Ronaldo, you said?"

This is appalling. She'll have to leave. I'll pack her bags myself the moment Patrizio has left.

"Calm down, Lorri, for heaven's sake." Maudie descends the stairs cautiously in her high-heeled mules. "Patrizio's going to put the phone in the *salotto*. Is that all right, he wants to know?"

"Of course it's all right. I've already asked him to do that."

"But we'll have to shift the furniture. We can't move in that wee room."

"We?" My blood is boiling. "Maudie, kindly leave this to me, will you."

"Whatever's the matter with you, Lorri? I'm only trying to help."

"Well, don't! Patrizio, *nel salotto, per favore.*"

And so the telephone wire is finally fed through a hole under the *salotto* window and the new beige cordless telephone is in place on the windowsill. Patrizio refuses money, but is happy to accept a bottle of *Rosso di Montalcino,* which Maudie offers him from my store on top of the kitchen cupboard.

"You didn't have to do that," I say, after he's left. "Vittorio will pay him."

"Why ever not? What are you keeping all this wine for?"

"Not for telephone men. And it's not your place to give it." And now it's time you're on your way, I can't bring myself to add.

* * * *

The midday post brings a letter with the heading *Studio Legale.* It's written in Italian, the only two comprehensible words being the name 'Richard Marsh'.

"It's from a lawyer in Siena. He's saying something about Richard."

Maudie is convinced she understands more than me because of her Italian classes in Devon. She sits at the kitchen table with a dictionary. "Don't look so worried. I'm sure it can't be that bad."

"I'm sure it can."

"He's saying something about his client wanting payment for professional work."

"Oh, no. I don't believe it!"

"And something else about adding his name to something."

"The deeds, he means the deeds. Oh my God, he wouldn't do that, would he?"

"I think Richard wants you to share the property with him."

"What? I won't do it!"

"Or - " Maudie stares hard at the print, "I think you may have to appear in court."

"I can't do that! He can't make me do that - can he?"

"You need advice, Lorri. Ask Ronaldo to help you? Or this Vittorio, you've told me about?"

"No, no, I don't want to drag them into it."

"Perhaps you should have given Richard back his furniture then none of this would have happened."

"Whatever do you mean? I did, at least - some of it."

"He said you gave him nothing."

"He lied."

"Why should he lie?"

"To gain feminine support. He wants to make out that I'm the villain of the piece."

"And aren't you?"

I stare at Maudie, aghast. "What's he been telling you? And why are you on his side?"

"I'm not on anybody's side. I thought that's what you wanted, for me to take a neutral standpoint."

"I do. But I don't want you supporting him."

"I'm trying to be objective, Lorri. You'll have to write to this man, and in Italian, which won't be easy. What will you say?"

"No! That should be easy enough to translate in any language."

"Be serious, Lorri."

"I've never been more serious."

"You'll have to think this through calmly. You don't want to find yourself in an Italian courtroom being accused of something you don't understand."

* * * *

It's a safe place, bed, somewhere to escape threats and lawyers. It was the same in Devon, hiding from the day in the king-size bed with the mail-order sheets, self-help books, the tea, scones and the cats. And as I drift into a troubled sleep . . .

I am back in the Kellands Row cottage in Devon, straightening the pink candlewick bedspread, tidying the heap of how-to-get-to-grips-with-your-life kind of books. It's a question of how to get through the day before switching on the electric blanket and crawling back into the warmth, tucked up with the books and the cats, insulated from the outside world.

I take my mug of tea out through the back door and stand on the sodden patch of grass. The owner wants to sell quickly, the agency said. The garden is small and a shed steals most of the space. A fruit tree casts shade over the garden, but as the sun never shines it doesn't matter. Snowdrops mass around the trunk. Wherever I look reminds me of the life I have lost. Seagulls shriek as I let myself back into the cottage . . .

"Wake up, Lorri. Wake up!"

I open my eyes and stare uncertainly up at damp wisps of orange hair.

"Vittorio's on the phone. He wants to speak to you."

"Where am I?"

"In bed. You've been asleep for the last hour."

"I've been dreaming. I thought I was back in Devon."

"Well you're not, you're in Italy. Come on now. He's asked us to dinner tonight."

"Who?"

"I've just told you, Vittorio."

"Tell him we're not going."

"I've already said we are. You can show him the letter and get his advice."

"I don't want his advice."

Maudie hands me the receiver.

"*Buonasera, cara.* What are you doing in that suffocating dog kennel in this heat?"

"I'm sleeping."

"You sleep when you are dead, *cara mia*. What is the problem?"

"There isn't one."

"*Brava!* That is what I like to hear. Patrizio tell me you have a beautiful friend."

"Oh, did he?"

"You come together with your friend to my house tonight, eh? Silka go in Germania to see her mother. Giuseppina prepare the dinner. We drink the good wine."

"I don't think so, Vittorio."

"Why not?" Maudie nudges me. "We've got nothing else on."

"My friend doesn't drink, Vittorio."

"We soon change her mind, *cara*. We eat the *prosciutto*, the good bread; we sit in the garden with the good people near. What more you want in the life?"

I hang up feeling a weight in the pit of my stomach. Events are racing recklessly out of control.

11
A confused heart

Saturday evening:

This journal is becoming top secret: I wouldn't want Maudie to read it – but what a relief it is to write it all down.

I'd hoped we'd go out and have a pizza, but Maudie said we'd been doing that every night and it was time for a little excitement. But I'm wary of the kind of excitement she wants, for when men appear her whole personality changes. I was quite enjoying her company until Patrizio arrived to install the phone. But I feel bad because she's so generous; she offers to pay for everything. The trouble is she makes me feel like a disapproving aunt. Like that night of the New Year party in Devon when she'd got drunk and I'd had to call a taxi and take her home. She'd tried to light a cigarette in the taxi, but her hand shook so much the match went out. I couldn't wait to get out and as far away from her as possible. "Will Julian be waiting up for you?" I asked, trying to be pleasant, even though I couldn't stand the sight of her mascara-smeared face.

"He'll be in bed," she said.

Yes, I thought, I can imagine him turning away in disgust as you fall in beside him.

When Maudie got out of the taxi she stumbled on her high-heels. I offered to walk her to the door. But she seemed not to hear and climbed up the steps before turning to look at me. I leaned back in the seat as the taxi pulled away. That look, I'll never forget it. It had been so lost, so vulnerable, until that moment I'd never realized how wounded she was. I knew then I couldn't turn my back on her completely. And besides, who was I to judge her?

* * * *

"They're so macho here, the men, what's the matter with them? I suppose they feel they've got to overtake a woman just for the sake of it."

It's seven forty-five. We are on our way to Vittorio's in Maudie's Fiat Panda. The evening air is hot and heavy. With my window half-open, I'm enjoying the wind on my face, watching the fields of sunflowers sweep past, their smiling yellow faces following the last of the sun. I turn my head to look through the rear window. "That white van's still following us."

"Oh, for heaven's sake." Maudie glances in the rear-view mirror. "You're becoming hopelessy paranoid, Lorri. There are white vans all over Europe; it doesn't mean Richard has to be in one of them. Anyway, he's in Germany, you said."

"As far as I *know*, yes."

"Oh, come on, all these characters you think are following you. There's Quasimodo in the alleyway, Vittorio's bodyguard and now poor Richard in his van. Are you sure you're not imagining some of this, Lorri?"

"I'm not inventing things, if that's what you mean." I feel a sudden sense of anger. I breathe in slowly, trying to control it. "You read the anonymous note and Richard's letter. That's not imagination. I only wish it was."

"I know, but you're always scribbling away in that precious notebook of yours which you won't let me see. I can't imagine what kind of journal you're writing. I think perhaps you read too much into things, is all I'm saying."

"I just said I thought there was somebody in the alleyway the other night. And if I receive a letter saying I'm a wicked woman to leave my ex and wicked things will happen to me, it's hardly reading too much into things. And now my ex wants to sue me. Am I reading too much into that?"

"Well, you did virtually push him into another woman's arms, didn't you?"

My jaw drops. "That wasn't your opinion a couple of days ago."

"I know, but I've had time to think and now I believe you should have accepted him back when he came with hope and good intentions. We all make mistakes. After all, haven't I made plenty?"

I fix my eyes on the road ahead. Best to say nothing.

"You still haven't learnt to forgive. Jesus says, in forgiving others we forgive ourselves."

I lower my window and gulp in air. I'm beginning to wonder if I can survive the evening.

"I don't take sides, you know that. I like to try and see both points of view fairly."

Very commendable: so why the feeling that treachery is afoot?

"Will the Mafioso flautist be there tonight?"

"Rocco? I hope not. Why do you ask?"

"I want to see these characters for myself. I want to see if they exist." Maudie changes up into third. "Do I turn right somewhere?"

"At the *Terme* sign. And they exist all right."

"Did you bring the lawyer's letter?"

"Yes. But I've no intention of showing it to anyone."

"So why bring it?"

"Just in case."

Maudie chuckles. "Well, you're out to meet your beau tonight. Think of him instead."

I've thought of nothing else. When I made up my face and dressed, my heart was beating so hard I'd pressed both hands on it for fear it might burst through my skin.

"How do you think Richard would react if he knew about your new love?"

"Is he likely to?" I look at her.

"Not from me he won't. But he could make things more difficult if he knew. Be discreet is all I'm saying."

Discreet? I try not to laugh out loud. When had Maudie ever been discreet in her entire adult life? She's wearing the black linen dress she arrived in, which makes her look slimmer than ever. How is it she never puts on weight? She's been eating pasta, pizza and ice cream by the tubload. And why, after a sleepless night, like the one before when we'd reminisced till dawn, she merely looks fragile instead of haggard? It's infuriating. Long silver nails on slim tanned hands, while my nails are broken stubs on hands scrubby with all the cleaning and shifting furniture about. And my blue linen skirt and white blouse that I made myself is hardly exotic. Homespun is how I feel beside the glamorous Maudie. I hold in my stomach. "Do I look all right?" For some reason Maudie's opinion is important to me.

"You look lovely," Maudie says, her eyes searching for the turn-off. "I don't know what you're worrying about." She swings right onto the dirt road, the car wheels spraying up clouds of sand. "Wherever are we going, in the desert? I don't fancy driving back here in the dark. I won't be able to see a thing."

"We don't have to stay late. We can leave early, before it gets too dark – whenever you want."

"We haven't got there yet and you're talking of leaving. Don't you want to see your heart's delight?"

"Of course I do." I sigh. I've never been able to understand why it is that whenever I meet someone I really like, I go to pieces. Had it been like that with Richard? I suspect it had. But such thoughts bring back feelings of regret and that's the last thing I want.

"Are you feeling quite well, Lorri?"

"Yes. Don't I look it?"

"You look grand, I keep telling you."

"You turn left there." I point out the little arrow in the trees and my heart thumps.

Every window of Vittorio's house glows with light. The *Maremmani* bound up to our car as we crunch across the driveway. Maudie parks next to a Range-Rover with German number-plates.

"Are the dogs safe?"

"Yes, they know me."

"It's me I'm thinking of."

"They won't hurt you."

I get out of the car, trying to stop the dogs from jumping up against my white blouse.

"Does he have guests?" Maudie asks, tentatively patting a furry head.

"He always has guests. They call all the time. For a glass of wine or something to eat."

"His poor wife."

"She's used to it."

Someone whistles. I look quickly round. The dogs are racing across to Sherif in his black suit waiting by the gates. I wave. After a moment he raises his hand in response. As I turn back, I spot a cream-colored Auto Bianchi parked further up the driveway under the trees. "Look," I cry, hurrying over to it. "This is the car I'm buying from Vittorio." I open the door and sit inside. The key is in the ignition. "It's got plaid seats, Maudie, look."

But Maudie is more interested in looking at her surroundings than the car. "What an incredible place. Does Vittorio own all this land?"

"Yes, and another house in the woods with two apartments, one in which Ronaldo lives and a bar underneath which he is about to open. Let's go."

I get out and stride across to the *loggia*, feeling hot and aggravated. I must unwind before we go any further. I take several deep breaths.

A doll minus its dress lies face down on the table. Has it only been three weeks since I sat there, unable to take it all in? A green lizard runs along the low wall and disappears into the foliage.

"Who was that man you waved to?" Maudie is behind me.

"The bodyguard."

"Bodyguard? Is he the one that followed you into Siena?"

"Yes."

"Does he have a name?"

"Sherif. His name is Sherif."

"I thought you said you never acknowledged him."

"It depends how I feel," I mutter, and hasten along the passageway behind the house, deeply regretting Maudie's intrusive presence. Then I pause and feel heat rush to my face. Ronaldo is rendering the garden wall; he has his back to me. Stripped to the waist, his muscles ripple as he bends and straightens up, flicking cement onto the bricks with a trowel.

I smile and step forward. "*Ciao*, Ronaldo."

He turns to look at me, surprised. "Lorri. I no know you come tonight."

"Didn't Vittorio tell you?"

"No say nothing to me."

"Oh. Well, I've brought my friend, Maudie. She's English. She's staying with me."

Ronaldo looks appraisingly at Maudie. "*Un piacere.* But now I work. I must to finish. Vittorio is down." He indicates the dance floor with his trowel. Then turns back to the wall without a word.

My smile fades. I'm not sure what to do. Have we been dismissed? "I-I think everyone's down here," I say to Maudie, heading down to the lower level of the garden.

"He didn't seem that pleased to see you." Maudie follows closely. "What have you done to upset him?"

I blink nervously. Then I hear laughter, children shrieking from the pool and water splashing; apprehensively, I step across the dance floor to where Vittorio, wearing a purple flowered shirt, is sitting at an iron table with his German friends.

He gets to his feet as we approach. Hans, red hair curling on his expansive chest, and Hilda, a towel round her head from swimming, remains seated at the table smiling up at me in recognition.

I kiss Vittorio on both cheeks. "This is my friend, Maudie."

Vittorio brushes Maudie's hand theatrically against his lips. "I hear that you have much thirst for the good wine, *Signora*."

Maudie giggles. "Who told you that?"

"The little birds."

"Did they also tell you that I only drink water?"

"No, they are clever. They know you don't come in Toscana to drink the water."

"Is the water undrinkable here then?"

"As I never drink the water, *bella signora,* how can I say? I use the water only to make the shave."

Everyone seems amused. I look round for a chair. Perhaps the evening will turn out well after all.

* * * *

Maudie is lowering her body into a plastic chair, the back leg of which is bending in slightly. Any minute it might collapse. I feel mean and try to smother my laughter with a cough and catch Vittorio's eye.

He looks at me, puzzled. "I am missing something? Or this is the British humor which no one understand, only the British."

Hans grins. Vittorio pours red wine into a cup and hands it to him. "My very good friend, Hans, he like always when he make the communion with the wine, but not the holy one, you understand?"

Everyone laughs.

Hans slaps Vittorio's shoulder playfully and I pull out a chair from the stack, glancing surreptitiously at the legs before sitting.

"For what reason you come to live in Tuscany?" Hilda asks me.

"I wanted to change my life."

"Is it now changed better?"

"Yes. Much better."

"And do you work?"

"I'm doing Bed and Breakfast for the English – "

"Her place is so small, she pass the bacon and the eggs up through the window to the tourists on the roof."

More laughter. Vittorio looks pleased. I laugh too, although I sense a touch of malice in his humor.

"And where are you coming from?" Hans asks Maudie.

"Devon. It's by the sea in England."

"The English seaside where it rain always?"

"It wasn't raining when I left." Maudie's chair begins sinking beneath her as the legs give way.

"Maudie," I cry, a second before she collapses.

Vittorio, on his feet, helps her up. He pulls another plastic chair from the stack and re-seats her between himself and Hans.

"*Grazie. Molto grazie.*"

"*Prego, signora.*" Vittorio is observing her thigh as she crosses her legs, allowing the split in her skirt to open.

Why didn't I warn her about the stupid chair? Now she's going to try and seduce Vittorio. I'm going to suggest leaving soon, before things get out of control. I turn to the bougainvillea, above which, on the higher ground, I can see Rolando working. And it is then that I notice a slight movement in the tree next to the bougainvillea. To my amazement, Sherif is half-hidden amongst the foliage. He is avidly watching Maudie. I sip several mouthfuls of wine too quickly and have a minor coughing fit. Reaching for the bottle of water, I look again. But he has gone.

"When will Silka return?" Hilda asks.

"Two, three weeks, I don't know what my wife stays doing. She bring her mother from Germania . . ."

I let the conversation drift over me until I hear Maudie's words:". . . it's all part of my inner journey, you see . . . "

Oh, *please,* not that again. The last thing anybody needs is to hear the ongoing saga of Maudie's journey, spiritual or otherwise. I'll find an excuse to wander off. Only then I can't watch Ronaldo's muscles rippling.

How I long to be alone with him, to tell him how I feel. "I must to finish," he'd said. Had that meant he would see me after he'd finished? And why hadn't he given me a kiss or a smile even? No word to say he would *definitely* see me after he'd finished his wretched wall. No look or signal to show he was even pleased to see me.

". . . and so then I returned to my roots by the sea in Devon. It's all part of my spiritual journey . . . "

I groan inwardly.

Vittorio pours wine into a plastic cup and hands it to Maudie.

"She doesn't drink!" The abruptness in my voice startles me. Everyone is staring curiously at me. I smile tensely. "It makes her ill, you see, to drink."

"Actually, Vittorio," Maudie lifts her empty cup, "she's right. I don't feel at all well on red wine. I prefer white."

"Maudie. You said you'd stopped." Here I go again – the disapproving aunt.

"I have stopped, Lorri. But everything in moderation, don't you think?"

"When did you ever do anything in moderation in your entire life?" The words are out before I can stop them.

Hans snorts with laughter.

Now Vittorio is laughing: "You don't come in Italia to do things in moderation, *cara*. If you prefer the white wine I have the *Fassati*. I call Sherif to bring it from the *cantina*." He whistles as though for a dog. But no Sherif appears.

"What work does Sherif do here, Vittorio?" I ask, as a way of distracting his attention from the wine.

"He do what work there is – now he make the garden. "

Maudie reaches for the bottle and fills her cup. She tips the wine down her throat as though it's water.

I give up. It's useless trying to help her. Let her do her worst; she will anyway. My eyes flick back to the bougainvillea, only to see with a little nervous shock that Ronaldo has gone.

"You are in hell or purgatory on this spiritual journey, *cara?*"

Maudie flutters a hand over her cup as Vittorio tries to re-fill it. "Oh no, please - "

"No, please? This is the English way to say, yes, please."

"Lorri says I have to be careful."

"Of what, *cara*?"

"Of men like you."

"Maudie, I *never* - "

Hans bellows with laughter.

"She make me the compliment." Vittorio lights a cigarette. "You know why Lorri compliment me? Because she know I understand how to live, to eat good, to drink the wine and to make the love under the moon. If you don't do these things once in your life you are better to die." He lights Maudie's cigarette as she leans forward to the flame, uncrossing her legs, revealing more of her thigh. "Lorri, she understand, she take the risk to come here alone. And that is not the only risk she take, eh? " He winks at me.

I flush. What does he mean? He must know something. Ronaldo wouldn't have told him. Would he?

"The little birds say we must be careful of the very clever people."

"Who are these little birds, Vittorio?" I ask.

"If I tell you then they don't sing more songs. I say only you are more clever than you want the people to think."

"Is this little bird's name Giuseppina, by any chance?" That's taken him by surprise. But he makes one of his comic faces and says nothing. Then at the sight of Ronaldo strolling toward us with a bottle of wine, he waves his arm. "*Ecco,* Ronaldo. He is also clever. True, *amico mio?*"

"Sometime. If I want." Ronaldo has changed into a clean shirt and cut-off jeans. He opens the bottle with a corkscrew strung around his waist. "I 'ear *la signora* want the *Fassati* so I bring from the *cantina*."

"*Bravo!* Ronaldo arrive always prepared. Not like you, Hans. You arrive with not the money to buy the wine. But still you want the wine to take away in Germania."

"No, Vittorio – " Hans's face is sweating; he seems annoyed – embarrassed, even. "You are always insisting I buy more cases than I need. I have no more the space in my cellar."

"Then you make the extension, my friend."

Hans smiles disconcertedly at Hilda. "We have no more the money to make extensions," she says. "It cost so much money to make such things. Hans, he work always . . ."

A sudden movement at the bougainvillea catches my attention again. Giuseppina is picking up Ronaldo's shirt from the dust and kissing it. I watch, holding my breath. And I know for certain now what I'd already guessed. She is hopelessy infatuated with Ronaldo. I stare uncertainly down into my empty cup.

Ronaldo places a chair beside me, when, with piercing shrieks, Valentina, in a pink bikini rushes toward us, pursued by Anna, naked, clutching a blue rubber ring. Valentina climbs onto Vittorio's lap, causing him to spill his wine over Maudie, who squeals and jumping up, throws herself onto Ronaldo's lap. Vittorio, holding one restraining hand on Valentina and the other gesturing wildly at Hans, whose face has now turned crimson with the effort of justifying whatever it is he's trying to say about his extension in his house in Germany.

Anna cries and the rubber ring falls to the ground. Valentina snatches it up and drops it over her head rotating her hips. "Ooola-ooola!" she yells. Anna screams hysterically and Hilda takes her hand and speaking softly in German, both she and Giusepinna, reappearing from behind the bougainvillea and still clutching Ronaldo's shirt, lead both girls away into the house.

Meanwhile, Maudie is still perched on Ronaldo's lap with her arm around his neck. "Thank you for the lovely white wine you brought specially for me, Ronaldo . . . "

I can't bear it!

Ronaldo tries to remove her arm, but she holds him tighter. "What do you think, Ronaldo? Do you like me? Is that what you want to say?"

Ronaldo rolls his eyes at me. "I must to go. I make something in the cook."

Maudie splutters with laughter. "You make something in the cook? What's the cook?"

"In the cook 'ouse. I no know 'ow you say."

"I think you're lovely, whatever you say. You're going to cook something for us? Good. I'm starving." She kisses him on the cheek. "Do you mind me kissing your man, Lorri? Yes, I can see by that dreadful fixed smile on your face that you do."

"I think you should add water to your wine, Maudie."

"Lorri thinks I should add water to my wine, Vittorio. Do *you* think I should add water to the wine?"

Thankfully, Vittorio is paying no attention to Maudie. He is lifting Hans to his feet; the German's face is wet with tears.

Maudie, refusing to be ignored, grabs a wine cork from the table. She throws it, hitting Vittorio smartly on the ear. He spins round at the same time Ronaldo pushes Maudie off his lap. The chair legs buckle and Maudie falls on top of him in a sprawl of legs and arms.

I'm on my feet. But Vittorio is quicker: he grabs Maudie, and yanking her up, bends her over the table, screaming, lifts her skirt, reveals her black lacy briefs and spanks her bottom hard, once, twice. But now Ronaldo is on his feet: he punches Vittorio on the shoulder. Vittorio lunges out and thankfully misses. Then Hans, holding Vittorio's arm in an iron grip, leads him away to the pool.

Maudie is sobbing, leaning against the table for support, one naked white breast popping out of her dress.

"It's time to leave," I say, pushing the breast firmly back in the dress.

But Maudie pulls away and totters into Ronaldo's arms. "Thank you, thank you, oh thank you," she whimpers.

It must be the sight of her arms snaking round his neck that makes me suddenly dash for the garden stairs. I have to escape before I do something I'll regret. Even when I hear Ronaldo calling out after me, I keep on running, across the driveway and up the track into the hills.

And now I'm here, alone, on the hillside, feeling absurd, trying to control my awful sickening jealous anger. I have to think: I must think things clearly through, try to understand, try to make sense of my own confused heart.

12
The Night Watchman Returns

The two white *Marimmanos* shoot ahead, male and female running as one, up the track, out of sight, high up into the hills. I pause a fraction, look back, hoping to see Ronaldo following me, about to ask me why I'm always running away. But there is no one, only the evening light rising vividly, as if from the earth. I inhale the scent of the bushes, *rosmarino* and *salvai*, as I walk, calmer now, trying to clear my system of the poison inside me.

The track leads past a ruined barn, the roof fallen in like a gaping wound. I step over clods of dry earth and scorched grass to a slab of stone at the door: it is somewhere to sit and think calmly. The door is off its hinges; I glance inside and see an old chair and a heap of sacking in the semi-dark. The stone feels warm under my skirt; it's good to be sitting up here on my own. My mind is clearing fast. I let out a long shuddering breath. All this passion, I'm not ready for it; it has crept up on me unexpectedly. I'm out of my depth, emotionally unprepared for it all.

Could it have happened in Devon? Unlikely. It's the magic of this place, the light, the heat, the wine; even the fireflies and crickets are accountable. I have been hopelessly bewitched and must try to make sense of the spell I'm under.

The problem is the language, I tell myself. How can you speak with your heart when you don't know the words? I feel as vulnerable as a three-year old stripped of my language, something I have always taken for granted. And speaking is one thing; only understanding thirty percent of anything said is another. But that, hopefully, will improve in time. What isn't improving is my communication with Ronaldo. Why hadn't I said, see you soon, *ci vidiamo*, I could manage that. And *come stai* when he'd sat next to me. Except Maudie plonking herself in his lap hadn't helped me to speak in any language.

My stomach lurches at the image of her sitting on his lap. I kick a clod of earth. Thank God she'll be gone in a few days. But Giusepinna, she wouldn't be gone and she could have children and that was everything in Italy. Which, of course, is why Vittorio is encouraging the match, seeing it as a chance to expand his own family. And though Ronaldo might have no interest in her, she's *there* in the house, near him, available, ironing his shirts and making his bed. How long will it be before she's *in* his bed?

The thought makes me feverish. I'm losing myself, not for the first time and probably not for the last; even so, now is the time to get a hold of myself. I wipe the sweat from my face with my skirt. "These torrid passions are what happens to English women in hot countries," I say aloud, trying to ridicule myself. But the sudden sound of my voice in the still air makes me feel uncomfortable, embarrassed, even, as though someone might be listening.

I get up and look around, then seeing no one, sit down again. How is it possible to be infatuated with someone and yet still love and feel the loss of someone else at the same time? How did these two emotions connect? Had one caused the other? Or else, accustomed to loving someone, had I fallen 'in love', if that's what it was, with the first man I'd met after Richard?

I take the lawyer's letter from my bag and re-read it. It's inconceivable that Richard should do such a thing after years of sharing our life together. Yet, I have been expecting it, only when it happens it's worse than I'd thought it would be. Like the letters he'd written to me in Devon: my stomach had contracted at the sight of the blue envelopes on the mat, the contents of which had been lists of items he wanted returned to furnish his life with Veronica, the other woman. I'd felt such rage build up inside me I'd hardly been able to hold the pen to write. What did he expect to achieve now with this letter? No one could force me to add his name to the deeds; it is my property, my home, my rightful place in the cosmos.

The Platters crooning 'Smoke gets in your Eyes' comes echoing up the hillside. Nine ten. Something is happening down there, Maudie in her lacy black briefs, dancing with Ronaldo. "No, don't let it be," I cry, and get up to leave. Then with a shock, I spot a dark figure moving stealthily up the track toward me. I duck into the barn.

I stand motionless behind the broken door, holding my breath. Then take a quick look. Sherif! I thought so. Beneath the trees now with his back to me, standing so still in the dusk he could almost be mistaken for a tree. Furtive, unpredictable; you never know what he might be capable of.

Taking my chance, I rush through the barn door and across the dried earth. Then stop to peer behind me, into the spaces between the trees. He's not there.

As far as I *know*. But he could be hiding somewhere waiting to spring out at me. I bolt down the track. Then slow down, breathless, half walking, half running. A few bright stars twinkle on the horizon.

Someone whistles. Sherif. The dogs begin barking up in the hills. I walk on uneasily, I've come further than I'd realized. And I've heard it said that *Marimmanos* are unpredictable, they can turn, you never know what they might do. I walk faster, the barking growing louder as the dogs gain on me.

I turn to face them. "Stop!" I yell.

But the dogs race past me down the track, scattering small stones with their paws as they go.

I trot on behind, inhaling the smell of wild mint, wondering what I might be capable of under certain circumstances.

'Red Sails in the Sunset' is playing from speakers on the *cantina* wall. The long refectory table stands in the center of the room with the remains of *prosciutto*, bread and empty wine bottles spotlit as if from a scene in a film. An overturned glass drips red wine onto a rolled-up mattress beneath the table. Vittorio laughs down from his photographs on the walls with friends in various smoke-filled rooms, images perhaps to convince himself that he has friends. The smell of cigarette smoke is strong in the room. I can feel the presence of the people who recently inhabited it. Maudie, a mixture of spice in the air, bitter sweet, a scent unique to her.

No one is in the garden, or by the pool. The lights are on in the kitchen, but no one is there either. Maudie's Fiat Panda stands in the driveway, along with the Range-Rover, the Lancia and the Auto

Bianchi. Where can they all be? I wait in the driveway, wondering what to do. The music has stopped; the only sound is the usual crickets beating their legs in a frenzied dance. Could she be with him? The thought makes me sick. He wouldn't do that, would he? Yet what do I know of him? No one ever knows what another is capable of doing.

The moon has not yet risen. In the diffused light of the stars the wood looks menacing. I pick up a long stick from the earth; it gives me courage to take the short cut to Ronaldo's house, the narrow path partly obscured in elongated tree shadows.

Arriving up through the trees and into the courtyard, I notice a spill of light through the open bar door. Hans is speaking Italian in a German accent. Then Vittorio's voice, deep, resonant: I look quickly in the doorway. Both men have their backs to me, seated at a low table, drinking. I step softly away.

A light is shining from Ronaldo's kitchen window. I creep round to his front door. It is locked. I knock gently. No response. I am about to knock harder when I hear a sound behind me. I turn sharply. Rocco is tramping up out of the wood with boxes of pizzas. He pauses in the courtyard for a minute to get his breath. Then walks through into the bar.

Retracing my steps, I hasten back down through the trees, dropping my stick only when I reach the driveway. A green Mercedes is parked alongside Maudie's Panda. Then I catch my breath. Sherif is waiting at the gates. On an impulse, I climb inside the Auto Bianchi. I shouldn't drive, I have no insurance, but I don't care at this moment. I turn the key in the ignition; there is enough petrol to get me home.

I reverse and spin the car round, wheels crunching on the gravel. Winding down my window, I call to the dark figure: "Sherif, would you tell Ronaldo - oh, never mind . . . "

I can't think of the words in Italian. I flick on the headlights and the little car bounces forward, through the gates, out along the dirt road.

I notice with a slight unease, the distant headlights behind me. It is unusual to see a car at this time of night on a deserted road. Once on the main road, I put my foot down and join other headlights on their way to dinner or some other Saturday-night reverie.

* * * *

I'm lying in bed under the sheet, my imagination on overdrive. I keep seeing Ronaldo in the wood with Maudie in his arms. She's been sick in Vittorio's apricot-colored bathroom, crouching in her black lace briefs over the apricot-colored lavatory. It must have been the red wine that did it. She sticks two fingers down her throat and the *Rosso di Montalcono* shoots down the apricot-colored bowl and then groping for the button on top of the cistern, she presses it and water gushes up, washing away all traces of the ruby-red wine, gurgling down the Tuscan drains into the dark interior where, no doubt, it will come up eventually and be re-bottled by Vittorio for the following exceptionally good year.

I turn over in bed: my thoughts race frantically on. There she is again, shivering in the wood, in spite of the warmth of the night. Ronaldo holds her close;

she can feel the heat from his hands burn into her skin. And when she opens her eyes and gazes into his, dark and glimmering with desire, she knows that however much her stomach hurts, her real reason for coming to Italy was to find something exactly like this.

I turn fitfully. Then listen. Vaguely I remember leaving Maudie's suitcase outside the front door with her things packed in it. I'm midway between waking and sleeping, still lingering in the dream when I think I see the bedroom door slowly opening.

Gasping, I fumble for the light switch and knock the lamp on the floor.

"Shhh - no 'ave the fear."

"What . . . "

"I search for you. I no see the Auto Bianchi, I think you take it and I come for you in the Lancia of Vittorio. I go up the *scarico* on to the roof and come in the window of the cook."

"*What?*"

"You 'ope for me or another?"

"For you, Ronaldo, for you. But . . . Maudie?"

"She go out."

"Where?"

"In the 'ead. Why you run like the rabbit? And when I call you no respond?"

"Why didn't you come after me?"

"I no run after no woman. I see you 'ave my rose. Now is dead. I bring another."

"But . . . I . . . thought - "

"You think too much. No speak more." He places his mouth on mine.

How can I speak when I'm melting under his kiss?

* * * *

I have always believed there is something about watching a house without the occupant knowing, that gives the watcher power. In his imagination he can see through the walls into the bedroom, he can visualize the occupant lying in bed, naked, available for him. Perhaps, it's better than reality. Perhaps the reality of confronting a naked woman in bed is not easy to deal with.

I'm trying to understand the mind of the watcher I've seen earlier sitting on the wall outside my bedroom window. It was too dark to see clearly. But he was large – too large, I would have thought, to scale the high wall. The small window above my bed is always open; I like the night air. Perhaps he visualized himself as being lighter than he is and springing across the wall, Tarzan-style, in through the window.

But how he got up there at all is a mystery. The old village wall is ten feet high. He must have climbed the plum tree on the other side, taken off from a branch and landed on top of the wall opposite my window, congratulating himself on having made such a perfect manoeuver.

It had been the terracotta oil jar that gave him away. He must have been startled by my face in the window and fallen off the wall onto the prickly foliage growing along the bottom, and then come into contact with the terracotta jar, which broke as it keeled over. I can imagine him stumbling through the bed of lettuces with a violently beating heart and a stone lodged in his shoe. What I can't understand, though, is how no one in the street heard him. Not even Ronaldo, leaving my place at five a.m. this morning, heard anything.

Now it's seven a.m. on Sunday morning and all is profoundly quiet. Only a cat is screeching in the alleyway.

It's when coming out of the bathroom several minutes later that I hear a sound at the front door. I'm poised at the top of the hall stairs, huddled in my dressing gown. If it's Maudie having found her suitcase outside, I'm ready for the confrontation.

Then I notice a piece of paper being slipped under the front door. I run down the rest of the stairs.

Written on it are the words:

'Credo lei sia una brava donna.'

As predicted, there is no one in the alleyway – no one to be seen anywhere. Maudie's suitcase has gone. So she left quietly, avoiding a confrontation that neither of us wanted. It's for the best. I re-read the note. It's written on the same lined notepaper as the first one. What have I done to merit becoming a courageous woman instead of a wicked one?

In the bedroom, I throw on clothes. This anonymous letter writer has to be found; I want to tell her that her talent is wasted.

Glancing up at Rosalba's shuttered window, I pass down the street steps. It can't be her, she says what she thinks and wouldn't be bothered to write it.

I look up along Via Ciro Pinsuti. Apart from the usual row of parked cars, the street is deserted: everyone preparing Sunday lunch with mothers, and fathers, aunties and uncles and fifteen noisy grandchildren: I feel thankful that I have only myself and two cats to think about.

I scrutinize the windows shuttered against the morning sun and balconies draped in washing. I'm not sure what I'm expecting to find; even if I had seen someone eyeing me from behind a beaded curtain, it doesn't mean they are the anonymous writer. The only way is to catch the person in the act, I think. But whoever it is moves fast. It couldn't have been more than a couple of minutes between seeing the note and opening the door. I have a last look round before climbing back up the street steps. And it is then that I notice something I'd missed at first. Maudie's Fiat Panda parked outside Martino's shop.

I stare at it without moving. Then I cross the street and look through the open car window. There is a map on the seat. I try the door but it's locked. Trust Maudie to lock the car but leave the window open. I spot an envelope on the dashboard with my name on it and reach inside.

Dear Lorri,

I don't know how to say this any other way than please have mercy on me. I didn't mean to be awful, although I don't remember much of what happened, I only know that everybody hates me and I feel wretched. When I saw my case outside the door I felt so desperately unhappy. I've gone to the little chapel behind Martino's to say a prayer. I can stay in the hotel tonight if you won't allow me in your house.

Maudie.

I drop the letter on the car seat. Then feeling hot and irritated, I walk past Martino's boxes of moldy fruit and along between the houses to the small chapel. I don't feel any mercy at all – I could wring her neck - probably will when I find her.

The streets are so narrow here; you could reach out of your window and touch the opposite building with a long pole. At night, it's easy to imagine oneself back in the dangerous torch-lit past, escaping with a thudding heart through the twisting putrid lanes that lead one into the other, never knowing who may be crouching in the dark ready to take your life for a pittance.

Even in the daytime the little streets are full of shadows. I pass under a Gothic arch. Trust Maudie to stage a dramatic farewell scene. A lamp juts from the wall at the end of a row of houses with broken steps and small iron balconies. I glance across the courtyard, at the steep stone steps leading up to the chapel door. And then I see her, lying in the entrance. "Maudie!" I hurry over to her.

Maudie lifts her head, looks at me and then lies back with a shuddering moan.

"For God's sake! Whatever's happened?"

"I was pushed."

"Pushed? Who by?"

"A man – big – grotesque – I could hardly look. He came toward me and I-I slipped and fell. I hit my head and . . . and . . . " She starts to cry. "All I wanted was to go into the chapel and pray. I was too frightened to come home . . . of what you'd say, I felt too ashamed."

"Oh, Maudie."

"Ronaldo hates me, he left me alone with Vittorio, they despise me, I know they do. And now you do."

"No, I don't. And no one despises you."

"I'm so sorry, really I am. I don't know what I'm doing when I drink. I beg you to forgive me. Will you?"

"Yes, of course. But can you stand? How long have you been here?"

"Hours."

"Oh, my God. Let's get you home."

I help Maudie to her feet and then with her leaning heavily on me, walk her slowly back under the Gothic arch, past Martino's and up the street steps, round into the alleyway and to my front door.

* * * *

It's Sunday evening: we're eating hard-boiled eggs and salad. We drink water. It hasn't been easy showing Maudie sympathy. I feel used somehow, dragged once again into another of her absurd melodramas, which I'm not entirely sure I believe, for she seems to have recovered remarkably quickly from her harrowing ordeal.

"Could Vittorio be behind it?" she asks, having showered and washed her hair. Now, she looks remarkably perky in my towelling bathrobe. "After last night I think he's capable of anything, including murder. That man I saw outside the chapel could well be one of his *Quasimodo* henchmen."

"I'm supposed to be the one with the over-active imagination, remember?"

"I never imagined it. And you'll never know how badly your friend Vittorio behaved."

"He's not my friend."

"He encouraged me to drink. And I think the wine was poisoned."

I roll my eyes.

"That last glass of white wine Giuseppina gave me had been doctored, I swear it."

"Why would she want to?"

"Not her, *him*, Vittorio, to have his wicked way with me."

"Oh, Maudie, *please*. You were plastered; he didn't have to dope your wine to do what he wanted. It was more likely Giuseppina. She was jealous. That's a motive for violent action."

"She's no reason to be jealous of me. I'm not in love with Ronaldo. You are. And he is with you. Sherif told me. He knows a lot of things that go on. Did you know Vittorio's wife doesn't allow him in his bed any more?"

"And how would Sherif know?"

"He's heard the aguments. They think that shut up like a dog on a mattress in the *cantina* he hears nothing, but he hears everything."

"And I suppose he told you this in English, did he?"

"Sherif speaks quite good English. If you hadn't ignored him you'd have found that out."

"I didn't ignore him; I just had no desire to communicate with him."

"You'd have found a jewel if you had. He's a deeply spiritual man, a lost soul amongst all these dysfunctional people. I feel uplifted because of him. Just imagine, Lorri, I have to come to Italy to fall in love with a gardener – very Lady Chatterley, don't you think?"

"Maudie, be serious."

"I've never been more serious. In fact, I'm going to put the house on the market the moment I get back."

"What for?

"I want to exorcize the past and find a new life like you've done."

"But I thought you loved the house."

"I do . . . "

"And is Julian also to be exorcized?"

"No more than you've exorcized Richard. Julian's given up hairdressing and wants to be an actor. Now I want to find a new life with Sherif."

"Oh, come *on* . . . You don't know the man."

"Sometimes, Lorri, you can meet someone for one evening and know more about them than someone you've lived with for years. He's the most sensitive man I've ever met. And he respects me, unlike that loathsome Vittorio and his German friend. He never took advantage of me, never laid a finger on me all night. It was so romantic, sleeping together under the trees. He carried me through the forest in his arms."

"Couldn't you walk?"

"I was ill, I keep telling you. He was protecting me from Vittorio. I can't mention his name without feeling ill again. He's an *animal* - "

"What did he do, exactly?"

"It's not what he . . . " Maudie sighed and put down her fork. "It was the degrading way he danced with me, sticking his thumbnail into my back, pushing his loathsome leg between mine while that German friend of his just laughed. Honest to God,

Lorri, I don't know how you can start a new life surrounded by such dysfunctional people."

"I'm hardly surrounded by them - they live a bus ride away. And they're not all dysfunctional."

"Poor Sherif, having to sleep with the dogs and never getting enough to eat. Thank heaven he's now sharing Ronaldo's apartment."

"I didn't know that."

"There's a lot you don't know, it seems."

"How do you know Sherif's not married with a family in Albania?"

"He would have told me."

"Not if he wants to get to England he wouldn't. He'd look for any excuse to get there."

"I'm not his excuse, if that's what you mean. He loves me. He told me so. And you can take that cynical look off your face."

"But it's so sudden."

"Lots of things are sudden in life. Your meeting Ronaldo was sudden. Sherif thinks he's the most honest person he's met in Italy. But I think you should be careful. He's a friend of Vittorio, so can he be trusted?"

"He's not a friend, he's working for him."

"I think he's attractive, completely different from Richard. But is this what you want? Sherif says Vittorio wants Ronaldo to marry Giuseppina. Do you think he will?"

"No."

"Would you like to marry him?"

"No."

"Oh, I don't know that I believe you, Lorri. I think you might. I'd marry Sherif if he asked. I believe in being spontaneous."

"So do I but not about things like this."

"Just about things like this. When something's right, you know it. Which is why I can't wait to see him tonight."

"But you're leaving for England tonight."

"I'm meeting him at the airport. On a late flight you can sometimes get a standby ticket. He wants to come to England and spend time with me so we can get to know each other. Oh, Lorri, your face is a picture. How could you imagine he could continue working for a man like Vittorio? Even if he wanted to, he couldn't, not now, not after Giuseppina's seen us together. She saw us lying in each other's arms. She's bound to tell Vittorio and then who knows what he'll do.

"But I'll tell you something else; Giuseppina was very kind to me. Everyone had gone off with the dogs when I arrived at the house wrapped in nothing but a bath towel in the morning. She ironed my dress, she made me toast and gave me a special herbal remedy to calm my stomach. I don't think she means any harm. Are you sure you're not reading too much into that as well, Lorri?"

13
In a State of Trust

I am travelling back in a stupor on the crowded bus from Siena. A robust woman with hairy armpits is sitting next to me taking up most of the seat. She has a basket of oranges on her lap that keeps nudging my thigh. I can smell the sickly odor of her sweat mixed with the scent of the oranges. I close my eyes, too exhausted to complain, and lean my head against the window. Sweat trickles down my face. Someone has opened the window behind me. I lift my hair up and air caresses the back of my neck.

"If you don't know what being in love is, you're not in it," Gerry Croft had said at lunch today at our favorite restaurant, the *Grattacielo*. "He called me his angel of delight," I'd said. "Is that a sign that he's in love, do you think?" She had laughed, rather bitterly, I'd thought. "Spare me the mush," she said. "Words, words, nothing but words, but there's nothing behind them with these Italian men. Only a lot of garlic breath. So much for the great Latin Lover!"

The bus stops: the woman with the oranges is on her feet, mercifully, shuffling to the door. I stretch out my legs - two seats for myself. A man in a black suit is easing his way through the crowd at the bus stop. I look round in surprise as the bus pulls away. But all I can see is the back of his dark head. I feel certain it was Sherif. But if so, what is he doing here? He should be in England with Maudie.

* * * *

Dear Lorri,

By now you should have received the solicitor's letter instructing you to add my name to the deeds making us therefore joint owners of 2 Vicolo della Mura.

The letter in the blue envelope was waiting for me when I arrived home. I read it with, as always, a sinking heart.

I put considerable value into the property in both time and money, probably to the value of £7,000 and I have a legal entitlement to that. From the point of view of marital law I am equally entitled to half of what we accumulated together, the furniture and possessions. I was shocked that you took it upon yourself to decide what was an equal division of our personal possessions. I am now in my own flat here in Frankfurt and have barely enough to furnish one room, I have no dining-table to eat off, I do not have crockery, sheets, towels, not to mention countless other things that are necessary for everyday living.

What had happened to the things I sent him? He must have received them, for Del of *Del Boy's Removals* had taken them out to Germany on a round trip and they were renowned for their reliability.

I was incensed by your insensitivity to me and our friends...

What friends? We didn't have any; he'd scared them all away. *I feel at least by sharing the property with me you can make up a little for the hurt you have caused me . . .*

I screw the letter up. For the first time, I begin to wonder whether Richard is quite all right in the head. He's turned everything round in his mind so that now I'm the guilty one - perhaps I am, but not in the way he's implying. I hadn't gone off to another country and then moved in with some man because of a housing shortage. Going off to Germany to work for a friend; I'd admired him at first for his courage, but when he'd explained about Veronica, and how he had to share her house and then eventually her bed, I'd been devastated. You don't understand the relationship, he'd written. What was there to understand? They'd probably been sitting up in bed together drinking tea and composing the letter. I grab the pen:

Richard,

Everyone hurts everyone in every relationship, it happens because people are growing and sometimes grow away from each other . . .

I throw down the pen. I want to shout and scream from sheer frustration. I get up from the table and swaying slightly, open the fridge to look for iced tea. None left. Maudie has drunk it all. I sit down again and smooth out Richard's letter. . . . *and I would very much appreciate it if you could put my white canvas shoes into a bag and leave them with Rosalba for me to collect on my next visit. . .*

Rosalba! She's the one writing the anonymous letters. They are in cahoots. She'd always favored Richard, put an extra little roasted bird on his plate at lunchtime. The trouble is, I have no proof. I shall find it, though.

I begin washing up. There'd been no time this morning. I'd overslept from the night before and rushed for the Siena bus anxious to arrive at the university on time.

Maudie's legs had been covered in little red scratches, I'd noticed, when she'd left for the airport. Carried through the forest indeed! I rinse out the coffee pot. She isn't happy unless she's starring in some extraordinary self-created drama. Like the time when she'd collapsed on the grass during my birthday party in England, saying that she'd seen a menacing shadow behind Roy, the man sitting next to her. And poor Roy, training to be a healer, had carried her upstairs to the bedroom demanding smelling salts with Julian, her young lover, ready to punch him on the nose and Roy's wife seething in the dining room. The guests had said they couldn't remember a better lunch party. But really it had all been about Maudie needing attention.

I stack the plates, cups and saucers in the cupboard. She had probably placed herself decoratively on the chapel steps waiting for me to find her and be instantly forgiven out of sympathy. Which is, of course, exactly what happened. It might be comic if the memory of her behaviour at Vittorio's wasn't so awful. What with that and Richard's demands and the anonymous letters, it's making me feel weak and muzzy with apprehension. I have to lie down and rest.

And that's when the dream begins:

I'm driving along the Devon coast road: the problem is that alleyway, I'm thinking. Potato peelings flung about and a rotten tomato outside next-door's dustbin. The walls need painting, flowers set out in tubs. But no one cares about the backs of the houses. Only the fronts look respectable, hedges trimmed, pebble paths leading from little gates to identical crocus beds on either side of identical front doors. Strange how in five weeks of living in Kellands Row I've never seen anyone else; lights come on in other houses at night, but I never hear a sound. I sometimes wonder if the lights are switched on and off automatically at certain hours and I'm the only person living in the row. But someone else must be there, if only to fling out the potato peelings.

I pull into the deserted car park of the Thurlstone Grand hotel, get out of the car and lock it. A light rain is falling. I step over puddles, my clothes already drenched. The reception is deserted. Could I be the only person in the hotel? I enter the spacious and empty lounge and settle myself in a flowered armchair near the window to wait for someone to come and set the scones, the cream and the jam before me.

No shortage of hotels, I'm thinking, gazing through the window at sky the color of curdled milk. I might try the Cottage Hotel in Hope Cove. Then there's the hotel I'd heard of in Bigbury Bay, which you could walk to when the tide's out. So many hotels in South Devon, so many cream teas - the choice is endless. No need to worry about having nothing to do. And so long as the Social Security gyros keep arriving I could start on North Devon, might even venture into Cornwall. But is this it? Is my life to be nothing more than a sequence of cream teas in various hotel lounges?

My eyes flutter open for a second: drenched in sweat, I turn over. I'm back in the dream:

A shimmering green light shimmers on the sea and the rain is falling, each drop separate, like glass beads upon a curtain.

Hope Cove is a wild and windy place; it calls to the wildness in me. Inner and Outer Hope, where huge rocks protect it from the southwest. There is no sound, apart from the sea and the relentless cry of the seagulls. The sea is streaked as red as the sky, making it difficult to know where one ends and the other begins. The jutting rocks, black against the evening sun, have a life of their own, prehistoric animals swimming in the blood-red sea.

Sunnyfield Cottage is small. The dilapidated thatch doesn't look up to surviving another winter. It's exactly what I want, though, so I knock on the door when I see the '*to let*' sign, hoping to find the owner. The place looks deserted. I peer through the leaded window into the sitting room. Dingy. But I could improve it and make it my home. *Home is inside yourself*; I hear Maudie's words. Maybe, but I have to start somewhere and escaping that miserable alleyway with the rotten tomato and potato peelings is surely the right start. I'd like to rent the cottage, I'm telling the estate agent. It's unfurnished, he says, dubiously. Even better. I can take the furniture out of store and save money. So I'm signing the contract for six months with the option to buy, though, with what I'll use for money, I have no idea. Now I am ringing *Del Boys's Removals* and they arrive the next day, bringing everything down from London, parking two wheels of the lorry up on the grass verge to allow the occasional car to pass . . .

I wake up feeling apprehensive. I get off the bed and go into the kitchen and splash cold water on my face at the tap. I stand in the *salotto*, furniture crowding about me like old friends from the past.

Everything had fitted superbly into that Devonshire cottage in Hope Cove: the tall clock, desk, reading lamp, dresser under the oval mirror, dining table against the flaking wall, the chintz chair and the green two-seater in front of the fire. It had been as if I had lifted up my home in London and planted it carefully down by the sea in Devon. All Richard's things I had given to *Del Boy's* to store. I'd watched them pass the rocking chair, Windsor chair, mirrors, standard lamp, several pictures and a warming-pan back into the lorry. Then I drove round to Kellands Row to collect the beloved cats and found a letter in a blue envelope that arrived that morning.

If there's anything you disagree with on this list of items to be returned I'm sure we can make a compromise then when I'm next in England I'll collect the furniture from Del's and take it all away.

It had been those words, *take it all away*, that had sent the blood to my head, made me rip up the letter and throw it into the dustpan. I had compromised enough with those stilted phone calls he'd made from Germany with *her* in the background banging pots and pans about as if to say, *I'm* here now, *I'm* the one preparing his supper.

Is this what ten years together has been all about? Fighting over chairs, pictures and warming-pans? It's the furniture so much as what it symbolizes. Our joint hopes and dreams, our life together, which, like the house when we'd left it, had been swept clean and thrown out with the dust.

There's no reason why we shouldn't continue to share our home in Sinalunga and enjoy it. So long as I know when you wish to visit then I'll make sure I'm not around and come for the occasional holiday without disturbing you.

Then my letter which had changed everything, saying I had decided to go and live in Sinalunga so unfortunately our home wouldn't be available for him to holiday in. What a shock it must have been for him to read that I intended going alone. An inspired idea, even though, of course, I had no intention then of doing any such thing. Why, the very idea of living alone in Italy, speaking only a few words of the language, was something that terrified me.

The tide had been coming in when I strode down to the Devon postbox to mail that fateful letter. The light had darkened on the horizon, seagulls dipping and wheeling across the water's edge. I'd run along the sand to the sea, crying out into the wind, "I'm free, I'm free." And the wind had whipped the words from my mouth, tossing them out to sea with the waves, tumbling and crashing them against the prehistoric rocks.

What had frightened me? The feeling that my life would change forever from the moment I sent the letter? Yes, that was frightening. I sit on the green two-seater sofa in the *salotto* and close my eyes. I must have drifted off, for there I am, in Hope Cove, re-living it all:

The sea closes me off from the shore, suddenly and perilously; spraying the rocks I crossed only minutes before. I'm walking quickly, water surging over my boots, sinking them into the sand. I tug them off, first one, then the other, then lose my balance, falling sideways into the foam. My heavy sheepskin jacket weighs me down; frantically, I unbutton it, sinking, rising, struggling out of it, thrashing the water, kicking my feet, trying to touch the bottom. But I am out of my depth, losing my breath, gasping and swallowing water in an attempt to keep my head up. And as the foaming water rushes over my face, I remind myself that I'm a good swimmer and strike boldly out against the current, swimming recklessly on into the freezing waves.

The dark and jagged rocks loom close. I'm swimming with all my might toward them and the current does the rest, thrusting me forward against the barnacled sides. I reach up desperately for a clump of seaweed, but it's slimy and I lose my grip. Waves crash over my head, engulfing me; my strength nearly gone. But up I come, scrabbling and grabbing for the rock. And in that terrifying moment, a decision was made. I have to survive, not just for the cats, but for myself. I must fight for my life with all my strength and spirit. And as another wave carries me forward up onto the rock's surface, I grip the seaweed that grows abundantly like a mane around a huge animal's neck. I pull myself higher, higher still, out of the water and onto the craggy head. My legs are bleeding, but I can feel nothing for the numbing cold. The sea crashes and roars in Hope Cove, shooting spray right up to where I crawl, inch by precarious inch, across the smaller rocks. I'm shaking so violently I can hardly hold on but if I fall I know I will never survive, I *have* to get to the road . . .

I open my eyes: I get up and go to the window. A strange greenish light had lit the Hope Cove sky that evening, as it is lighting the Sinalunga sky this evening. I remember how the intense joy of being alive had infused me with an energy that had driven me in a direction I wasn't sure I'd wanted to go. But I knew I must trust, and then, like the current, it would propel me forward to fulfil my destiny wherever that may be.

14
The Tea Party

Someone has trampled over Martino's lettuces in the night. And not content with that, they've broken the antique terracotta oil jar that belonged to his mother: *"nienti sicuro."*

Nothing is secure. Sinalunga is not the safe haven it had once been when doors could be left open and people trusted each other. I buy two loaves of bread from Martino and depart with a sense of unease. It must have been Quasimodo when he fell off the wall opposite my bedroom window. He probably stumbled through the lettuces to get to the street. I should report it to the *carabinieri*. Only I don't want to make a fuss. It would be simpler to get a light fixed outside my door then I can see who is in the alleyway before entering.

I understood almost everything Martino said, for he speaks Italian slowly and loudly to me. We must lock our doors, he'd said, waving his finger at me. For we never know who could be waiting in the night to surprise us.

I decide to call on Tonina immediately to see if she knows someone who can fix the light for me. Tonina opens her door and hugs me. But when I ask her about the light she looks worried. She says something about electricians not wanting to do small jobs. *"Che si fa? Aspettiamo."*

What is one to do? We wait. That seems to be the response to everything here. Which means things never get done. It's the same story with the plumber, never available to plumb in Tonina's new washing machine. And what is one to do about that? Then she carries on about a cousin in Arezzo whose brother knows an electrician who owes a favor to somebody or other, and from there on I'm lost. It will end with me having to ring Vittorio who will send someone round the next day. And what price will I be expected to pay for that, I wonder.

On Thursday Vittorio telephoned to say I must pay fifty *euros* for the two dinners I ate in his house and ten *euros* for Rocco's concert. At first, I'd laughed, thinking he was joking. Then when I realized he was serious, I asked if it was the custom in Italy to invite a guest to dinner then ask them to pay for it. He hadn't understood – or pretended not to, and then Silka came to the phone and invited me to a tea party on Sunday to meet her mother. And how much will that cost? I'd asked. Silka hadn't understood, either. But I've already guessed the price, for it has been hinted at a week ago: to teach Valentina English.

The phone is ringing as I open the front door. I climb the stairs two at a time.

"What you stay doing?"

"I stay shopping."

"I stay to work."

There is a brief pause: then he says *ciao* and hangs up.

I stare at the phone in misery. What kind of fool must Ronaldo think I am? There's so much I *want* to say to him but still don't know how. I like to think I'm understanding the language better. But I'm speaking less, even though I've returned to school and trying hard to catch up with what I've missed. It's a fear of making mistakes, Rudolfo, the *professore* says. I only know whenever I try to speak to Ronaldo I seem to forget every damned word I've learned. How I long for the time when I'll be able to talk intelligently to him, instead of like a three-year old.

But tomorrow I will see him. And tonight I shall think of him. I'll sit on the roof with the cats as I've done most nights, gazing out at the lights of Sinalunga, the distant lights of Cortona, Lucignano, Torrita, Bettolle, Montefollonico; it looks as though the earth is littered with stars.

* * * *

It's four days since Maudie's welcome departure: the hottest Wednesday on record, I'm told. And this Saturday, 23rd July, threatens to be even hotter. I'm expecting a honeymoon couple from Hertfordshire later today. That means six sweltering nights under the desk.

I'm on my way to Vittorio's, cycling across his driveway, a white cyclamen in my front basket. I can see him heading up the path toward Ronaldo's apartment with a bottle of wine. He looks round at the sound of my tires on the gravel, then comes gliding back down the path with long strides. He takes a swig of wine: there's the sound of women's laughter from the kitchen as he heads across the driveway toward me.

"Where are you going, *bella signora*?"

"I've come for tea."

"Ah, the English woman who come to drink the English tea?"

"Isn't that the idea, a tea party?"

"I've no idea what the idea is, *cara mia.* I know only that I don't drink the tea." He stares appraisingly at me. "Not many women go pink like you," he says. "I cannot remember when I have last seen such a strange *fenomeno.* It must be because you have the guilt to take the Auto Bianchi without the insurance?"

"I'm sorry - I explained on your answering machine what happened."

"I don't want the explanations. I want that you insure the car."

"I have the money to *buy* the car, not just insure it," I say. I reach inside my bag for the envelope of money. "It's all here in cash."

Vittorio laughs. "What would you say if I tell you that I don't want your money, eh?"

"I'd say that then I couldn't take the car."

He stands lopsidedly regarding me astride the bicycle. These undressing-me-with-his-eyes kind of stares make me feel uncomfortable. He'd stared at me in the same way in the Corner Bar in Sinalunga ten years ago. I'd had paint in my hair and was dirty from all the decorating I'd been doing. I couldn't understand his interest in me. He'd talked to Richard first at the counter then joined us at the table, introducing himself, saying how he liked to meet English people. He'd ordered champagne, which, of course, Richard paid for.

"I think sometimes you see into my heart," he's now saying. "It disturbed me once, and it still does. A woman like you can ensnare a man, especially one like Ronaldo who is open: before he know more he will be caught like the fish on the hook."

"I'm not trying to catch anybody on any hook," I say. "Can we get back to the money?"

"Why you insist always to speak of money?"

Can he be serious? It's one of his favorite subjects. "I'm not aware that I do," I say. "But now I want to. Which reminds me - " I draw another envelope from my bag. "I owe you for my dinner and Rocco's concert."

"You are like the *grand ragioniere, cara*," he says, opening the envelope and pocketing the fifty *euros*. He hands me back the empty envelope. "*Va bene.* But I no take nothing for the car. Or are you too proud to accept a present?"

"A present?" I don't like the sound of this. "No, I'm not too proud. Only - I'd prefer to pay, that's all. But thank you for the generous offer."

He makes a face as though to say, don't waste my time with your stupidity, and walks away.

"Just a minute, Vittorio." I wheel the bike after him and withdraw the lawyer's letter from my bag.

"You have more money to give me in your envelopes? What you think, I am, *un grande prostituto?*"

I ignore that. "I'd value your advice. I'm not sure what to do about this."

Vittorio takes the letter, his mouth turning down at the corners as he reads. "Ricardo don't think you show this to me? What Ricardo stay thinking?"

"I'm not sure what Ricardo's thinking these days."

"Come, we go."

"Where?"

"To drink the wine."

"But I've come for tea." I lift the cyclamen from the bicycle basket.

Vittorio grabs the bicycle and dumps it on the ground. Then taking my arm, he leads me firmly up to the terrace where Giuseppina is setting the table with rose-patterned china. He fills a plastic cup with red wine and drinks it himself. Then picks another from the stack on the table and pours one for me. "You put your money away before you lose," he says, grabbing the envelope of money and stuffing it back into my bag. "Now you don't worry more. Everything okay?"

No. It isn't. And the last thing I want is wine. A glass of iced-tea would be welcome. I place the cyclamen on the table. Then become aware of Giuseppina watching me. That too adds to the general feeling of anxiety.

"You are always in agitation when you come in my house," Vittorio says, leaning back in his deck chair regarding me. He slaps a mosquito on his leg, a curiously hairless leg, I notice. Then he frowns at Giuseppina watching us and she moves sullenly away.

"So what you think?"

"What do I think about what?" He's put his wraparound sunglasses on; it's disconcerting not to see his eyes.

"What we must to do in this situation, eh?"

"I don't know. That's why I'm asking you."

"I tell you what I do. I give this letter to Rocco."

"Rocco? Whatever for? I don't want him involved."

"Rocco understand the law. He take good care of this lawyer."

"What do you mean - good care?"

Vittorio looks across me. "*Ecco*, Ronaldo. He take my new shirt. He is the true *prostituto*. He take all and pretend it is for the love."

Sun-streaked hair freshly washed, beige silk shirt open at the neck, crumpled navy cotton trousers and the same old cowboy boots with the dusty toes turned up. Ronaldo smells of the shower, soap and cologne. He touches my shoulder fleetingly as he pulls a chair beside me.

From now on I'm finding it difficult to concentrate on a single word that's being said. Is this falling in love? Losing your mind, no longer having control over yourself? If so, I must be very much in love, because I can't remember ever feeling quite like it. Perhaps I have, and perhaps each time it's been different, so that each time has felt like the first time. No matter the answer, it is an unhealthy state to be in for if he moves away I might cease to exist.

Now Ronaldo is reading the letter. He makes a gesture that could mean anything and hands it back to Vittorio. The dogs bark and race after a battered gray Peugeot drawing up in the driveway. "I keep for now and we speak later," Vittorio says, winking meaningfully at me and tucking the letter into his shirt pocket.

Lisa, the sari-clad English woman I saw at the concert, is emerging from the Peugeot, this time in a flowing green sari. She's carrying a biscuit box. Her skin looks unhealthily white in the sun. Then a robust woman in Bermuda shorts and gray-cropped hair appears in the kitchen doorway, carrying an enormous bowl of potato salad. She marches across the courtyard on wrestler's legs and plants it down in the center of the pink flowered tablecloth. "I am Gretta," she announces. "I am the mother of Silka. And who might you be?"

"Lorri."

"Lorri who?"

"Just Lorri will do."

"How long for you remain in Tuscany, Lorri?"

"Forever."

"That is too long to remain anywhere."

"I'm happy here."

"You will not remain so."

"Oh? Why not?"

"The Anglo-Saxon mentality goes not well in a Latin country. We have a different idea of family values."

We are off to an excellent start: sitting round the table on the terrace, me between Ronaldo and Lisa, the irascible Gretta opposite. With Silka on her right, her granddaughters on the other side, she is trying, in between snatches of conversation, to predict their every need: water for Valli? Gretta is there; glass in hand. A plate for Anna? A fresh napkin for Silka? Now lunging to the drinks trolley, her massive backside almost splitting the seams of her shorts as she bends to collect a rose-patterned plate and pink paper napkin. Everything has to be attended to: everything, it seems, is under Gretta's control, even the mournful looking dogs know their place, tethered on long leashes to the nearest tree trunk.

"I'm not entirely convinced the mentality is all that different," I say. I help myself to a slice of pumpernickel spread with Gretta's special carrot and celery paté. "Or the culture. We all seem to like the same things, good food and wine and plenty of sunshine."

"Obviously, you have little experience," Gretta says. "When you have been here more long you will understand how different it is. First of all, the Italians do not listen. They want only to talk."

Not unlike yourself, I think.

Lisa, forking sauerkraut into her mouth, nods in agreement. Ronaldo rolls his eyes. His only motive for being at the table was to sit next to me, he explained later. Vittorio, refusing to join the tea party, sits apart in his deckchair, drinking wine from the bottle.

"So, what have you seen of the grand art since you have been in Italy?" Gretta asks me.

"Not enough," I say. "I don't seem to have had enough time to do anything yet."

"If you are interested you make the time. Otherwise, why are you coming in Italy?"

"To find a life. I can study the art afterwards."

"*Posso?*" Valentina reaches for one of Lisa's homemade biscuits. Gretta taps her on the arm. Valentina smiles demurely at her and speaks in German. "No." Gretta says. "We speak English with our English guests. What do you say if you want a cookie?"

Valentina giggles. "I want – " she begins, looking round at everyone, happy to be the center of attention. "I want that." She points at the biscuits and wiggles her tongue. Everyone laughs and Gretta offers her the plate of biscuits. Valentina decorously eating biscuits in her pink frilly dress, playing the good little grand daughter, accepting all that her grandmother puts before her. I grimace. How long will she be able to keep it up?

"You will speak good English, Valli, and also you, Anna, when Lorri teaches you," Silka is saying. Then repeats it to them in German.

I stare apprehensively at her. "Well, I'm not a teacher, you know." I look at Ronaldo for support. But he's gazing up into the vines, lost in thought.

"You don't have to be a teacher," Gretta says. "Only to talk the mother language. Do you think you are talking your language good?"

"I hope so." I try to catch Ronaldo's eye. I want to talk to him, but what can I say in front of these people? For now, it's enough that he is close and I munch steadily on into my pumpernickel. But Giuseppina is beginning to annoy me, for whenever she collects the dirty plates she makes a point of leaning over Ronaldo and touching his ear with her breast then repeating the gesture when setting out the clean plates. If she does it again I might well push her face into what remains of the sauerkraut!

"It is us strangers what keep the old houses going. We are the ones what are caring for these old places, not the Italians. They are not caring if they fall down. What is your opinion, Lorri? Now you are changing your life and living here, you must have some opinion about these things?"

Gretta is looking earnestly at me. As I've been only half-listening and am not at this moment remotely interested whether houses fall down or stay up and am more concerned as to when Giuseppina's iced tea will arrive to quench my thirst, I'm uncertain how to respond. "What do I think about what, exactly?" I ask.

"You are an expat, are you not? What are you expats thinking about these old houses?"

"I love old houses, I live in one and it's not falling down – as far as I know. And, out of interest, I don't see myself as an ex-anything. An ex-wife perhaps, but not an expat."

Lisa gives a snort of laughter.

"But you have left your country. You are on foreign earth. You must have an opinion."

"I've just given it. And I don't think of myself as an expat. I'm still a British citizen."

"What are you meaning by that?"

"I mean, I could go back to England tomorrow if I wished. In fact, I think I could go almost anywhere in the world now and pick up my life again."

"Ach! You English. You are so arrogant."

I flush. "No, not arrogant," I say, controlling my anger. "Free, free as air. I feel as though I'm flying above the world looking down on it." I turn to Lisa. "My consciousness has expanded since I came to live in Tuscany."

"I always thought you were stoned. What is it you're on, that's what I want to know."

"On the light and color, the smell, the warmth and generosity of the people. I've been stoned ever since I arrived. Who could fail not to be?"

"My husband could. He's a night receptionist in a hotel in Siena. He sleeps most of the day so doesn't get much chance to see the light or color. There's another side to *bella Toscana*; surviving here isn't easy if you haven't got money."

"Well, I haven't any money either. But I'm hoping to survive for as long as I can."

"You've got your own place. That makes a big difference. Our rented cottage in the wood has a leaking roof that the owner refuses to fix and working for the Italians is no joke. They screw you for all the hours they get out of you and pay as little as possible. I'm sorry, Ronaldo, but it's true."

Ronaldo is staring at her. I'm not sure if he has understood. Perhaps it's better if he hasn't. I'm sure it's not true, anyway. From what I see of Lisa, I would say she's inclined to exaggerate.

"You don't know how fortunate you are to own you own flat and work for yourself."

I nod. "I know I am. For as long as it continues."

"But *why* Ronaldo, you cannot do the restoration is what I am asking?" Gretta's voice is beginning to rise in anguish. "You are the right man for the job, are you not? Who else is there to do it? *Why* you are so negative about this old barn?"

I look from Gretta to Ronaldo. What old barn? What is she on about now?

Ronaldo lights a cigarette. "*No sono mai negativo.*" He rises abruptly and to my disappointment, moves across to Vittorio.

"He has to finish the bar, *Mutter.*" Poor Silka is looking strained.

"The bar, the bar, this crazy bar!" Gretta spoons fruit salad into glass bowls. "All I hear of is this bar. And who is coming in this bar, I want to know?"

Silka, with mouse-like movements, hands round the bowls of her special fruit salad made with kiwi, oranges and apples, sweetened with honey. She seems to have shrunk into herself since the arrival of her mother. She nibbles food, sips water and hardly speaks a syllable to anyone.

"All the way in the dark woods for a drink? Ach!" Gretta shudders with mock horror. "Why would a person go there when he could go in a bar in the town, is what I am asking?"

Gretta is addressing her remarks, in the main, to the back of Vittorio's head. Now she turns and stares intently at Lisa who stares unblinkingly back. "Do you think the people are coming to a bar in the dark woods?" she asks her.

I put my hand over my mouth. I have a horrible feeling I'm going to laugh.

Lisa smiles politely. She's not sure what to make of Silka's mother, she told me earlier. She doesn't like her, even though it has to be said, she seems to be having a positive effect on the children who aren't running round screaming for a change: everything looks clean and orderly and we are drinking water out of crystal glasses instead of plastic cups and eating off porcelain plates. "It's not really *in* the wood," Lisa explains, "it's more on the edge. And some people like that kind of rustic thing. I know we do." Lisa darts little glances at Vittorio as she speaks, as if hoping he can hear and understand she isn't against him. He ignored her when she arrived. But as he seems to be ignoring everyone, it's obviously not personal. Lisa had been surprised that she'd been invited to the tea party, she'd confided. After telling

Silka that she couldn't teach Valentina English because she had enough students already, Silka stopped ringing her.

"And what have you got to say about this, Lorri?" Gretta is addressing me again.

"About what?" Why is she so concerned with what I think?

"The bar? Will you want to go in this bar in the woods?"

"I might," I say, and turn away.

Lisa is watching me; I can see her from the corner of my eye. She observes me quite a lot, I notice, especially when I'm looking at Ronaldo. I must try not to be so transparent. She gives a knowing laugh and reaches for her over-size handbag. "Now I know what you're on," she jokes. "I'm surprised I haven't seen it before. But I don't envy you. You've got your hands full with that one. In my case, it's simpler; a special little ciggy is all I need to help get me through the afternoon." She gets up and clutches her leather bag, the size of a holdall. I watch her walk into the kitchen, wondering what she means. I'll make a point of asking her later.

Gretta is talking to Silka in German. The girls are crumbling biscuits into the fruit salad. The dogs are asleep under the tree, and Giuseppina, hopefully, is in the kitchen preparing the *tè freddo*, which, I'm told, is her speciality: a little muslin bag for each glass filled with aromatic herbs hand picked in the woods before the sun comes up.

15
Tè Freddo of a Different Kind

The dirty plates, the remains of the sauerkrout and potato salad have been carried back into the kitchen. Gretta's sugared apple cake now dominates the center of the table. "And what is your Grandmother Rosa doing for you?"

Gretta is speaking to the children slowly and deliberately in English. But every so often, she addresses the back of Vittorio's head, as if hoping by the force of her will to turn it round, for any reaction is better than being ignored, which he has done for most of the afternoon. "Does she come here to see you? Does she make apple cakes and biscuits and good jams?"

The children are looking at her, puzzled, understanding nothing. They look at Silka then at Gretta. Valentina giggles behind her hand. "She sings," Gretta continues, seemingly unconcerned whether they understand her or not, "Arias from Tosca, your mother tells me."

"*Mutter.*" Silka sits rigidly upright on her chair, staring intently at Gretta. "It is not good to speak of the mother of Vittorio. He does not like it." She then rattles off something in German. But Gretta carries on regardless. "And always she sing with no ears for the music." Gretta gives a hard laugh. I look apprehensively across at Vittorio, uncertain whether he is taking this in and what he will do if he is.

Gretta's voice is rising in pitch as Giuseppina finally emerges from the kitchen carrying a tray with five tall glasses jiggling with ice and fruit. The dogs stir restlessly in their corner. The female whimpers, eyes following Giuseppina as she sets her tray carefully on the table, a safe distance from Gretta who is now brandishing the cake knife. "Grandmother Rosa," she says, as she slices through the apple cake with sharp decisive cuts, "she is a simple woman. She does not know how to do things in the way what is – "

"*Basta!*"

Oh, my goodness, now for it!

Gretta, relieved to have Vittorio's attention at last, lays down the knife. "What is wrong with you? I say only that your mother is a simple woman, Vittorio. I am not speaking bad of your mother."

But Vittorio is on his feet, and drunk, by the looks of it. He stumbles against the chair.

"I am not speaking against her . . . I say only that she do not know how to sing the arias from Tosca."

"*Basta!* You are too ignorant to know anything about Tosca. What you know, eh?"

"I am not ignorant, Vittorio. And I did not say I know anything about Tosca."

"*Bene.* Because you don't know nothing."

"I repeat – " Gretta is making a supreme effort to keep calm. "I did not say – "

"You think my mother is stupid because she is simple?"

"I did not say she was stupid, Vittorio. I said – "

"Because, I tell you this, my mother is many times more the woman of you."

"Vittorio . . . I do not want this –"

"It is *you* who is stupid, because if you were clever you would understand you don't come in my house and insult my mother."

"I am not insulting – "

"You know, I tell you what you are, you are *arrogante e presuntuosa*. You don't speak never of my mother. You don't speak never of nothing more in my house. Now, you listen to me, you take your *marmallata*, your cakes and your little biscuits that even the dogs no want and leave my house this moment."

I held my hands to my face, part of me thrilled to see Gretta put in her place; yet appalled by the threatening violence.

"Vittorio, no." Poor Silka is flapping her hands in a helpless gesture. Ronaldo catches Vittorio's arm and leads him away, mumbling something to him in Italian. Things may have calmed down then if only Gretta, her ruddy complexion turning a worrying shade of crimson, hadn't continued with: "I am not leaving and you cannot force me to leave. You are an Italian *bastard!*"

I gasp and get to my feet.

Vittorio shakes Ronaldo off and advances on Gretta. Silka screams as he grabs Gretta's robust arm and shoves her against the table, knocking into Giuseppina's tray, upsetting two glasses of tea, one toppling into a pot of geraniums, the other to the ground, shards of glass scattered everywhere.

With a howl, Silka darts between Vittorio and Gretta. Ronaldo places a hand firmly on Vittorio's shoulder. "I don't want this woman in my house!" Vittorio yells, struggling to release himself. "She donna stay more in my house! *Capito?* Or I have to make the translation?"

Gretta is too shocked to speak. She clutches the table edge, then says in a rasping voice: "I understand well it is your house, Vittorio. But who paid for the house is what I am asking? *I* paid. It is *my* money what has paid for your house." Silka lifts a sobbing Anna into her arms, Valentina dodges behind her. "And *'this woman'* as you call me has kept everything going on here. Otherwise you would still be in the cowshed you brought my daughter to live in when you married her."

There is a deathly hush. Then Lisa coughs from the kitchen doorway and Gretta continues in the same voice: "I have never said no because of my daughter and I never will. But you have taken advantage of me for all these years, Vittorio. You have taken much advantage of me."

Now it's Vittorio's turn: "You think *I* have done nothing? I have made a life for your daughter here in Toscana. Given her two beautiful daughters, built a *palazzo* with all my ideas and the creativity of Ronaldo."

Suddenly he breaks into a flow of wild Italian, shouting the words, roaring with the rage of an animal. Then grabbing at the table, he lifts it and turns it over, sending glass, china, cake, forks and teaspoons flying. Then he falls back, losing his balance, and Ronaldo supports him. Ronaldo leads him stumbling down to the *cantina*, leaving us to stare after them in shocked silence. Then we hear a heavy door slam shut.

Nobody seems to know what to do for a moment. Giuseppina stands guarding the three remaining glasses of tea on the trolley. Lisa says something about final straws and Silka drops to her knees grasping at the bits of devastation surrounding her. "He's destroyed all *mutter's* china," she sobs. "All my best glasses, he's destroyed everything . . . he's destroyed my life, oh . . . oh."

Gretta pulls Silka up into her arms and rocks her like a child with Valentina clinging on behind and Anna crying with her hand in Lisa's. I kneel to gather the glass and the male dog breaks his leash and runs forward to sniff at the bits of cake on the ground.

"Giuseppina!" Silka shrieks over her mother's shoulder. "Keep the dogs away from the broken glass."

Two pairs of hands reach simultaneously to the trolly to clasp two of the three remaining glasses of tea. Two English women thinking alike, tea will calm, restore sanity. But Giuseppina, whose attention has been momentarily distracted by the dogs, cries out when she sees Lisa sipping the tea. She cries out again, only louder, when Lisa shares her tea with Valentina and Anna. "*No, no, no. . .*" She waves her hands, crying hysterically.

"Giuseppina, stop that noise! Fetch a brush and clean up here."

But Giuseppina ignores Gretta. "*No, no, no, no...*" She continues to wave her hands and cry.

"Do as my mother says. Bring plastic bags and a brush."

But Giuseppina ignores Silka too. She gazes at the third glass on the trolley and reaches for it; but

Gretta picks it up and holds it against her temples, and then thirstily gulps down the rosy-pink tea enhanced with bobbing slices of peach. "*Aaaah, no. . .*" Giuseppina turns on sandaled feet and runs back into the house like someone demented.

"What's gone wrong with *her*?" I ask, offering my tea to Anna who takes a few tentative sips. "Should we call a doctor?" But no one answers, for Gretta, trying to grab the dog by its collar, falls against Vittorio's deckchair and clings to Silka who strokes her arm and speaks reassuringly to her in German. "Should we call a doctor?" I ask again. "Is there anything we can do to help?"

"There is nothing anyone can do," Silka says, her arm around Gretta. "I must do what my mother said I should do a long time ago. I must divorce myself from Vittorio."

Valentina wails, which sets Anna off and the female dog breaks her leash and lopes forward to join the huddled women, howling, wailing, all moving unsteadily together into the kitchen.

"What can be done?" I ask. "It's like a Greek tragedy."

"Nothing. Sit down and drink your tea," Lisa says. "It's best to leave them to it, you'll only get in the way. It's not the first time I've witnessed something like this. Two years ago Vittorio held a knife to the throat of one of the German guests because he thought he was having it off with Silka. It took two strong men and a dog to hold him down."

"And was he?"

"What?"

"Having it off with Silka?"

Lisa shrugs. "I doubt it. But who knows? It was all forgotten the next day, whatever the truth was. As I'm sure this will be. Blood rushes to the head here. People threaten to kill each other one day, then carry on as though nothing has happened the next. We Brits keep everything inside until it festers. You only have to raise your voice at someone in England and they don't speak to you for ten years."

"Is it true that Gretta paid for the house?"

"She paid for the renovations. Vittorio lives on what he earns from the wine and his teacher's pension, which isn't as much as it might have been because he retired early. He's hoping Gretta will pop off soon and they'll inherit. And knowing Vittorio, I wouldn't be surprised if hasn't laid a few trip-wires about the place." Lisa inhales on her roll-up. "Some of us think Giuseppina's his illegitimate daughter."

"What?"

"Yes, her mother was an old flame, so the story goes. In these families there's usually a skeleton in the cupboard. I think Vittorio's hoping to marry her off to Ronaldo then he'll have the son he's always wanted."

I pick out a slice of peach from the bottom of my glass and eat it. "Does Giuseppina know?"

"That she's his daughter? I doubt it. Anyway, it's only a rumor."

"Some rumor. How did it start?"

"The ex-girlfriend came here once, Silka told me. She tried to demand money from Vittorio. There was a violent row in the *cantina* between them. She hit him apparently and Silka fled back to her mother in Germany, threatening divorce. But it all calmed down and when Silka returned, Giuseppina was installed as a home help."

"And Silka accepted that?"

"It was what she wanted, a girl to help with the children. It never occurred to her there might be something more to it. She's very naïve. She believed Vittorio was trying to make life easier for her, and in a way he was, as well as for himself. And Giuseppina's no threat to Silka. Or you," Lisa adds as an afterthought.

The tea has an unusually sweet and sour taste. I drain the glass. "Whatever one may think about Giuseppina," I say, "she can certainly make an excellent *tè freddo.*"

* * * *

Ronaldo drives the Lancia fast along the dirt road, a cloud of dust spraying up around the wheels.

"We are like on Safari." He turns on the radio and sings along with the Country and Western music, miming the guitar with his right hand, steering with his left. He looks at me. "You are sad?"

"No. Thoughtful."

"Yes, I know why. After today who is 'appy? But is more good they say what they feel. Tis better not to keep inside the feelings. But you are 'appy to be with me?"

"Oh yes," I assure him. "*Very* happy."

He switches the music off and we drive in silence. It's better not to talk, I suspect there are too many thoughts in his head, and in mine too, better not to try and discuss them in a foreign language. Yet, he needs to talk, I can sense his agitation. So I ask what happened in the *cantina* with Vittorio and he says Vittorio cried when he'd talked of his love for Silka. "Silka and her mother, they *succhiano la forza*," he explains.

"They suck the strength?"

"*Esatto.* They want to take *les filles*, the 'ouse, they take all and 'e 'ave nothing. And 'e say I am 'is only true friend in this life and the other one."

"What other one?"

"The next one – you know - the life what come after."

"Oh, *that* life. It's a bit dramatic, isn't it? But then, of course he is."

"But I no want to be 'is one true friend in this life or another, *è troppa responsibilità.*"

"Yes, I imagine it would be."

"But when 'e say 'e no 'ave nothing I laugh, because 'e 'ave much, 'e 'ave the *appartamento* where to live, and the bar to make the money. This is no nothing. You must not to trust the Anglo-Saxon mentality, 'e say. They no 'ave the sense of the family."

"Well, he would say that, wouldn't he?"

And it isn't true. I have a strong sense of family, even if it is only for the cats, their food served up on time with care and affection.

"And 'e say that you no speak my language never."

Also not true. In time I will learn Italian, I already understand many words; it's a question of putting them together in the right order. Things will work out. I'll make sure of it, in spite of Vittorio.

"I say I like the woman who no speak too much."

He places his hand possessively on my thigh. "You are *la bella donna Inglese,* who come from *Inghilterra* with two *gatti inglesi* to give Ronaldo Salvi the love and *sicurezza* I no 'ave never." He gives my thigh a squeeze and makes me jump.

He turns off the main road to a vineyard shelted by oak trees, some a hundred years old, he says. It had belonged to his Uncle Eugenio many years ago and he'd played there as a boy. Now it belongs to a wealthy *Romano* who hardly ever visits and never knows how often he, Ronaldo, sits amongst the vines reading *Hercule Poirot.* He likes to imagine how it would be if he owned such a vineyard and made wine to sell to the tourists. Vittorio had tried to buy it once, he tells me: they'd had plans to go into business together, the wine was to be called *Vino del Paese.* Wine of the Country. Ronaldo had designed the label, he pulls out a copy stuffed under papers in the glove department, a man floating face up, smiling in a wine glass. But the idea came to nothing when the bank refused to finance it. "Now is the good moment to visit the *vigna* again to make the renting in the summer. I bring friends to pick the grapes and then we make the wine together and I bring the tourists to buy the wine. What you think? Is a wonderful idea?"

"Er - *si,*" I say, tentatively. I'm not sure what he means by '*we*'. I don't fancy squashing grapes underfoot all summer long. Besides which, I can't. I've got my own tourists to consider.

We get out of the car and walk slowly amongst the vines. Their shoots knot across the wires between one row of posts and the next. On a leafy patch he throws himself onto the earth and pulls me down beside him under the vine leaves. We lie shaded from the sun and breathe in the smell of leafy mold. "This is better than my 'ouse," he says. Even though he'd cleaned it since Sherif had gone leaving his few possessions behind. He brushes his mouth against mine.

"I can't stay for long," I say. "I have to get back to look after my honeymoon couple, they're here for a week."

"But if they make the 'oneymoon they want to be alone. Like me with you."

"How do you know?" I kiss his ear playfully.

"'Ow I know what?"

"That they want to be alone?"

"Because 'e want to do like me now." He kisses my neck. "You want to be my woman?"

"Yes," I breathe. This is like something out of a film, I can't help thinking. I would never have believed it could happen.

"And when I give to you the rose you no think more it come from Patrizio?"

"He handed it to me. What was I to think?"

"You think too much and not always is good. Why you 'ave the fear?"

"I fear that you will go away."

He holds his eye against mine, eyeball to eyeball, our sweat trickling together; I have taken him to a place inside myself where he will remain for always.

We walk back to the car without speaking. Around us in the evening heat the vineyard whispers, secretive and primitive. The warm air enfolds us as we sink exhausted into the Lancia. He lights a cigarette; after several inhalations he stubs it out in the overflowing ashtray, leans across to wind back my seat and kisses me, urgently, forcefully again.

He follows the car ahead; on any other occasion he would have overtaken, now he seems content to drive slowly. He plucks cigarettes and a lighter from his shirt pocket and hands them to me. "Now I taste you and no the cigarette," he says, when I light it in my mouth and then place it in his. He puts his arm around me. "You are sure is finished with Ricardo?"

I look at him, surprised. "Yes, quite sure. Why do you ask?"

He slews his eyes round to me. "I must to be sure you are free."

"I am free. There is no other man in my life. Only friends, platonic friends."

"With the men is not possible?"

"Yes, it is - sometimes."

"Is no good. If I make my life with you I want no *uomo platonico* to come close."

I study him. It's hard to believe that he should care so much for me, older than him and unable to communicate that well. How long can it possibly last?

"Why you look?"

"Because you're good to look at."

"Also you. You are my angel of light." He tosses his cigarette out of the window. "We pick together the grapes, Lorri. I make the wine and you sell. What you say?"

I lean over and kiss him. It's all so wonderfully crazy. Then after a pause I ask: "Are you free also, Ronaldo?"

"Why?"

"Because   - I hear that you might marry Giuseppina."

"Giuseppina!" He gives a mocking laugh. "Who say that?"

"Vittorio."

"Vittorio say the stupid things."

She's infatuated with you. She looks at me as though she hates me. I'm jealous. I've never felt jealous in my life like this. I want to say this. But fortunately, I only think it.

Ronaldo puts his foot down, roars past two cars and speeds along the empty road. I feel a sudden coldness. I wonder how much he's understood.

"Giuseppina *è molto giovane, ha solo diciassette anni,* Lorri. We must to 'ave the passions."

"You mean the patience?"

"*Si, si.*"

"Why? I wonder. Being seventeen doesn't justify bad behaviour."

"Vittorio make the promise to 'er mother to give the work. You understand now?"

No, not really. And does he believe she's Vittorio's illegitimate daughter? Better change the subject. But still, I can't help asking: "Do you like her?"

He shrugs. "I no think of 'er."

"She thinks of you."

An ambulance, siren blaring, blue light flashing, tears past on the opposite side of the road. Ronaldo brakes. "You worry for Giuseppina and I worry for Rocco. I think 'e try to visit in your 'ouse."

"Rocco?" I almost laugh. "I wouldn't let him in. Anyway, I've not seen him since the night of the concert."

"Rocco wait always."

"What for?"

"The good moment."

It occurs to me for a wild second that Rocco could be *Quasimodo*. But it's absurd. I haven't told Ronaldo how I'd seen someone on the wall trying to see into my bedroom window. He'd insist on my closing all the windows and I'd die of suffocation.

"I think 'e come in the school in Siena."

I shake my head. "I've never seen him there."

"'Ow more long you stay in the school?"

"Another week."

"If you see 'im you call the *carabinieri*."

"Why? Is he dangerous?"

"All is dangerous who 'ave the *obsessione*. They no know the limits."

By the time we reach Sinalunga, he has begun a discussion about Gretta not knowing the limits. "She speak always too much, say the bad things with Silka, two women in the 'ouse, do nothing but cook the cabbage and make the bla-bla-bla. Then come Lisa who go always like the Indian and smoke the drugs. I come today for to see you, *altrimenti*, I no come. I stay good to eat with Sherif."

"Sherif? I thought he'd left for England."

"*Non, non.*"

"I think I saw him in Siena."

"*Si,* Sherif go in the *Questura per i documenti*, 'e want to bring the family in Italia."

"Family?"

"There is the wife and three sons."

Poor Maudie, I think.

Cars line either side of Via Ciro Pinsuti, making the narrow street even narrower. "Where is your leetle car?"

"In Martino's garage. I can't leave it on the street uninsured."

"I 'ope you no take without to pay."

"I want to pay. But Vittorio won't take the money."

Ronaldo parks the Lancia at the bottom of the street steps. He gets out and lifts my cycle out of the boot.

"Why does Vittorio call you a prostitute, Ronaldo?" I ask, jokingly.

He looks at me in surprise. "Because is jealous. 'E no want for us to be together."

"Everyone seems to be jealous. Including me."

"You no 'ave reason."

He kisses me goodbye and I watch the back of his head through the car rear window as he drives away. I almost told him I loved him. But fortunately, the words got stuck in my mouth. I'm not even sure I know what it means any more. I feel I have given too much and taken too much. I need time alone. Hopefully, the honeymooners will be out seeing the sights and I can shower; sit on the roof with the cats and find what remains of myself.

But when I open my front door, I hear voices. I sigh. The honeymooners have let themselves in with the key I left in the flowerpot. I shouldn't grumble, I need the money. I climb the stairs, and then pause in the kitchen doorway. Three people look up at me from around the table, Peter and Kim, the honeymooners, and Maudie's ex, Julian Bain.

16
The Interloper

Julian, in knee-length shorts, a red T-shirt, his long black hair tied back and one silver earring in his left ear, kisses me on the cheek. "I bet you didn't expect to see me, did you?"

"That's what Maudie said when she arrived," I say, eyeing the two empty wine bottles on the table.

"You look great. Coming here was definitely the right idea. And you've met a new fella, I hear."

"Not exactly, no. Who told you? Maudie, I expect. Well, you've mistimed things, Julian. She left on Monday."

"It's not Maudie I've come to see, it's you."

"Oh?" I smile anxiously at the honeymooners. "You've met Peter and Kim Craze, then?"

"Oh, I think you could say that." Julian laughs. "We've been putting the world to rights, haven't we, Peter?"

Peter, a flushed-faced young man, begins explaining, apologetically. "We'd just arrived back from Siena, you see, when your friend here – er, arrived at the same time. We were exhausted and thought a glass of, er - "

"My special red wine would revive you? Yes, I understand perfectly."

"Er, well – yes . . . I hope you don't mind?"

"It was my idea," Julian cuts in. "Can I offer you a glass of your special red wine, Lorri?"

"No, thank you."

"We'll replenish your store before we leave, won't we, Kimmy?" Peter says, and his Chinese wife smiles serenely up at me.

"I'm surprised you've got any bottles left after Maudie's visit."

"She's given it up, Julian."

"Oh yes?" He laughs cynically. "For how long?"

"For as long as she wants to."

I sit at the table feeling confused and mildly startled. He'll have to go, and as soon as possible. I can't conduct my love life with Julian around. "I hope you enjoyed your visit to Siena," I say to the honeymooners, trying to sound welcoming. So far, I've hardly had a chance to speak to them. When they'd arrived in the early afternoon, I'd handed them the key, vaguely explained where things were before cycling rapidly off to Rapolano. "And if there's anything you need, you have only to ask."

"Are you saying she actually didn't drink *anything* while she was here?" Julian asks, taking a glass from the cupboard.

"She drank iced tea." I watch him pour water into the glass. He hands it to me, and then empties the ashtray full of his cheroot stubs into the bin under the sink. He seems to know his way around.

"How did you find me?"

"The *carabinieri*. They thought I was your lover."

"Oh my God!"

"Does it matter?"

"Of course it does."

"Why? Are you not supposed to have a lover in Italy?"

The honeymooners laugh.

"Where are you staying, Julian?" I'm trying to keep the irritation from my voice. But this is too much. If Ronaldo hears about it – better not to even think of it.

"I thought – here, if possible?"

"No, no. That's not possible, Julian, I'm sorry. There's only one bedroom."

"And in there?" He jerks his thumb at the closed *salotto* door.

"T-that's my study. And I sleep in there, with the cats."

As if on cue, Billy and Gertie appear at the window as though they'd been listening and now felt it time to make their presence felt. Gertie flees at the sight of so many people. But Billy stands his ground on the top step.

Julian salutes him.

Billy regards him with yellow-eyed hostility.

"Okay, I won't take your bed," he says to the cat. "I'll sleep on the kitchen floor." Everyone seems to find it funny, except me, and Billy, who, tail flicking with annoyance, disappears out onto the roof.

"And if you folks want a cooked breakfast before you leave for further sightseeing in the morning, let me know."

"Julian, just a minute - " My voice quavers. I take a breath. "There's a hotel in the village. You can go there." Everyone looks at me as though I'm the wicked witch. "There's no room here, is there?" I laugh awkwardly. "You can see that for yourselves."

Julian grins at the honeymooners. "Do you mind if I crash here for a night or two?"

"Makes no difference to us," Peter says. "We can work the bathroom routine between us. We're going to Trasameno in the morning. We'll be off early, then it's all yours."

"Great. No problem. I'm a late sleeper. I wouldn't mind jumping in the shower now if that's all right with you, Pete?"

"Feel free. And don't worry about breakfast. We can handle that, can't we, Kimmy?"

I stare incredulously at them. Things are going horribly wrong. Under normal circumstances I would never be so feeble. But feeling dazed and exhausted from so much – well, lovemaking, I'm at a loss to know how to handle events. I am about to speak when the telephone rings. I stare in dismay at the *salotto* door, listening to the ringing. I can't respond in case they see inside the room.

"Aren't you going to answer it?" Julian asks. "It rang before but the door was locked."

"I always keep it locked."

"Why? Who are you hiding in there?"

More laughter from the honeymooners: feeling foolish, I take the key from behind the milk jug in the cupboard, unlock the door and slip inside the room, careful to close the door behind me.

I lift the receiver.

"Have you seen him?"

"What? Oh, it's you, Maudie."

"Do you know where he could be?"

"I've no idea. Listen, I – "

The *salotto* door opens. I dart forward to try and close it, pulling the telephone from the windowsill and sending a pile of books to the floor. Julian and the honeymooners ease themselves into the room, gazing round in amazement at all the furniture, clock, books and pictures. "Oh, look," Kimmy squeals with delight. "The little cat's bed under the desk, how sweet."

"So where's your bed?"

The game's up! "I sleep in the cat's bed, Julian," I say, resigned. "We all sleep together in a row."

They laugh. They don't believe me. The church bells begin clanging in the *piazza* and Julian, climbing over the sofa to help me pick up the books, trips over the chair leg and lurches forward, sending yet more books to the floor. I ease past Kimmy to the door. "Can we all get out of here now."

"There's a woman opposite staring at me. Shall I wave?"

"No, Julian!"

"Are any of these things for sale?" Peter is examining my desk.

"No! Now can we *please* get out of here before we all die of heat."

* * * *

"I can't afford to stay in a hotel," Julian is saying after the honeymooners have gone out shopping. "Surely I can crash here for a few days; I'll be no trouble. I can help you. I'll cook for your guests and you can tell the neighbors I'm your brother."

"They wouldn't believe it, Julian. And I don't want you cooking for my guests. I want them out of here as much as possible. I need my own space, there's little enough of it as it is."

"But I'll be here for you when you get back from your school, the place clean, the cats fed and Peter and Kim out of the way."

"Out of the way? What do you intend doing with them?"

"I'll tell them all the things they've got to see. I've been studying the guide books."

"Julian, you can't come here and start taking over."

"I'm not trying to, honestly I'm not. But I've got to talk to you and now they've gone out this is the only opportunity I'll have."

"What about?"

He smiles conspiratorially. "Running a drama school in Tuscany. What do you say about that?"

I stare at him. I can think of nothing to say.

"I've thought of little else," he carries on, "since I failed the Royal Academy of Art exam."

"Yes, I know, Maudie told me. I'm sorry."

"An ex-Glaswegian hairdresser with no experience of theater, reciting Hamlet before the board of examiners for the Royal Academy of Dramatic Art. Do you not think that takes nerve?"

"Yes, I'm sure it does. But you still can't stay, Julian."

"I want to change my life like you've done," he persists, as though I haven't spoken. "I want to search the world, discover what's out there. But in the meantime, I've found students who want to come to Tuscany and study drama for three months in the summer."

"Really? And where will they stay?"

"I thought you could put them up here, perhaps?"

"Here?" I give a burst of laughter.

"You could teach them. Think of the money you'd make. They could sleep on the floor in sleeping bags."

"I can't believe you're being serious, Julian."

"Or we could rent a farmhouse."

"What with? I haven't any money. And I wouldn't know how to teach drama."

"What with all your experience as an actress?"

"*Ex*-actress."

"But you could contact your old drama school – London Academy, wasn't it? They'd send out students if you asked them."

"They wouldn't even remember me. It was too long ago. And anyway I'm not interested in teaching drama."

"You could let this place off in the summer and make enough money to rent an old house and have somewhere to put the students and all this furniture cluttering up the place."

"Julian, I've only just got myself here and I'm trying to survive through next week. My survival here depends on finding B&Bs. I've only got one more couple after the honeymooners, then I've got to find the money for another advert. I'm trying to learn another language, another mentality and a new relationship, as well as coping with an ex who's demanding money I haven't got. It's a full-time enterprise in itself. Now you turn up and try and move me into a derelict farmhouse and run a drama school."

"It doesn't have to be derelict, pet. We could find something that needs doing up a bit and I'll do that."

"You? You're a builder now, are you?"

"Aren't we all when we have to be? Just think, poetry readings in people's villas on summer evenings round the pool. We can travel all over Tuscany and Umbria searching out the English and Americans, there are plenty of them by all accounts. We could call ourselves the 'Strolling Tuscan Players'."

"The Strolling Tuscan Players? Julian, listen to me. It's a fascinating idea, but I can't get involved - "

"Don't worry. We'll talk about it over dinner. And I want to hear all about this new fella. How did you meet him?"

"That's the reason you can't stay. He's very jealous."

"He won't know. I'll be gone in no time."

"You don't understand, everybody makes a point of knowing everybody's business here. And now you say the *carabinieri* think you're my lover?"

"I was joking. You worry too much. Now are we eating out? Or if you're nervous about being seen with me, I could prepare you something here. Then I'll go to the *piazza* and buy an ice cream, no one will know I'm bringing it back for you. And after that, I'll tuck you up in the cat's bed. That's if you'll allow me stay?"

I shake my head. This is impossible. But also mildly comforting to have someone offer to buy me an ice cream and tuck me up in bed. He'll be reading bedtime stories next. Am I worrying too much? I'm where I want to be, aren't I? Following the hand of destiny, as Maudie said over dinner one night. She's right in a way. I'd felt it from the moment of arrival – destiny taking its course. And now even more so - the air is thick with the smell of it. Or is it only the cigarette fumes she's left behind?

Julian's clothes for going out for a pizza are a purple shirt and jeans so threadbare across the thighs you can see his skin through the latticework of threads. It will doubtless be the cause of more wagging tongues, which haven't stopped since Maudie's departure. *Un' attrice,* Martino had said, a twinkle in his eye. *Una modella?* Ornelia had asked. *Una* show girl? *Una* ballerina*?:* the ever-continuing portable theater. I accept the inevitability of it. So long as no gossip reaches Ronaldo's ears. He'll never believe Julian is only a friend. He might even finish things between us and the thought of that gives me a crippling sense of anxiety.

We are on our way out of the house when I hear the phone ring. Better ignore it. If it's him I don't have to make excuses as to why I can't see him. Little did I know then that Ronaldo had telephoned with an urgent message about Silka's mother, Gretta.

* * * *

Forms are being handed round the class to be completed by those who wish to continue their studies in the autumn. The Japanese are filling in theirs, the Germans are returning to Munich, Gerry Croft, the only other English woman in the class beside myself, will stay with her estate agent brother in Umbria and is undecided; the Hungarian girls dropped out several weeks ago.

I can't afford further tuition. So, sadly, this is my last day at the university. Our teacher, Rudolfo, offered me private lessons for an hour every week for a moderate price. But I still had to decline. Sinalunga will have to be my school. I will learn from the people, ask them to correct me when I make mistakes, which, so far, they have seemed only too happy to do. I've learned more in Martino's shop than in the University. For he speaks slowly and points at things: my vocabulary has improved tremendously.

Julian's one-night stay has become three nights without either of us realizing it. He's been good company and in a way I'll miss him when he leaves later today. But the concern of having to explain him to Ronaldo, who might turn up unannounced and who doesn't believe in platonic friendships, has taken the edge off the pleasure.

I've driven Julian into Siena to catch the afternoon train to Pisa airport. By the time we'd finished lunch at the *Gratticello* it had begun to rain, softly at first, then heavily, the dusty streets awash with rivers of rain cascading into the gutters as we ran for cover. In dodging from one doorway to the next, I spotted Gerry Croft waving from a shop doorway further down the street. But we'd rushed on, there was no time to stop; Julian wanted his last *cappuccino* in the Piazza del Campo before catching the train.

And now here we are, sitting outside the bar with the yellow umbrellas, in spite of the rain. With his long dark hair and tanned face, Julian looks more like a Sicilian than a Glaswegian. People in Sinalunga think so too. Stories are spreading, according to

Tonina, of how I've taken up with a young *gitano* and how is it possible that I could go around with a man who can't afford a decent pair of trousers? I had explained that he was Maudie's *fidanzato*, who had mistimed his visit. But it's a question of believing what they want to believe, and the more notorious the story, the happier they seem. Whatever rumors may reach Ronaldo's ears, they can hopefully be explained by saying he's a tourist: he can see the sleeping bag in the kitchen for himself. But it may be difficult to believe if he'd seen Julian bringing me a mug of Horlicks under the desk every night.

The rain has stopped. The Piazza del Campo is as busy as ever: people strolling past with umbrellas: the English in silly straw hats, overweight Americans in baseball caps, then the Italians, you can spot them from far: the woman in short skirts and perfect legs, the men strutting in over-tight jeans.

Now the sun is coming out, hot as ever, spicy odors lingering in the air: it smells as if the Campo has become one big cake shop.

"*Prosecco?*" Julian gathers his still damp hair back into an elastic band. No money to stay in a hotel, but always enough in his pocket to spend on wine and cakes from the local bakery. However, that's Julian: takes a lot, but gives a lot. And I'm lucky enough to be sitting in my favorite place on earth and he will be gone soon, along with the honeymooners, and then I'll have the luxury of sleeping in my own bed again.

The waiter takes the order while I look around: this is the bar that Vittorio frequents and I glance nervously over my shoulder, half expecting to see him in his white jacket and black shirt. He wouldn't hesitate in telling Ronaldo that he'd seen me in the Campo drinking champagne with a Sicilian gypsy.

"So you thought you'd given me the slip, did you?"

I start and look up at long tanned legs. Oh God, Gerry Croft. I force a smile. I don't want Julian's departure delayed. He'll be only too happy to miss the train to Pisa. "No one's giving you the slip, Gerry," I say. "We were trying to get out of the rain. That's why we ran past you. This is Julian, an old friend."

Her eyes dilate at the sight of Julian. "Not satisfied with one Italian, you have to have two on the go."

"Julian's not Italian and yes, he is on the go. About to return to England, as a matter of fact."

"Too bad." Gerry pulls a chair up to the table. "I can't believe you're not Italian. Is your tan real, or does it come out of a bottle? I've never seen such a dark skin on an Englishman."

Julian grins. "Actually, I'm a Glaswegian." He gets to his feet. "What would you like?"

"I'll have what you're having." Gerry's eyes drop to the latticework thighs of his jeans. "Wow!" she says, as he walks away. "Where did you find him?"

"I didn't find him anywhere. I told you, he's an old friend."

"I can imagine." She raises an eyebrow. "How long have you been old friends, then?"

"Years."

"Lucky you. How old is he?"

"Twenty-six."

"Oh, wow. How do you do it?"

"Do what?"

"It must be something to do with having blue eyes."

"Gerry, he's a friend, I keep telling you. Nothing more. We're like brother and sister."

"Oh yeah? Tell me another." Gerry cranes her neck to watch Julian weaving his way back through the tables.

I grab my bag and make for the lavatory. "Don't be long," Julian mutters as we pass. "She'll devour me."

I study my face in the cracked mirror above the basin. I look strained. Julian's presence has disturbed me; I've lain awake at night wishing he wasn't there in his sleeping bag on the kitchen floor. It would have been wiser to tell Ronaldo, especially as I have nothing to hide. And at the memory of his touch, my hand trembles. I comb my hair. How much simpler to be in love with Julian who was totally uncomplicated and kind, preparing me breakfast when the honeymooners had left for the day: freshly squeezed orange juice, toast, a boiled egg and tea. Had Richard done that? Perhaps he had. I suspect Ronaldo never will; he isn't the type. He'll want everything done for him. And I might even do it, given half a chance! I drop my comb into my bag. He'll never believe Julian is only a friend, no matter how much I'll try and convince him if necessary.

Someone rattles the door handle. I close my bag. There's a queue outside the toilet. I slip past, slightly embarrassed at having taken so long.

I can see Julian through the spaces people are making as they get up from the tables. He's leaning toward Gerry in animated conversation. I pass a group of hefty Germans waiting for chairs. "All I need is the right location to bring the students," Julian is saying.

It's then that I spot Vittorio. My stomach gives a lurch. He's standing by the fountain, surveying me over the rim of his wraparounds. "I'll be right back . . ." But neither Julian nor Gerry look up.

I hurry through the milling Japanese tourists waving flags. "Vittorio!" I call. "What a surprise. It's the last day of school. I'm here with a couple of friends." I see a dark-suited man with Vittorio, an older version of Sherif. He looks uncertainly back.

"*Adesso, parli italiano correntemente?*"

"No, Vittorio, you know I don't speak Italian fluently."

"What I tell you, *cara*? This is Agron, the brother of Sherif." Vittorio slaps the man hard on the shoulder, making him wince. "He also don't know how to speak Italian."

"Do you know where Sherif is?" I ask.

"He say only *si signor*. I hope he is not learnin' to say *no signor*. You speak with Ronaldo? He try to call you but you are not there."

"Oh. Why?"

"Gretta go in the hospital."

"What happened?"

"She has the heart attack, too much of the stress, the doctor say. But what of *my* stress? I ask him. You must to give to me the new heart with all the stress I have."

"How terrible. Is it serious?"

Vittorio shrugs. "*Si, terribile.* All is *terribile.* Silka, she stay in the hospital with her. That too is *terribile.* Now I have to make the documents for Agron to work in Italy. We go now to see Rocco. He make things good. And you don't think more for to buy the car. I don't make the present, Rocco make you the present to you."

"*What?*"

"He pay me for the car, so you don't pay nothing. Don't be so proud to accept the present in the life, *cara mia.* We go first to buy the cigarettes then you present me to your friends, eh?"

"Oh, no, w-we're just leaving. My friend's got a train to catch."

"We come soon."

"No . . . "

I hasten back to the table as Vittorio and Agron cross the crowded *piazza* in the direction of the *tobac.* "Hi," Julian says, when he sees me. "Guess what. Gerry's invited me to stay in her brother's house in Umbria. And I've accepted. Now I won't be catching that train to Pisa."

"Fine," I say. "But I must go. Ring me from Umbria."

I head for the stairs leading off the Campo to the Banca di Sopra. Best to leave them to it. Gerry has a car; she'll be delighted to have Julian to herself. They won't miss me. I need to escape before Vittorio re-appears.

* * * *

"Please don't hang up on me this time. I need to talk about changing my life. I couldn't get Sherif a ticket that last night so I gave him the money to buy one the next day, or whenever. But I've still heard nothing. He has my phone number - why doesn't he ring? I'm so worried. Do you think Vittorio's told the *caribinieri* he hasn't any papers and they've arrested him? He said Ronaldo was the only friend he had. Could you ask him? He followed you in Siena trying to ask you to teach him English. But apparently you walked off with your nose in the air. And when he saw you on the hillside, you ran away as though he was a monster. He asked if all English women behave like you and I said they probably do but as I'm Scottish, I wouldn't know. Well, you could at least *speak,* Lorri, couldn't you?"

Maudie hangs up before I have a chance to say a word.

17
Treachery Afoot

It is Saturday evening: I'm cycling along the one-way street, curving round onto the main Asciano road. I get off the bike and wheel it down to the old town. The new B&Bs, Stacy and Harry Gibbs, an elderly American couple from Boston, arrived soon after lunch, leaving me free for the rest of the afternoon.

Having only been to Rocco's house on the night of the concert, in the rain, in Silka's car, and direction not being my strong point, I'm just hoping I can find his house. I looked up the name Miullo in the telephone directory and found three, none of whom live in Asciano. I could have asked Silka but then she'd have asked why I wanted Rocco's address which meant I must tell her my intentions and the less she and Vittorio know of them, the better.

I pause by a bar with tables and chairs outside on the flagstones. Several elderly men are sitting together at a nearby table, drinking wine. If I ask for Rocco Miullo's house I'd probably be directed straight to it. But I walk on and pass *Matilda's Beauty Shop* and the *Alimentari* and a paper shop with pornographic magazines displayed in the window. Discretion is the best option. Otherwise, it could be like a bush telegraph, announcing my visit before I arrive.

The shops are still closed at ten to four. Apart from a youth on a motor scooter zipping past and an old woman on a bicycle, hardly anyone is about. I mount my cycle and pedal halfway up a street to the left before I realize it's the wrong one. I distinctly remember there being a row of villas all resembling each other. I ride back the way I've come and cycle up the parallel street, Via della Luce.

This will have to be handled sympathetically; it's not every day that someone offers to give you a car as a present. Dear Rocco, I've written, thank you for your generous gift. But I am unable to accept it because I cannot offer you anything in return. Perhaps I should have said more. But it's too late; the envelope is sealed with the money inside. It will have to do. It clearly states my intentions. I'll drop it in Rocco's letterbox and make a hasty retreat. I like the thought of the Auto Bianchi in Martino's garage; it's almost mine. I'll get it insured and then off I go, to wherever I want.

The row of ochre villas on the left-hand side of the street all look alike. I walk the bike across the road, and then stop outside a heavy oak front door with ring-shaped brass handles. The name Miullo is engraved on the polished brass plaque: just as I remember it, on the wall with the plaster flaking off.

I lean the bike against the street railings. No sign of life at the shuttered windows. Carefully, I lift the letterbox lid and am about to drop the letter in, when I hear the sound of the front door opening. I look up. The old lady in overalls, the same who'd been pushing chairs about on the night of the concert, eyes me suspiciously.

"*Si?*"

"*Buonasera.*" I smile and hand her the letter. "*Per favore, puo dare questa lettera al Signor Miullo?*"

"*Prego.*"

"*Grazie.*" I glimpse a section of black and white tiles as the heavy door swings to.

I pedal along Via della Luce, wobble precariously round into the main street and let out a sigh of relief. The dreaded deed is done!

* * * *

Raised voices can be heard as I cycle across the driveway. Nothing unusual in that, lengthy discussions are often in progress in Vittorio's house with neither party listening to anything the other has to say. The dogs come barking, tails wagging furiously, escorting me to a space between Silka's Punto and Vittorio's Lancia.

I can hear Silka sobbing. I prop the bike against a cypress. The sobbing is getting louder as I cross the terrace.

Silka sits at the table, her head in her hands. I put my arm around her. She looks up at me. "*Mia madre sta male, è in ospedale.*"

* * * *

When I lift my clothes off the floor, he reaches for my hand, his eyes luminous in the moonlit room. "Why you go now?"

"I'm not going," I whisper, and I pull the sheet over us. But at four a.m. I rise quietly and dress. It's pointless lying here listening to the sound of his breathing, my breathing, and the humming of the generator. Sometimes, on the edge of sleep, I can't make out which is which. Earlier, the subject of Rocco came up and it had made Ronaldo angry. "Never you must to go alone to 'is 'ouse," he said. "It is no correct." And when I'd asked him what I should have done, he said I should have given *him* the money to give to Rocco and we had sat at the window looking up at the moon without saying a word. And when we went to bed he lay apart from me. *"Non facciamo l'amori ci sono troppe cose che disturbono. Tutto é cambiato."*

Too many disturbing things? Everything is changed? What did he mean? What had changed? I'd wanted to say that making love didn't matter, being together was more important. But as usual the Italian words hadn't come when I needed them, so I'd reached across the spacious bed to kiss him goodnight. But he was asleep, or pretending to be, and I'd stared up into the dark, listening to the generator humming relentlessly on into the dawn.

I let myself softly out through the front door, moving as though in slow motion through the trees. The moonlight streams through the leafy branches, making silver cutout shapes on the earth. I step over them, walking deeper into the wood, feeling pine needles crush beneath my sandals.

His words worry me. Is everything about to change because Silka's mother is in hospital? Why should that affect us?

I pause and look around. Every tree looks the same. Nothing gives any indication of what direction to go in. I make my way back along the way I've come then turn down through the trees, starting each time a branch snaps underfoot.

With a sudden shock, I stop. Something dark is sprawled on the ground. A black jacket: I touch it with my sandal, then pick it up and shake it free of earth and pine needles. I feel in the pockets. Nothing. It looks like Sherif's. Has something sinister happened to him? Has Rocco taken care of him too? I want to laugh at the absurdity of it. But is it absurd? I'm beginning to think almost anything is possible in Italy. I drop the jacket on the ground and hurry on.

Under the branches in the direction of one particularly tall tree, then I dart left where I think I recognize the wild rosemary bush I'd picked a stem from on that first night with Ronaldo, that magical night when I could have pulled the stars from the sky. Down, down, I run, to the driveway where my cycle waits like a faithful steed against the cypress, ready to carry me home.

The dogs come running, licking, panting. "Shhh," I say. They must have understood for they don't make a sound, as my wheels crunch over the gravel, tails wagging, accompanying me to the gate.

I pedal fast along the track, my front light dimmed by the brightness of the moon. Why has Sherif not returned for his things? And what motive could Vittorio or Rocco have for harming him - or worse, *murdering* him? The full moon is affecting my thoughts.

I brake in alarm. A scurrying figure is pulling a suitcase along the track ahead of me.

I pedal up alongside. "Giuseppina. Where are you going? *Dove vai?*"

"*Vado alla stazione.*"

"*Perche?*"

"*Perche, torno a Napoli con la mia mamma.*"

She squeezes back tears, and rubs her eyes. Then she cries. I regard her for a couple of minutes in her black T-shirt and jeans. I'm not convinced her tears are genuine. "*Che successo?*" I ask. "What's happened,

Guiseppina?" I can't bring myself to put my arm round her.

With a few hesitant English words, and many Italian, the story stumbles out: the gist seems to be that she has slipped out of the house before the girls were awake, only the dogs watching her leave. There would be no Mass this morning; Silka and Vittorio would sleep till midday. Then he would make his espresso and light his first cigarette. Giuseppina wipes her tears away with the back of her hand. He's been like a father to her, she says. Then she hesitates, as if noticing the bicycle for the first time, and the sobs rise up in her throat again and she sits on her case on the side of the track to recover.

She had seen my cycle in the driveway when she left the house, she says, and guessed what it meant. How could Ronaldo want me when he'd made her believe *she* was special to him. Why had he kissed her on the terrace when no one was there and told her she had expressive eyes and how eyes were the most important features for him in a woman? He had touched her hair and said she should brush it more to make it shine and she had brushed it and brushed it until it had fluffed out like a dark halo round her head.

At least, that's what I imagine she said, but perhaps it isn't quite like that. But now she's sobbing again, loudly into the stillness and asking me why life is so cruel? She has worked for Vittorio's family as best as she could. She promised her mother to obey him like a father, save her money, go to Confession and not think dirty thoughts.

Lifting the bike, I balance her small suitcase on the front basket.

"*Che cosa fai?*"

"Get on behind."

Giuseppina stares at me in disbelief. "We go slowly. Come on, *andiamo, piano piano.*"

She climbs reluctantly onto half the bicycle seat behind me and holds me tightly round the waist. We go slowly, slowly to the main road. I secure the case with one hand and weave along the almost deserted road to *la stazione* in Rapolano, where she will take the train to Chuisi and another all the way back to Napoli.

When Giuseppina looks out of the train window, I wave enthusiastically and blow several kisses and she waves back, minus kisses. "*Mi dispiace. Mi dispiace tanto . . .*"

Yes, I'm thinking, I'm sure she is very sorry. But I can't remember ever feeling so glad to see someone leave. And in spite of feeling sad for Silka and bad about her mother, Gretta, I do a little skip on the platform.

It is six forty-five when I return to Vicolo della Mura. The Gibbs have taken the early train to Rome. They've left a note on the kitchen table along with two nights' money.

We have a Peeping Tom! A large man was sitting on the wall at 5 o'clock this morning trying to see into the bedroom window above the bed. Harry told him to get lost which he did. But we think you should inform the carabinieri.

* * * *

Dearest Richard,

I returned from Italy last week having had an amazing time. I can understand your love for Tuscany. It certainly has a most seductive energy. Which brings me to Lorri. I have to tell you she's having an affair with Vittorio's builder. His name is Ronaldo. He's penniless and I can't see him being of any help to her in her new life. I believe she still loves you. She talked of you all the time; she couldn't walk down a street, she said, without thinking of you.

As for the B&B business, it's a joke! She sleeps under the desk in the sitting room when people arrive and the room's so full of furniture you can't move without falling over something. She doesn't understand how unstable her situation is. And what concerns me most are the dysfunctional people she has around her, someone writing poison pen notes and a Quasimodo character in the alleyway. It's not surprising Lorri's become unstable living there. Can you believe, she goes to church and thinks she's having conversations with the Virgin Mary?

My advice is to return to Tuscany quickly. Talk calmly to her, I'm sure this builder infatuation is no more than a passing fancy. But go before it's too late. Nothing would make me happier than to see you both reunited.

I mean that with all my heart.

All love always,
Maudie xxxx

I let out my breath. Then read the other letter enclosed in the envelope.

Dear Lorri,

I felt it necessary to send you a copy of Maudie's letter. I suspected you might be seeing someone but didn't expect to have it confirmed in writing. I seem to remember Ronaldo, Vittorio pointed him out to me once in a bar, a scruffy young man who'd promised to rebuild his house and create a bar in the cantina where everyone would come from miles around to drink his wine. But that's Vittorio, has to appear to be the great Don Corrado when really he's nothing more than a petty scrounger. And what's this about going to church and talking to the Virgin Mary? You've never been religious. What kind of effect is Italy having on you?

I assume Maudie's alluding to Vittorio and his cronies as the dysfunctional people. I always showed him generosity and went along with his stories of how he knew all the padrones of the best restaurants and then when the bill came, conveniently vanished.

I believe he was partly responsible for our break-up, causing bad feeling between us. Then the recession did the rest, business gone to the wall, having to sell the house. And that fool of an accountant, driving up twice a week in her Porsche to muddle my head with senseless facts and figures, finally giving me the wrong advice. And then my father dying and disinheriting me. That has been the straw that has broken me; leaving a letter saying, treat my son Richard as though he is dead. . .

As with most of Richard's letters, they are too painful to finish. But I read on: *Maudie believes you still love me. Because of that I'm cancelling the legal action against you. I've tried telephoning Avvocato Benocci but the line's dead. So I've written to him instead.*

Looking round the flat I'm renting and the few pieces of furniture you returned to me, it's the missing items which I had particularly wanted that make themselves felt the most. Like the table that I'd changed the legs of, redwood legs, rounded with claw feet, which had made the chestnut dining table so attractive. You sold it, you'd said, to pay the phone bill. But you had no right to sell it. It had meant a lot to me that table. It was as if you'd stolen it from me. And now my home in Italy too, which you've plundered, refusing to add my name to the deeds. You've stolen my chance of happiness; you've stolen my dreams as well as my table . . .

I can't read any more. I fold the letter back into its envelope. I feel numb. There is nothing I can say or do in response to such a letter. That's the answer, of course: don't respond.

A sweet smell of vanilla, honey and fruit wafts up through the window. This is what I'm responding to: Ornelia, my downstairs neighbor, is baking her 'match-making cakes'. That means there'll be another invitation for Sunday morning coffee with Domenico, the builder, which, so far, I've managed to avoid.

* * * *

Ronaldo seems to be moving in. He brings his clothes, a jacket one day, jeans, two dirty shirts and a tie the next, no socks, no pants, he doesn't wear any: he brings them in a pillowcase, he doesn't have a suitcase. What kind of a man is this?

Lisa chuckles as she sets her tobacco tin on the kitchen table. "So what are you going to do, the two of you? You can't both live here and do your Bed and Breakfast. I can't see him agreeing to sleep under that desk with you, no matter how much he loves you. He's not the obliging type, I would have thought."

"Yes, you hinted at that before. He's a handful, you said. What did you mean?"

"He's had a difficult life."

"So have a lot of people."

"Yes, but he has no family. He was turned out onto the street when he was very young, apparently."

"I know. Vittorio told me he was brought up by the priests."

"Well, God knows what went on there."

"You can't be sure of that. Not all priests are bad."

"Do you know any good ones?"

"Yes, I do. The priest here, Don Giuliano, is very kind. He seems pleased that Ronaldo is seeing me. He's invited himself for dinner one evening."

"I'm sure he has. He'll drink you out of house and home."

"Well, so what. I'm crazily happy and I don't care. I want to make *him* happy. But I don't know how. He has such peculiar moods. He hardly ate any of the chicken casserole I made him last night with tender loving care. What's wrong with it? I asked. But he wouldn't say, just withdrew into himself and read the paper. I wanted to hit him on the head. But that would have finished things and then where would I be?"

"Well, that's just it. Where would you be?"

Lisa deftly rolls a line of tobacco between a cigarette paper. "I think you're making yourself too vulnerable," she says. "I'm not sure this infatuation stuff is such a good thing. I'm worried about you."

"No, no," I say, and laugh rather wildly. "I feel like a teenager, it's wonderful. And a lot seems to be happening that I'm uncertain about. Like Richard threatening to descend on me again. I don't know what to do about that, I can tell you."

Lisa licks along the line of paper. "I've heard it said that when people first separate from long relationships they go a little crazy. I think you're in danger of that. You need to be more practical. I mean…" she holds a match to her cigarette, and then gulps in smoke. "… have you thought of selling this place and buying something larger? Or why not let the whole of it and move in with Ronaldo for a while? That way you could make more money."

"Vittorio's let Ronaldo's place to German tourists. He's sleeping in Silka's house in the children's room while she and Vittorio are in Germany visiting Silka's mother, Gretta. The other two bedrooms are let as well, the place is full of German tourists."

"You could advertise in a German newspaper. They're buying everything up these days. Ask Silka to help you." Lisa inhales another lungful of smoke then stubs the cigarette out in her saucer. "Have you told Ronaldo about the Peeping Tom?"

"Good God, no. It would only upset him. He's already said I mustn't walk around in my underwear in case the *carabinieri* see me Even hinted that I *wanted* them to see me. He's obsessively jealous. I'm not mentioning it to the *carabinieri*, the less they know about my business the better."

"I think you should tell them, even so."

"There's no need. Ronaldo's fixed a light up outside the front door. Now I can see who is in the alleyway."

I've also hung a curtain over the small window above the bed. It never occurred to me that someone would climb a high wall in the middle of the night to see into my bedroom.

* * * *

I've been thinking most of the night about selling this place: a daunting prospect, but it might be the solution. I have one last couple of tourists and then that's it! No more money coming in. I'm trying not to panic. But if we are to live together, we have to move on, start our life well, with more space to move around in.

The phone rings: *"Pronto?"*

"I've found the perfect old castle to create a drama school. Gerry's brother, Roger, thinks it's a great idea. A drama center's what's needed here, he said."

"Wait, Julian. What castle, where?" I lower my voice. Ronaldo is still in bed and if he hears me speaking on the phone he'll want to know who it is and every word of the conversation.

"It's in Umbria, near Città di Castello. There's a lot of English in the area, we could perform to an invited audience; Roger knows everyone. There's a courtyard with a tree in the center, it would make a wonderful stage. When can you get over?"

"I can't. Not right now."

"We can pick you up from Trestina."

"It's not as easy as that." I glance through the kitchen: no sign of movement from the bedroom. "It's not the best time, I've er – got my friend staying with me. The people he works for have gone to Germany. It's all a bit tense, and I've got my last B&Bs in a week's time and nowhere to put them."

"Bring them here. Roger will find you a place, he's an estate agent."

"I know. I've met him. Roger Croft. He tried to find a house for Richard and me before we split up.

He won't know me. It's Marsh he may remember. But don't say anything, it's better he doesn't know too much. The name of his house is *Casa Schine*, isn't it?"

"That's the one. Roger's leaving for England in a couple of days so we'll have the place to ourselves for a month. Bring your friend and stay a while. Oh, by the way, I rang Maudie. I said I'm staying with friends of yours in Umbria. She's got a buyer for the house. Did you know she's selling it?"

"She mentioned it, yes."

"I can't think why she wants to."

"She wants to change her life."

"Don't we all. Listen, I can offer you money – or Roger can, if you agree to teach the students for three months. I'll bring them over for the autumn term, September, October and November. It will be good for business, Roger says. It will be good for all of us. Listen, I've got to drift. I'm glad you're getting it together with – er – what's his name?"

"Ronaldo."

"How's it going?"

"I'm not sure yet. Time will tell."

* * * *

Back to the journal:

He's gone to get his television. Could be he means to stay. He seems to have recovered from whatever it was that annoyed him. He kissed me and I felt whole again. Dangerous!

Lisa rang and asked me to tea this afternoon but I can't go as the bike has a puncture.

'Come in the Auto Bianchi,' she said.

'I can't,' I said.

'It's still uninsured.'

'So get it insured. You shouldn't lose your means of escape.'

'Suppose I don't want to escape?' I said.

She said she'd consult her crystal. 'It'll swing to the right for yes and to the left for no. So ask a question while you're on the phone.'

'Will it work out?'

It swung to the right, apparently. 'Yes!'

* * * *

"I no turn back tonight."

"What?" I jam the receiver to my ear. "I'm not sure what you mean."

"*Non torno stasera.* I make the *promessa* to Vittorio to stay 'ere."

"For how long?"

"I must no to leave the 'ouse with nobody."

"But Sherif's brother, Agron, is there with the dogs, isn't he? And what about the tourists?"

"Agron no understand nothing. I want that I come one day soon to you but I must to remain for the Germany people. *Ciao amore.*"

One day soon? My heart sinks. How long does that mean? I hang up, feeling confused and anxious. Perhaps he'll never come back. The thought fills me with a sickening pain in my stomach. Some vital part of me has been stolen – I have to recover it or go insane.

Later in the evening I call on Tonina to ask if she knows someone who would like to have an English couple to stay for a week. She suggests Ornelia who often goes to the sea to stay with her daughter. "*Ha bisogna di soldi.*" She winks at me in a conspiratorial way.

But Ornelia, it seems, is more interested in discussing my friendship with Ronaldo than making money from tourists. "*Molto affascinante e stimolanti*," she says, bringing out Martino's special *Vin Santo* and *cantucci* biscuits. She wants to know where I met him, and did I know that the house where he was born is at the end of my street, Via della Mura? And did I also know that his mother, who was no better than a prostitute, had run away from her family at the age of fifteen to marry his father, a man twenty years older than herself, then ran away from him, abandoning Ronaldo, her firstborn, because she wanted to be an actress?

I dip my *cantucci* biscuit into the *vin santo* and concentrate hard, trying to understand as much as possible of this intriguing dialogue. Over a second glass of the heady wine, there's a long animated monologue about how he'd stood at his bedroom window, whether 'he' is Ronaldo or his father isn't clear, but whoever it is – or was – had been able to see into the window of my *salotto*. From what I can make out, the locals seem to make a habit of trying to see into my windows.

"*Non capisco bene quando lui parla*," I say. I don't understand well enough when he speaks. "*Parla troppo rapidamente*," I struggle on. "And . . . *Io voglio sapere*. . . and I want to know all about him," I burst out in English, knowing I won't be understood, but unable to stop myself. "I don't want to keep learning everything second hand. How long will it be before he can share his past with me, however painful?"

"*Destino! Destino!*" Ornelia, not having understood a word, embraces me, plants two wet

kisses on either cheek. *"Tutto è possible con patienza."*
All is possible with patience. Well, we'll see.

Now finally, I move the conversation round from destiny to tourists staying in her apartment. *"Sarebbe – possible portare I touristi qui?"*

"Chi sa?"

Who knows? Well, I want to know, and as soon as possible, otherwise they'll be sharing the bed with Ronaldo and me.

Dusk has settled by the time I walk back down the alley to my front door. All is possible with patience, Ornelia said. And faith in myself, I add. Not to mention, a very great deal of hard work.

I switch on the new outside light that Ronaldo has put up. Nothing. Typical. The lightbulb must have blown. I reach up into the glass shade to unscrew it. But it isn't there. Who has removed it? I insert the key into the lock when I hear someone cough behind me. I jerk round.

A large man is leaning against the far wall, watching me. He walks foward.

"Hello, Rocco," I say, warily.

"I am disturbing you?" He is carrying what I think, for one mad second, is a gun case.

"Y-you gave me a shock."

"I also have the shock." He withdraws a familiar white envelope from his jacket pocket. "Why you cannot to accept my present?"

I stare at him for several minutes: I hadn't expected this. "For the reason I explained in the letter," I say. "I can't – offer you anything in return."

He shakes his head and tuts, as if what I've said is too stupid to take seriously. "I want only that you accept. If you return these monies you are insulting me."

"I have no wish to do that." I glance nervously along the alley behind him. "I'd no intention of insulting you, Rocco. Believe me, that was never in my mind."

"You want now to take these monies?"

"No. I want *you* to have them – it. I want to buy the car for myself"

"Then you are destroying my good feelings for you."

"But I made it clear to Vittorio that I wanted to..."

He presses the envelope of money into my hands. "I am not wanting to speak of Vittorio. I am only wanting to *offer* something to you and now I hope you are accepting what I am wanting to give."

"Oh, dear. Listen, Rocco – "

"I am *begging* that I give to you. I want to telephone to you, but I do not know well how to speak and I am wanting to speak of many things. " His voice is becoming louder, more impassioned. I shoot another furtive glance along the alley. "I am speaking with my students of my music all the day. I am speaking with my clients of the law, but with you I am not finding the *words* to speaking."

"Yes, yes, I see what you mean," I say, in a hushed voice. I don't want my neighbors to hear. There'll be another letter on the mat by tomorrow.

"This is why I must to play. I am *speaking* in my music; I make the *present* of my music. Will you now return my music to me?"

"No, no, of course not. But I thought we were talking about . . . "

"Then you will allow me to play for you?"

"Yes, of course."

"Then I can to begin?"

I stare at him. "W-where? Now, *here*, you mean?" I sense an almost unnatural silence, as though the walls and the alleyway itself are waiting for the music to begin. "Perhaps you better come in for a minute." I open the front door and lead the way quickly up the stairs.

* * * *

We stand facing each other awkwardly in the kitchen; the cats have fled at the sight of Rocco.

"I am speaking with the lawyer from Montepulciano," he says, placing the black case on the table. He takes off his jacket and drapes it round a chair back.

"What did he say?" I ask, eyeing the jacket dubiously, wondering how long he intends staying.

"He is no more the problem."

"What have you done with him?"

Either he hasn't heard or he chooses not to. He opens the case and draws out a flute to my relief. "This is speaking all the words for me."

He places the instrument between his lips and plays a few shrill notes, sausage fingers tapping up and down the instrument with extraordinary agility. I imagine them tapping up and down me for a second and shudder. He notices the shudder and must think the practice notes are affecting me even before he's begun to play the piece. He smiles at me in an odd kind of way. Then closing his eyes, he fills the room with quavering notes, which soar around the ceiling, ascending out through the windows and across the rooftops, then come trembling back even more yearningly into the kitchen.

I listen, watching the perspiration run down his fleshy cheeks, the matted black chest hair thrusting up under his open-necked shirt. A discouraging sight, no matter how talented a musician he may be.

After some time, it's impossible to know exactly how long, an hour, maybe more, he stops playing and lays the flute on the table, the mouthpiece dripping with saliva. I applaud and he bows. Then he draws a white handkerchief, the size of a napkin, from his trouser pocket and wipes his face. It is now that I become aware of the voices in the street.

Out of the *salotto* window, I see Rosalba at her window with her husband, Giovanni: Tosca, Ornelia, and others are gathering on the street steps, Tonina with Martino, the tall good-looking *carabiniere*. They begin to applaud. Then along Via della Mura comes *Don* Giuliano, the priest, and Livensa from the paper shop. They stand under my window and call for *la musicista* who plays such magical music through *la staniera's* window. Then to the mounting pleasure of his audience, Rocco, pushing his bulk round the sofa and sending books slithering in all directions, appears at the window beside me. He gives a bow to another enthusiastic burst of applause.

But to be trapped behind the sofa with Rocco is unwise. Having no other means of passing him, I climb over it, stepping on clothes and blankets. At the kitchen sink I pour myself a glass of water. I'm beginning to feel at a loss to know where fantasy ends and reality begins.

"The people here are accepting me," Rocco is saying, reappearing in the kitchen.

"Yes, they are, Rocco, they are."

"And you are now accepting me?"

"Of course I am."

"And you accept what I give to you?"

"The car, you mean?"

"No!" he shouts. "I am not speaking of the car. I am making the present of my *feelings,* my emotions."

"Oh, I see – yes, I see."

"And you accept?"

"I accept your music. I love your music."

"Then you love also me? For we are not separated."

"No - I didn't say that . . . "

"Then you are dividing me from my music?"

"No, I don't think . . . "

"Because we are not separated. My music is the best of me, it is speaking *all* for me."

"Yes . . . "

"You speak yes, yes, but you are not understanding what I am speaking to you and how important it is that I can to express what I *feel.* How is it possible to communicate with you if I can not do with my music?"

I'm beginning to feel alarmed. Saliva is frothing up on his tongue as he speaks. I must find the right words to pacify him. Then get him out of the place as quickly as possible. "I understand, Rocco, I really do." I take his jacket from the chair as a hint that he should leave. "You're a wonderful musician; I don't understand why you don't play professionally. Have you never thought of that?"

But the copper pots above his head have now caught his attention. "They are English, like you?" he asks.

"Yes, they are. Do you like them?"

"I like very much."

I'm on the point of offering him one – the whole lot if he'll leave. But that might be misunderstood. I hand him his jacket and watch him struggle into it. His bulk fills the kitchen. How am I ever to get him out? Ronaldo would say I'd encouraged him by inviting him in, which I suppose is true. I edge my way into the hall. "Unfortunately, I have an appointment, Rocco. I have to go out soon."

But he is staring over my shoulder, through the open bedroom door, at the double bed, the sheet pulled invitingly back. I begin descending the stairs. Perhaps the only way to get rid of him is for me to leave. "I have to go out, Rocco," I call. "I'm already late."

Silence.

I creep back up the stairs. To my dismay, I see he is now in the bedroom staring up at the small window. "Rocco, this is the way out," I say, with a calm I don't feel. "I'd like you to leave *now*. This minute, Rocco, please."

He rears round toward me. Then with a strange strangled sob, lowers himself awkwardly onto his knees and begins kissing and licking my sandaled feet, first one and then the other. The silence surrounding us seems to have an energy of its own, watching attentively, while I watch, appalled, the dark head with the small circular bald patch.

"Rocco - " I move my feet away, but he holds on to my ankles. "That's enough, Rocco!" I speak with a force that makes him look up.

He groans and struggling to his feet, swings round like a colossal bear, back into the bedroom and collapses heavily onto the bed. He lies on his back with his arms stretched out, saliva dribbling from the corner of his mouth.

I need help. He's not well. There's no knowing what he might do. I race down the stairs, tug open the front door and fly along the alleyway and am immediately encircled by the group of people still talking outside Ornelia's door. When they learn that the *musicista* is ill everyone pushes back along the alleyway and crowd through my front door, up the stairs and in to the hallway forming a bottleneck at the bedroom door. I push my way into the room, past the priest, Rosalbo, Ornelia and several people I'd never seen before.

This is the cue for everyone to follow me into the bedroom and gaze in wonder at the *musicista* lying on *la straneira's* bed with his eyes closed, fully dressed and with his boots on. Everyone tries to wake him without success. Then it's back and forth, up and down the stairs, along the alleyway fetching medicines, in and out of the kitchen carrying water jugs, people running from everywhere, shouting and arguing as to what should be done to help *il bravo musicista*. The priest slips a spoon under Rocco's tongue. "*Epilessia,*" he says, and heads nod in solemn agreement.

I stand helplessly by trying in vain to follow what people are saying. Rocco is alive, I know that, for Ornelia is holding a mirror to his mouth and we've all seen his breath on it.

Now the *carabinieri* arrive. This is terrible. They climb the stairs, stamping their feet. The short fat one I saw on my first day of arrival, he recognizes me: he begins asking me questions. I can't understand, I can hardly get a word out, I'm so distressed.

The people gather in the Via Ciro Pinsuti to watch Rocco being carried down the street steps on a stretcher and lifted into the ambulance. Several women cross themselves. And even after it has driven away people remain in the street discussing the extraordinary event of the *musicista* comatose on *la straniera's* bed. And when the *carabinieri* returns with the *maresciallo* in his high peaked hat and glistening medals, I tremble. What can I say to the chief of the *carabinieri*? If only I hadn't invited Rocco in, such a disaster would never have happened.

* * * *

It was later when everyone had walked to the *piazza* to continue the discussion that I noticed the envelope of money had disappeared from the kitchen table.

18
Strange Fits of Passion

"Why 'e is in your bed?"

"On my bed, Ronaldo. Not *in* it. There's a difference."

"But why you invite Rocco in the 'ouse?"

"Because he came to return the money for the car and then began playing the flute outside the door and I didn't want everyone listening, which they eventually did anyway, and so I took him upstairs."

"I no understand nothing you say."

I sigh with exasperation. I have given up any attempt to try and explain to Ronaldo in Italian what happened. The more I'd tried, even in English, the more unreal the story sounded. But there the flute is on the kitchen table beside its black case as proof of the awful reality.

I'd telephoned Ronaldo for help and he'd returned tired and fractious from trying to explain in English to the German guests why Vittorio and Silka weren't there to welcome them. And when Silka had telephoned him to learn what was happening, he'd refused to speak of tourists and had hung up on her. He was concerned only with what Rocco may have done and what he would do to Rocco if he'd even so much as breathed on me.

"I no know what I can to believe," he says now, looking down at me looking up at him from the kitchen chair.

"But I'm telling you the truth, Ronaldo," I say. "*Please*, you must believe me."

"I 'ave much problems of Vittorio, and now with you. I no want these problems, Lorri."

"Neither do I, but sometimes it happens in life, you know."

It's ten forty-five. We haven't eaten. But food is the last thing on our minds.

"*Com'è possible avere fiduca in te?*"

"What do you mean, how is it possible to trust me? Of course you can. You *can* trust me - oh God, this bloody language!"

"*Non capisco Io!*"

"What don't you understand, Ronaldo, tell me?"

"*Perche hai invitato lui a letto?*"

"Oh, Ronaldo." I almost laugh, it's so ridiculous. "I didn't invite him to bed. He lay down because he wasn't feeling well."

"I no understand. *Dimmi cosa dovrei immaginare?*"

"I don't understand what you're saying either, Ronaldo. Speak English."

"No, *you* must to speak Italian."

"If I could, I would."

"What now I must to imagine?"

"The worst, you're imagining the worst, like everyone else. I think he's an epileptic. That's why he collapsed on the bed. Do you understand what I'm saying? No, of course you don't."

"You are in Italy. *Parla Italiano!*"

"I can't say all that in Italian. But please believe me, I'm telling you the truth exactly as it happened. Rocco – he - he was kissing my feet."

"*Cosa?*"

"Then I went to get help. Why is it when you tell the truth no one believes you?"

"And the Mercedes?"

"What about the Mercedes?"

"Where is he?"

"I don't know. Isn't he - it outside in the street?"

"*Non!*"

"Perhaps he, Rocco I mean, came in a taxi."

Ronaldo, exasperated now, goes down to speak to Ornelia. Then *Il maresciallo*, who speaks a little English, telephones me to say that *Signore* Miullo has been taken home from the hospital and is now under the care of his housekeeper. Then there's the question of the Peeping Tom and the missing lightbulb.

"Never mind all that. What about the missing money?"

But it appears Ornelia had seen the half-open envelope of money on my kitchen while fetching water for Rocco and took it downstairs to the safety of her kitchen. I'm on the point of asking *il maresciallo* how he knows, but realize the foolishness of such a question. For everybody knows everyone's business in Sinalunga.

"Why you no say me of the money what go missing?"

"Because I didn't want to create problems."

"But you create more the problems, Lorri, if you say nothing. Now we go again to the *carabinieri.*"

"Oh, no. Do we have to, Ronaldo?"

Documents had to be signed in the *carabinieri's* office across the street and awkward questions asked. Had I seen the man watching from the wall? How many light bulbs had been stolen? Why was *Signor*

Miullo bringing me money? Then Ronaldo took over and recounted the story of how Rocco had presented me with a gift of a car that I didn't wish to accept. Vittorio's name and address was taken down along with the car's previous owner, a butcher living in Croce and suddenly the whole picture had become more complex.

The short fat *carabiniere* fingers the gun at his belt. He explains that the locals are good honest people, and there's never been any report before of anyone stealing light bulbs or watching women undress. But if the shutters are left open then how could you blame a man for looking?

"I want much to believe you," Ronaldo says when we are alone.

"Then do so," I tell him, my arms around him. "Trust me. *Fidati di me.*"

"You see, you can to speak Italian."

"Sometimes."

"When you want."

* * * *

We have spent most of Saturday and Sunday together. We've read and watched the television. I washed the only two shirts and cotton trousers he possesses and hung them out to dry. He suspended a rope from the kitchen window to the bedroom. One minute pegging Richard's shirts on a line in an English garden, another, pegging Ronaldo's across a Tuscan rooftop; and both names beginning with R. What a strange life. Time seems to have slipped: past into present.

Rosalba, no doubt, will announce to all that I have a new man. Then Domenico, the builder, who waved frantically from a rooftop yesterday, will finally accept that all hope is lost. And Ornelia, with her matchmaking coffee mornings, will sigh with relief. *La donna Inglese* is no longer a threat to everyone's husband. And little Tosca will smile her toothless smile and thank the Holy Mother for sending me a good Italian man to replace the gypsy in the torn trousers.

For this weekend, the outside world has ceased to exist. I hurried out in the morning only to buy food then hurried back to the seclusion of our love nest to cook it; when Ronaldo allows me to, for he prefers to cook. "Then I know what I can to eat," he'd said, chopping onions and *prezzimolo* with a professional touch.

I hang his two clean shirts in the wardrobe, remembering how I'd seen Giuseppina kissing his shirt in Vittorio's garden. It's a relief she's gone. Now, hopefully, there will be no one to come between us. I close the wardrobe door, hoping the faint but lingering smell of his skin and cologne will rub off on my own clothes. And Gertie, the black and white cat, she too, seems, intoxicated. She sat on the bed earlier and gazed into his face while he slept, occasionally licking his nose. "*No, Gerti,*" he'd said, pushing her gently away. But back she came to gaze at him for the rest of the morning. And Billy, who has become 'Billii the Keed', from his place on top of the kitchen steps, listens to every word Ronaldo says to him in Italian, as though he understands the language perfectly and has been waiting all his life to converse in it.

Why is it sometimes, maybe once in a lifetime, you meet someone and know that from then your life has turned on its head, pulled in every direction you never expected it to go in?

* * * *

The cats' heads jerk up. They're the first to hear the key turn in the lock. Now it's too late. Julian walks into the kitchen as we're having breakfast.

He looks startled at the sight of Ronaldo in my towelling bathrobe. "Hey, I'm sorry," he says. "I didn't know you had company, Lorri. I've brought your spare key back." He drops the key on the kitchen table.

"*Buongiorno,*" Ronaldo says. "You 'ave the key to the 'ouse?"

"Hi, I'm Julian."

"Ronaldo – " I get to my feet. "This is Julian – oh, but - " I give a laugh. "You know that already. I didn't expect you, Julian. What's happened? Have you fallen out with Gerry?"

"Not at all. I wanted to talk about the school. I've been in touch with a friend in Glasgow who teaches elocution. He's dead keen to send the students out. He says the parents will pay. I was hoping to crash for the night. But if it's not convenient I can take myself off."

"*Che diceva, lui?*"

We look at each other, uncertain what to say. Then Julian says, "I think I'd better go. I can see I'm interrupting."

"You come to see Lorri?"

"I have, yes. But, no problem, I can see this isn't the best time."

Ronaldo pushes the key across the table toward him. "But you must stay together, of course. Take you key. I go. *Ciao!*"

"Ronaldo!"

"Hey - " Julian catches Ronaldo's arm at the door. "You stay. I can come back later."

"No, Julian, don't say that!"

"*Si,*" Ronaldo throws off the bathrobe and walks naked into the bedroom. "Yes, you come later. When you want, you come."

"You're making a mistake, Ronaldo. It's all very simple."

But for Ronaldo nothing is simple, especially cheating in love and being made a fool of. "You come, of course," he calls from the bedroom, zipping up his jeans. He slaps Julian hard across the shoulder on his way out of the bedroom. "I want that you come, I see you are *simpatico*. I understand why Lorri like you."

"Hey, you've got it wrong, man. Lorri and I are friends – I mean . . . Look - I think it's better if I shoot off. I'm really sorry if I've upset things." He sprints down the stairs and lets himself out through the front door.

"Ronaldo, Julian is *un amico platonico,* nothing more." I watch him putting on one of his newly ironed shirts and feel my stomach lurch. "Where are you going? You don't need to leave, *è molto semplice.*"

He ignores me and pulls his other shirt off its hanger and flings it onto the bed.

"W-what are you doing, Ronaldo?"

Then he suddenly begins to shout, his voice rising higher and louder, incomprehensible Italian words tumbling one over the other. The ironed shirt stuffed into the pillowcase with a pair of dirty trainers on top: the pillowcase will split, it already has a tear in it, and all the time his voice is ranting and the frustration, hurts and pain of a lifetime come pouring forth without restraint.

I retreat into the kitchen remembering the Bach Rescue Drops in the cupboard. I unscrew the top, and shake four drops onto my tongue; six, ten, twelve, overdosing will do no harm; it's a natural product. I sit at the table. I'll be all right. He will go and I will recover.

Still he is shouting. No pause between the words. What can he be saying? There's nothing I can say or do to stop him leaving. If I told him I loved him, he'd laugh in my face. Better let him go. But *please* go quickly. Then I can pick my stomach off the floor. Maybe I could take the cats and leave too. But where? I have no other place to go. Vittorio would laugh; I can hear his dry cackle in my head. What I tell you? The English woman with her English mentality, she don't understand the life here. Giuseppina will return and there'll be a match made in hell. There may even be an invitation to the wedding.

I'm aware of a hostile silence. It speaks more than the shouting. The cats appear briefly at the window, then vanish as the voice starts up again from the kitchen doorway, rising into a crescendo, face distorted like a gargoyle with pain and fury.

"Please go," I say, in a voice that sounds a long way off. I clasp my hands between my thighs, aware of a strange numbness creeping over me. The rescue drops are working.

Another silence, more hostile than before. He's staring down at me coldly, disdainfully. "Why you give 'im the key?"

"Because he needed it," is all I can think of saying. "He stayed here for a while with my tourists. He asked for a key, so I gave it to him."

He drops his key on the table; it slides off onto the floor.

I close my eyes. The biggest mistake I made was in not telling him about Julian. If only I could go back in time and do it differently. I hear his feet descend the stairs. Now it's too late, I lack the strength to call him. If someone prodded me, I would fall to the floor. The front door opens – I hold my breath: when it closes that will be the finality. It will be over.

But I hear nothing. Julian must have left the door open. I rise shakily; I'll close it later. Now all I can do is make for the bed, lie curled up on my side. The taste of violets in my mouth is not unpleasant; neither is the relaxing numbness spreading through my limbs, it makes me feel detached, able to close my mind on all that is happening.

* * * *

I dream Ronaldo is hastening along the alley and down the street steps, counting them as he goes, nine, ten, eleven, twelve, one for each month of the year. He is drenched in sweat and a violent hammering in his head makes him feel like vomiting. He moves along Via Ciro Pinsuti to where he's parked the Lancia and, opening the door, he collapses onto the seat. He will have to return to collect his Leonardo da Vinci art books; he'll leave the television, but he wants his precious books. He turns on the ignition.

But to drive away now would be to end everything. He would never come back, never had in the past. He'd always got out before the pain went too deep. Why should this time be any different?

Yet this time is different. He has never cared that much in the past, now he cares so much he has a wound inside like a knife has gutted him. He leans his face against the steering wheel, feeling faint with heat and apprehension; a nervous tic flutters in his eyelid. With an unsteady hand, he lights a cigarette, inhaling the smoke up through his nostrils. He knows that if he walks away this time it will be like throwing his life away.

Now he begins to think. A memory leaps up of his mother banging the shutters, telling him to go, that he gave her too much pain. He can see those closed shutters in his mind with a curious clarity, dark green with paint peeling off. "*Mamma, ho fame,*" he'd called, too young to understand what she'd meant. But those shutters had remained closed against him.

He climbs out of the car and tosses his cigarette against a wall in a shower of sparks. He treks back along Ciro Pinsuti and mounts the street steps. At the top he pauses. Wiser to call in on Ornelia first, she would make him a strong black coffee with a little brandy, the way he likes it, and she'd give him a couple of aspirins to calm the pain in his head.

He parts the beaded curtain. "Ornelia . . . "

* * * *

I have no idea how much time has passed before I wake and hear voices in the alleyway. My watch has stopped. It could have been ten minutes; it could have

- 265 -

been an hour. I get off the bed, feeling drained of energy, and stumble into the kitchen. The voices are at the front door now, laughing, traveling up the stairs to the kitchen. I hold onto the table for support.

"*Amore,*" Ronaldo calls, entering the kitchen as though nothing has happened. "Ornelia say me you bring the tourists in 'er 'ouse. She go in Grosseto to see her daughter. What you say?"

I stare at him in disbelief.

"*Complimenti!*" Ornelia is gazing round the kitchen. "*Tanti complimenti davvero.*"

"*La stile Inglese è elegante?*"

"*Molto.*"

"Lorri, we go to see the 'ouse of Ornelia. No is *elegante* like yours, but is good."

Holding me firmly by the arm, he leads me downstairs and out of the house as though I'm an invalid. We follow Ornelia along the alley, round the corner and through the beaded curtain into the kitchen-diner of her two-bedroom apartment. Fresh coffee is prepared, strong and black with plenty of sugar, accompanied by the *Vin Santo* bottle placed in the center of the flowered plastic tablecloth with a dish of *cantucci* biscuits to be dipped into the wine and softened before eating.

I look at Ronaldo and then at Ornelia. They're both smiling expectantly at me. "You like the good idea, or no?" Ronaldo says. "You must to say yes of course, *amore.*"

I'm not sure what I'm supposed to say yes to. Ornelia is going to Grosseto, or is her daughter coming here? It hurts my head to think. He'd left, hadn't he? Everything is over between us. Now here we all are, laughing round a *Vin Santo* bottle, at least, *they* are laughing, while I nibble a biscuit, wondering if I'm in danger of losing my mind.

The church bells in the *piazza* begin clanging as we stand up to leave. Clang - Dong – Dang - slowly, sadly. It means someone has died when they clang like that. Now I'm back from the dead, being thrust through the beaded curtain, looking up at Rosalba looking down at me from her window. Soon she will move round to the front window, or is it the front in the morning and the back in the evening, like a big blonde sun with the windows rotating round her?

"We go to eat the fish, Lorri."

"Fish?" The last thing I want on top of rescue drops and *Vin Santo* is fish. But if I disagree, it could all go wrong again. "I thought you'd left, Ronaldo," I say.

"I am turned back now."

"Oh, you are. Why?"

"Why you say always why, Lorri? *Ho fame.* I 'ave the unger."

Best to leave it at that and avoid any in-depth explanations. I haven't the energy to listen: he's back; until the next time, when he might leave again; maybe for good. I can either accept the situation or tell him to bugger off! But to live near him, to occasionally see him and not be with him is unthinkable.

Halfway up the stairs I notice the bulging pillowcase partly concealed behind the hall curtain. And then the truth dawns on me. He had never intended leaving. Otherwise he would have done so. It had all been part of the non-stop Italian theater, the need for the passionate drama, after which, having nearly destroyed me, he feels fine.

"Ronaldo," I say in the restaurant. "I want you to know something."

"I know what you want to say."

"You do?"

"Of course, *amore*. When you say you give to your friend the key I understand you are direct, you are 'onest. If you want to say the lie you make the story with more *fantasia*. No make *complicazione*, Lorri. You must to be simple, like me."

* * * *

Later with the journal:

Tonight in the restaurant I hardly ate a thing because what happened left me feeling weak, frightened and alone. And when he asked me to explain what I felt for him I couldn't. It's difficult enough sometimes explaining how you feel in English, in Italian it's a lost cause. And then he went all moody because I didn't tell him what he wanted to hear.

Perhaps I should send him packing with his pillowcase. But it would be like throwing away a jewel no matter how complicated the package it comes in.

19
The Plot Thickens

September:

It's a fresh sunny Monday morning. I head along the *Superstrada* in my now fully insured Auto Bianchi, turn off at Cortona and drive up the hill in the direction of Città di Castello. It will be a long winding stretch to Trestina.

The hotel *Mercurio* is the meeting point. Not quite the grand *castello* I've been led to expect would be our work place. But it will only be temporary, Julian assures me. "The students will sleep in the hotel while the castle's being restored," he'd said. "Then after, they'll have spacious rooms where you can work on plays, both modern and Shakespearean. And did I tell you there's a great little theater in Città di Castello? I'm hoping the Central School of Speech and Drama may help us financially."

With Julian it's difficult to know quite what to believe. He gets carried away with his enthusiasm, a quality Maudie at first had loved, but later found difficult to share. When I met him five years ago, he'd had a dream of opening up a hairdressing salon–cum café. Then failing to get the financial backing required, he'd had another idea: he put advertisement in the local paper, offering himself as a home visiting personal stylist. But when women saw his picture, it wasn't hair styling they had in mind. There had been several more colorful ventures, but with only one problem, money, or the lack of it, to back them.

Make sure you get paid, Lisa had warned, when I'd asked her advice. A lot of people come here with big ideas then run out of money in the first two weeks. Even so, a regular income for four days a week is more than welcome. Having raised money from Gerry Croft's estate agent brother, Roger, Julian offered two hundred *euros* a week including petrol. I asked for four, we settled on three.

Climbing steeply now, the Auto Bianchi snakes round the bends, dangerously close to the edge where the land drops sharply through shrubs and dense forest. Smoke rises languidly from a distant bonfire. It's difficult keeping my eyes on the road for the grandeur of it all. I swing round another bend, speed across two stone bridges and then begin curving down the other side of the Umbrian mountain, my back wheels skidding on the leaves that border either side of the narrow road. I slow down; a car could skid over the side, hurtle down through trees and thickets and be lost for weeks before anyone found it. Doing this journey in November and December will not be fun.

The five students are gathered in the hotel reception. Julian, with a wide grin, dressed in tight black jeans and a black T-shirt, is saying how there's an atmosphere of something special in the air. I shake hands rather solemnly with three nervous looking youths and two girls. Then Tonino, the hotel manager, says, *andiamo,* and we all follow him past a Chinese screen into the cocktail bar. "Fino *a mezzogiorno,*" he says, before he and Julian dart off behind the screen.

Until midday: I glance at my watch. That gives us two hours. "They've got to learn to love Shakespeare," Julian had stressed. "So I'm depending on you to drill it into them."

"That's not the way to make them love anything," I'd said. "They'll end up hating it."

Julian had laughed, slightly hysterically, and gone on about how I must choose the play and teach them how to perform well. Everything depends on it," he'd insisted. "Two drama schools have promised to view the production in December and might offer a grant if the students show enough promise."

Having never taught anything, I'm not sure I can do it and had said so when offered the work. "But you were an actress," Julian had insisted. "In many Shakespearean productions."

"True," I'd said. "But that doesn't mean I can teach it."

Five young hopefuls face me round a Formica table in the cocktail bar. There's Eddie from the Wirral, 20, cropped hair, leather jacket, "looks aggressive," I scribble in my notebook; Hamish, 19, green-eyed, fair-haired, "romantic type"; Malcolm, 23, tall, hefty and "vulnerable." Then Tina, 21, with "squeaky voice" and Mary, 18, mousy, "needs bringing out of herself."

"As we've now got less than two hours," I begin, "I'd like you to look at the person next to you, think how you feel about them."

Smiles all round; we're off to a good start. "What sort of parts do you see yourself playing?" I ask them, one at a time.

Eddie wants to be a hard-nosed cop in a television serial. Hamish sees himself as another Mel Gibson, leading an army of blood-curdling Scots against the English – I'm wrong about him. Tall, awkward Malcolm longs to play Burns in a one-man show around Scotland. Tina, already a great Shakespearean actress in her opinion, dreams of playing Titania in *The Midsummer Night's Dream* and Mary doesn't know what she wants.

"Interesting," I say. "Now let me tell you something about me. I'm not here to teach you how to act. I'm here to teach you how *not* to act . . . "

And so it continued until lunchtime. I've escaped to an out-of-the-way bar. I need time alone to work out what I'm going to do with them in the afternoon. Halfway through my *panini*, Julian appears. "They said you were here," he says. "They think you're wonderful."

"I haven't done anything yet."

"It's what they told me. They never heard anyone talk like you, they said. They can't wait for more. Now – " He pulls out a chair and sits opposite. "Can you direct them in a Shakespearean play for October?"

"A Shakespearean play?" I'm not sure I've heard correctly.

"Scenes from a play. It doesn't have to be a full scale production." He chooses this moment to slap a bundle of money on the table. "First week's wages. I've added a bit extra to give you incentive. By the way, how's your friend taking it?"

I look at him.

"Working for me? It can't be easy, dealing with his possessiveness."

"He's fine. He seems to have calmed down since we've been living together. But let's talk about us: I'm here to teach drama, not direct it. And I've still got my tourists to think of."

"But the season's finished, you said. Come on, you can do it; I know you can. And what's the alternative, Lorri?"

The first day hasn't passed and now suddenly I'm a director as well as a teacher, with a bunch of inexperienced students and only a month to prepare them in Shakespearean scenes for their stage debut.

There is no alternative; it's simple, I need to earn money. I can't work in a shop because I don't speak the language well enough. I could teach English, but students have to be found and that takes time and in the meantime I have to live. So I shall stick it out with Julian and see where it leads.

* * * *

The afternoon passed quickly. The cocktail bar is closed after three so we worked in the hotel dining room. Walking up and down between the tables, swinging their arms, holding hands, embracing, flushed faces drawing close, the intention being to loosen up, free themselves of tension and inhibition.

Everyone seemed to enjoy the class, including poor shy Mary, who flung her arms wide and spun like a dervish, knocking into one of the tables, sending the cutlery flying and finally collapsing into the arms of Eddie, who stretched her out on two dining chairs to recover.

I leave for home before it starts to get dark. It will be a long lonely journey high up over the mountain, all the way down to Cortona and then straight on to Sinalunga.

* * * *

It's Tuesday: a day to myself before it all starts again on Wednesday. I've invited Silka round to translate an advert I've written for a German newspaper. *'Appealing two-bedroom Tuscan cottage to let with magnificent views across the village.'*

It's better than 'apartment' or flat - even worse. For who wants to stay in either down a dark alley, Tuscan or otherwise?

Silka arrives with a suitcase, looking exhausted. With the heat of summer, hotter than any she can remember, Ronaldo's continual building in progress, the dust, the dirt, and the garden wall still unfinished, it's even getting Vittorio down, apparently, who normally enjoys the creativity going on around him.

Ronaldo's ideas are changing every week, according to Silka: a door into the bar one day, a Gothic arch another. And something else; he's different, she says. He's become more aggressive, taking a stand against Vittorio instead of supporting him as he'd done in the past. The discord between the three of them has been getting worse since the day they returned from Germany with the children. "What influence do you have on him?" she asks me.

I watch her flop into a chair, her suitcase at her feet. I'm about to tell her what little influence I think I have on Ronaldo when, to my distress, she bursts into tears.

It's the thought of her mother, Gretta, in hospital unable to speak because of the heart attack, that has brought on the tears. Vittorio being no support, how he'd hated coming to the hospital in Germany and how he'd slumped onto the bed in her mother's apartment and thrown his rolled up socks against the wall.

"I said to him, why did you come if you hate my mother so much? I lose count of how many times I have told him how my father died and left so little money that my mother had to work much to pay for my schooling and give me a good life. But Vittorio only laugh. It's your father you should feel sorry for, he say. Your mother drove him to his death. And you don't understand the word poor. And then he begin to tell of his mother in *Napoli* who had nothing and I ran out of the room with my hands over my ears. I don't want to hear the story of *his* mother again. Even to *think* of Rosa is too much for me: my mother is right; we never like each other from the moment that we meet. She think always that I am the German woman who is no good enough for her son."

"Most mother-in-laws think like that, Silka."

"And now Vittorio is smiling because he think that when my mother die he have all her money."

"And will he?"

"*I* will have the money. Not him. And I will not more have the *need* of him."

She begins to cry again. I hand her a tissue. She blows her nose. Her new kitchen with the avocado green cupboards that she'd wanted so much: Vittorio had been generous there, she says. He may not have had the money to pay for it, but he hadn't interfered with what she'd wanted as he'd always done in the past, saying that his taste was superior to hers. Then at the mention of the wrought iron staircase, she blows her nose again. He'd insisted on installing that and she'd hated it. Ronaldo said it would take up half the room and he'd been right, it had. Dead greenery hanging over the balustrade because Valentina hadn't watered the plants as she'd promised to do when Giuseppina left. Now she must do *that* job as well. Surely marriage has more to offer than watering dead plants and cleaning up after children and a husband who did nothing but criticize? They had made love the night before, she confides. The first time in ages. In spite of a genuine headache, she'd needed the comfort of physical contact. But he'd fallen asleep straight after and she moved away to the far side of the bed.

"I ask him if he believes in our marriage. And you know he respond by asking me why I ask such a question. We have two beautiful daughters, he say, a magnificent house and your mother's money. What is there not to believe in?"

She lets out a howl and I hold her close, feeling at a loss for words at such an outpouring.

"If only he had told me that he love me," she carries on, between sobs. "It would have made a difference. I cannot to remember when he last tell me that. Once there'd been flowers and many passionate words, then when I am pregnant all that stopped. He is sure of me. I belong to him, the woman and the house. Only in my case it had been the woman and six broken walls, no roof, no toilet and cold water from a tap in the garden. But then I am young. We had sleeping bags together on the dirty floor, and I think it is so romantic. Dreaming of the work we do on the house and how so wonderful it is going to be. Even in winter when we are freezing together on the floor, to collect the wood from the forest to light a fire is so very magic. Then Valentina is born, Anna shortly after, and then I have a miscarriage and going home to my mother who blame Vittorio. What do you think? You listen so much when I speak, Lorri. You are so wise always."

I laugh. "That's the last thing I am."

"But Lorri, there is a selfish and unselfish partner in most marriages, do you not think?"

"It depends on what you mean by selfish."

"I know what it means, one person making demands and the other person giving always in. But I am not selfish. I like to give something to you, Lorri."

"Really? Well, there is something I need – " I slide the advert across the table to her. "I was wondering if – "

But Silka is opening her suitcase and lifting out several brightly colored silk dresses, which she drapes over the chair back. "Vittorio buy me these. You take, please. I have not the use for them now."

* * * *

I'm photographing Ornelia's downstairs two-bedroom apartment. I plan to make brochures to send to people if and when they respond to my advertisement in the German newspaper.

The telephone is ringing in my apartment upstairs. Pointless trying to answer it: by the time I've run along the alley and up the stairs it will have stopped. Besides, it's too hot for running. I open the shutters of Ornelia's stuffy larger bedroom, which looks out across the village. Sunlight streams across the matrimonial bed draped now with the white linen cover from my own bed. Fresh flowers on the bedside table, lace cushions scattered against the mahogany headrest. On the other small table I've placed a bottle of wine and two glasses. I stand back to view the room through the camera lens. The small touches have transformed a dull bedroom into something promising romantic possibilities.

Ornelia has given me the key to her place until the end of September and told me to go ahead and bring the tourists. As from the following spring, the place will be mine to work with because she wants to live with her daughter in Grosseto. The extra money, she'd said, would be useful. We have agreed on a price, though somewhat lower than Ornelia had in mind, twenty percent of the profit for me and we will share the price of the publicity. Also, Margo Speller of *Holiday Homes*, who has seen my advertisement in the *Telegraph* for B&B in a Tuscan Village, telephoned to offer a year's advertising in her new company on the Internet at a special low price. It will be the same price as a week in the newspaper. Six photographs are needed with a short description of the area, not forgetting the intrepid Martino waiting to tempt the weary traveler with his *vino, prosciutto, pecorino,* and - somewhat moldy fruit.

Removing the plastic cloth on the kitchen table, I replace it with a blue cotton one, place a bowl of fruit in the center and take shots from various angles. Outside there's nothing to alter; it's already beautiful with the old stone and brick walls, a profusion of scarlet geraniums trailing from terracotta pots. Tosca, watching from under the washing, sticks her hand on a scrawny hip and cackles. I photograph her. She'll add local color.

Locking Ornelia's front door as I leave, I hear Rosalba's shutters opening and dive into the alleyway before she demands that she too should be photographed for the Internet.

The telephone rings again as I open my front door. I climb the stairs two at a time.

"No, Ronaldo, I cannot come and cook for three hungry men."

"But Silka is in the bed. She stay sleeping."

"Well, you must cook – or Vittorio. I have other things to do right now which are very important."

I put the phone down with a thumping heart: I will not allow myself to be manipulated, whatever the consequences.

* * * *

There are functions in the hotel dining room for the rest of this week. So it's back to the cocktail bar where this morning I had everyone read scenes from Shakespeare's *A Midsummr Night's Dream*. My heart sank as I listened to them struggle through the text. It'll take a month to get them to pronounce the words properly, let alone perform.

"Why that play?" Julian asked me this morning. "I would've thought maybe *Richard the Third*. Tina would make a great Lady Anne."

"We'll have to see. What's the matter with her voice? It sounds like a tin can opening."

"Oh, she's very talented, they all are; don't you think?"

"Well – er, they're going to need a lot of working on."

"What about *Macbeth*?"

"What about him?"

"That's a good play, isn't it?"

"They're all good plays, Julian, but I'm not doing anything complicated. I've been in *The Dream*, I'm sticking to what I know.'

* * * *

Friday morning. I'm on my way out through the door when the post woman hands me a letter:

Dear Lorri,

I thought you'd like to know that I've had several offers for the house. But I don't know what to do because I still haven't heard from Sherif. I'd write to him but I've no address other than Vittorio's and I don't dare send it there in case he reads it. I have a dreadful suspicion that something bad has happened to him. I don't want to ring the house in case Vittorio answers. What do you think I should do? Julian doesn't know about Sherif and I hope you won't tell him because he's still madly in love with me and can't bear the thought of losing me. Let me have news please as soon as you can. I've tried ringing but you're never there.

I feel muddled and distressed.

Love always,
Maudie.

PS. I rang Richard and he said that he has nothing to eat off. Can't you at least let him have his table back?

* * * *

The following Tuesday:

Dear Maudie,

Sherif has probably returned to his wife and family in Albania by now. Sorry to break it to you like this, but it's what Ronaldo told me. Put it behind you as a holiday adventure. Julian is setting up a drama school in Umbria. As for my own business, a couple are arriving for a week and staying downstairs in Ornelia's apartment, which I have the use of and now 'Lorri's Tuscan Cottage' is on the Internet.

Vittorio's wife's mother has died and Silka (his wife) has inherited a lot of money. She's left Vittorio and taken the children to Germany. I don't know what will happen to the house, it's in her name and she might sell it. Vittorio, who thought he was set up for life has been left with nothing – well, not nothing, he has the bar and two apartments above, one to live in, one to let. Silka told me she suspects her mother's heart attack was brought on by a violent row she had with Vittorio. Giuseppina made tè freddo on the day of Silka's tea party, which we all drank. Could one have been doctored? I wonder, sometimes, if it was meant for me and the mother drank it by mistake. We'll never know.

The lawyer, since Rocco promised to 'take care' of him, seems to have disappeared. Which brings me to Quasimodo. I think it was Rocco. The police found his Mercedes outside Martino's vegetable garden. I won't go into the story, only to say that I now have a light outside the front door.

As for Richard's table, don't worry about such things and concentrate on your own household.

Good luck with the sale of your house.

L.

I made a point of not mentioning how Julian is cosily ensconced with Gerry. That might be too painful. "We're not exactly an item," he stressed. "We're just together for now with no pressure on either side. She's found a good dentist to fix her teeth and she wants me to hold her hand."

And Maudie? Who will hold her hand? Over the years it has usually been me picking up the pieces of her life. But from now she must go it alone, for escaping her is crucial: letting the past go, which isn't easy when it's all around me, seeping into the present like water through cracks in a wall.

* * * *

On the Wednesday of the second week we moved between the cocktail bar and the hotel garden. I wanted to work outside in order to show them how to look at things, how to see.

"Yes, but when are they going to start learning the words?" Julian asks. "We've only go three weeks, remember."

"They've already started. And we'll get back to that as soon as possible. Now it's important to get the feel of the open space, flowers, trees and grass. It's a play set in a forest, after all."

We huddle together under the trees watching Julian drive off in Gerry Croft's red Saab, going about his business - whatever that is. He has become curiously guarded on the subject. But I'm still receiving a full pay packet and for now that's all that matters.

"Imagine," I begin, "this is the first time you've seen grass. Show how you would react. Study each blade, the flowers each petal, the leaves and the insects."

"Eeek," squeals Tina. "I hate insects."

"And I'm sure they hate you too," Mary rounds on her.

Eddie flings himself face down on the grass. Hamish drops on all fours and sniffs the earth. The girls giggle.

"And not a sound," I say. "Let only Nature speak."

An hour passes: Eddie on his knees now, staring transfixed at a geranium leaf, Hamish in a trance holding up a stick of wood, Malcolm, stroking the bark of a cypress, and Mary weeping behind a rose bush; moved by the beauty of it all, perhaps. Tina, too, appears to be absorbed, even if it is only with her toes, hunched over, staring intently at her chipped nail varnish.

By Thursday, they're embracing each other in the garden without embarrassed giggling. "We're here for each other," I tell them. "You must find the trust in each other to make mistakes without fear of being judged, to take wild risks, to know you're safe, that you're free to be what you will."

On Friday evening I drove home later than usual. I felt uplifted by the student's trust and enthusiasm. They were bringing out something in me, a longing to break the kernel that holds us in check, to burst through into a space where the creative energy lies buried.

The sun is sinking as I follow the winding road. I must not allow my mind to wander, think only of the journey and keep well in to the side of the rock, allowing space for other cars. Except there are no other cars, I'm in my own isolated world up here on the shadowy mountainside with only the wind for company. And as though for the first time, I notice a purple curtain drawing across the pink lamp of the sun. The darkening landscape undulating beneath a crimson sky streaked with slashes of silver and green. I stop the car and get out. This is the true drama, being performed right here in front of me, greater than anything I could ever teach.

* * * *

Ronaldo left this Saturday afternoon in Vittorio's Lancia. He's using his car more regularly now; if Vittorio couldn't pay him wages then he'd have to pay in other ways. Supplying the materials needed to build my fireplace is one way. Drawings have been in progress for several weeks, spread over the entire surface of the kitchen table while he sits most mornings in my bathrobe gazing into the distance, smoking, stroking the cats and finishing off the wine store.

"I must to invent in the mind," he says. "When you think I do nothing I do much."

* * * *

It's Thursday afternoon: I am driving down the hill toward the station. I turn left at the bottom and head for the garage on the *Superstrada* the only place selling cheap petrol and chilled mint tea in the Sandy Bar.

It's while drinking tea after filling the tank that I notice something familiar about the white jacket the barman is wearing. "You like?" he asks in English. "I find under the trees, someone throw away good jacket."

I'm vaguely aware of the barman's puzzled smile when I pay for the tea and leave. If by some extraordinary chance, it's Richard's jacket, why would he throw it away? And in the garage of all places: and what about Sherif's jacket – if it was his, and I'm beginning to believe it might have been, why was it dumped in the forest? Is he buried somewhere in the forest? Then the thought that something may have happened to Richard is so appalling I can barely hold it in my head. Surely it's too much of a coincidence; people don't go around throwing jackets away. I should have asked the barman when he'd found the jacket, and I'm on the point of returning when I realize all I have to do is ring Germany and find out. But then the thought of hearing Richard's voice coming down the phone is so unnerving I'm not sure I can do it.

I drive back up the hill then ease along Ciro Pinsuti and slip the Auto Bianchi into a parking space opposite the street steps. On letting myself through the front door, I climb the stairs and go straight to the desk drawer in the *solotto* and take out my address book. But instead of Richard it's his ex-lady friend's number, Veronica, with the snappy teeth that I find. I won't be troubling her, that's for sure!

The only other people who might have his new number are the lawyer and Maudie who keeps in touch with him for reasons of her own. I try the lawyer first. No answer. But at least the line is connected. I'm on the point of dialing Maudie when the phone rings, making me start. After a moments' hesitation, I pick it up.

"Lorri?"

"How extraordinary. I was just about to ring you."

"I don't believe what you said in the letter about Sherif being married with children. You're making it up."

"Why would I do that?"

"To put me off him."

"Don't be absurd. You have to believe it because it's the truth."

"Is that what you were going to ring me about?"

"No. I need Richard's new phone number."

"Has it changed then?"

"Come on, Maudie, you know it has. You said in your letter that you'd rung him and he'd talked about his table."

"Are you going to give it back to him?"

"Can I have Richard's number, please?"

"Even if Sherif is married he still wanted to be with me."

"The number?"

"I don't know that I still have it."

"Could you look, it's important."

"Has something happened?"

"No. I just need to speak to him, that's all."

"Do you think Vittorio's bumped Silka's mother off to get his hands on the money?"

"No, Maudie, I don't. Are you going to give me the number?"

"He could have got his Quasimodo cousin to bump Sherif off too. Because I don't believe he's gone back to Albania."

I close my eyes in exasperation.

I look at the number I've scribbled on a piece of paper. What on earth can I say? The barman was wearing your jacket and I thought someone had bumped you off, ha-ha. It may not be his, of course. And yet, somehow, I know it is. The hem of the breast pocket was coming unstitched. Something I'd always meant to do and never got round to. I'd noticed the small detail immediately.

I lift the receiver, telling myself that the reason for ringing is to know that he is all right, not to make lighthearted conversation. I'll hang up the moment I hear his voice. But after several rings he speaks on the answering machine telling me to leave my name and number and he'll get back to me as soon as possible.

My hand trembles as I replace the receiver. The sound of his voice has brought his presence too strongly into the room.

* * * *

"It is excellent that you are now extending the drama into Umbria. But where is this young man, Giulianno, finding the money?"

"Roger, the estate agent, I think – I'm not sure."

"Estate agents do not usually have the money to finance Shakespearean productions in a castle or elsewhere – except you say, there is no castle and you are practising the play in a cocktail bar? Huh! It sounds wonderfully crazy to me."

"It does to me. But at least I'm being paid."

"For now. But for how much longer, I wonder. And now you have another drama with the barman wearing Richard's jacket." Lionello chuckles. "This is a good addition to the story, I like it very much."

"But he's never there when I ring . . . "

"I don't think it's so strange. He is away somewhere, perhaps in Italy, about to pay you another visit."

"But what do you think it means?"

"The jacket thrown away?" Lionello waves his hand in the air. "I presume he was tired of it. Or it was too hot, or it reminded him of you – who knows?"

"But it's so unlike him. Richard would never throw his clothes away, especially under the trees in a garage. And not a good jacket, even if it did remind him of me. It's out of character. He used to walk down a street fastidiously picking up bits of paper and putting them into the bin. He hated to see things thrown away."

"But perhaps his personality has changed, become more expansive in the sun? In the heat we do things we would not normally do, and especially in Tuscany. I am sure Richard will do things here that he has only dreamt of doing in the cold of England or Germany. And as for the missing Albanian leaving his jacket in the forest – I am sure by now someone is wearing that too. But if you are seriously concerned why not ask the *carabinieri* for their help?"

"I don't want to involve them if I can avoid it."

"But they will find out if the missing Albanian is still in Italy."

"I wouldn't want to make trouble for him."

Lionello leans contentedly back in his chintz-covered sofa and sighs with pleasure. "I have been waiting with much anticipation for more of this wonderful theater. I was dying of boredom in my cousin's house in the mountains; I believe it is possible to die of such a thing. I have too many complaining relatives. They come to see me with all their aches and pains I don't want to be reminded of.

Here, I feel young again. I have returned from the dead. And now tell me, I want to know more about this curious young man in your life. Surely he is not living with you, is he? How can you do your bed and breakfast with him in the bed?"

"I'm using Ornelia's apartment while she's away."

"Ah, very clever, you are making use of your neighbors. And now tell me something else, does he make you happy, this young man, who you say has no money and is impossible to be with."

I lean back in my chintz-covered chair and sigh. Being in Lionello's house again, with the smell of roses, the dusty summer smell of faded linen and freshly brewed coffee, gives me a sense of happiness and security. "Sometimes he makes me happy," I say. "But sometimes he makes me very unhappy. He's possessive and jealous and totally unpredictable. And yet, I'm happier than I've ever been. It's impossible to explain how I feel, because I don't understand my feelings."

"And you are loving every moment of it?"

"No, I'm hating it!"

"Huh!" Lionello laughs as he pours coffee unsteadily into little blue cups. "Then my dear young lady, you are in love and there is no point to explain anything."

"But he's taking my life over, he's crowding me out of my space. And he now has no work and lies in bed all morning stroking the cat."

"Then you are to blame for allowing him to do so. You must push him out to earn the money and tell him not to return until he does."

The prospect of doing anything so drastic fills me with alarm. He may not return. "Well, he is working in a way," I explain, and sip my coffee. "He's building me a fireplace in the kitchen. Something Richard never had time to do. So I suppose you could say he's putting value on the property."

"And what has become of Richard's lawyer?"

"When I rung before the line was dead. Now it rings but no one answers. He's either moved. Or something sinister has happened to him too."

"The plot is thickening and I am enjoying every moment of it. Now someone, yourself perhaps, will find another jacket – on a train, with a torn paper in the pocket – blood-stained, of course, on which is written the name of the *Avvocato.*" Lionello reaches for the telephone book. "I am becoming like Hercule Poirot. What is his name, this lawyer?"

"Benocci."

Lionello leafs through the pages. "*Avvocato* Benocci of Montepulciano?"

"That's him."

Lionello picks up the phone and dials the number. After a moment he speaks and I lean forward to hear better and try and understand. The conversation continues for some time, as it always does in Italy. But the gist of it is the telephone line has been out of order due to works going on in the street. The discussion carries on rapidly about one thing or another, and then Lionello mentions Richard's name and I lean further forward.

"It appears that Richard wants to drop the case against you," Lionello says, replacing the receiver. "And Benocci has received a letter from an *Avvocato*

Miullo who says he is acting on your behalf. I did not know that you too have a lawyer."

"Neither did I – well, not exactly."

"Miullo says that Richard cannot have claim on your property unless his name is on the deeds. And if you decide to sell it and offer him money for his work then that is up to you."

"That's Rocco, the man I told you about who played the flute in my house."

"Rocco Miullo is the flute player who collapsed on your bed?"

I nod.

"*Santa Maria!* Nothing like this has ever happened in Sinalunga in all the years I have been living here. You must promise never to leave."

"Well, I probably won't – if things work out."

"Everything will work out if you want it to."

"I do – I do. Did he say where Richard is?"

"It would appear that he is in Italy."

"No! Where?"

"He had a postcard from him two days ago. He's in Umbria, buying a house."

"I don't believe it!"

"So, there we are. Perhaps he hopes you will join him in this new house."

"Never!"

But when I return home and find bags of cement outside my front door, yet more jammed in the hallway, dusty footprints and paw prints leading up the stairs, then another bag of cement pressed against the kitchen door, barring my entrance due to works being carried out within, I begin to look forward to returning to Umbria to continue the drama unfolding there.

20
Confronting the Phantom

I'm driving over the mountain, passing villages, small bars and the occasional restaurant, on and up into dusty green woodlands. Longed-for space at last: there is little enough in my flat; the whole place has been taken over with the building of the fireplace. I had wanted something simple; a rustic beam for a mantelpiece and a stone hearth upon which to stand a basket of wood.

But nothing so simple for Ronaldo: he's envisaged a sloping hood in the traditional Tuscan style, under which two sculptured heads, the Father and the Son, will face each other from either side of the flames. "But there's nowhere to stand my brass candlesticks," I'd protested. He shrugged and said something about how I was in Italy now and that a traditional Tuscan farmhouse fireplace was the only thing he was prepared to build. I pointed out that my tiny flat isn't a farmhouse and that his fireplace, although doubtless impressive, would steal space from the room.

I had paused at the front door as he called out after me: "I make the angel for you when you turn back." I left the house nervously, unsure what he meant. But he seems happy in his work, which is a relief, and he hasn't suggested coming with me, an even bigger relief, because I find it difficult to be myself when he's around. Yet who that 'self' is, I'm still in the process of finding out.

Ornelia's apartment comes to mind as I drive and all the things I can do to improve it. I had glanced at it possessively on my way down the steps to the car this morning. It feels like mine, even though it isn't. The five-day booking for a couple worked out well. They liked the place and promised to tell their friends. But now I definitely have to find another house, for when Ornelia returns at the end of September, my B&B earnings will cease until the spring of next year. I've asked the local housing agent for advice on selling my flat. But my request for eighty thousand euros was met with gales of scornful laughter. The place is pretty, they said, but with no central heating and only sixty square meters, the most I could hope to receive is sixty-five thousand and they would take two percent. Which is why I've decided to go it alone.

My hopes now lie with Silka who has taken my 'For Sale' advertisement to Germany with her and promised to put it into the Saturday edition of *Der Spiegel*. An old village house with a small garden or terrace that needs work on and doesn't cost more than seventy-five thousand is what I hope to find. Then with luck, I could borrow enough from the Abbey National in Milan to restore it and pay every month with my B&B money and hopefully drama teaching income. Ronaldo has said that he would do the renovation work. A gamble, I know, but one worth taking.

How I have changed since that first exhilarating evening when I set out in Lionello's Alpha Romeo, lost my way, and almost didn't make it to Vittorio's house. "You are a fish *in* water," Lionello says. It pleases me every time I think of it.

I have arranged to meet Julian at ten in the car park of the *Mercurio* hotel in Trestina. It's now ten-fifteen; the journey is taking longer than I anticipated. The plan is to go to Gerry's house for lunch and discuss the renovation of the castle. "She's met Richard," Julian said on the phone. "She's sold him a house – a kind of house; a tobacco tower in the forest with a tree growing through the roof. There's a lot of work to be done, and all the land around is his. When he saw it, he went into raptures, apparently, and said at last he'd found his Shangri-La."

I see Julian climbing out of the red Saab as I drive into the hotel car park. "I was beginning to wonder if you'd got lost," he says. "Leave your car here. We'll go in mine."

"*Your* car?"

"Well, almost." He winks at me and I inwardly laugh. Julian is turning out to be more ambitious than I ever realized. He kisses me. "You okay? How's the boyfriend?"

"Fine. And you? How's it going with Gerry?"

"Great. She's had her teeth fixed, makes all the difference." He turns the key in the ignition. "Have you been to Roger's house before?"

"Once, with Richard."

"Gerry thinks we could hold the classes there if the castle doesn't work out."

"I thought you said the castle's nearly finished."

"I thought so too. But the owner appears to have run out of money. That's why I want you to see Roger's house. It's perfect for teaching drama. I've written to all the drama schools in London, laying out my plans, sending them photos of the house, the grounds and surrounding area . . . "

His words come and go in snatches. It isn't easy concentrating, my eyes strain to see across the hazy landscape, parched with dryness, receding into hilly slopes dotted with vines and mauve patches of vegetation. I scaled every one of these hills with Richard, searching for a house and every ruin we'd seen had been the ideal home in the making. And now he'd done it without me. I feel a hollow sense of loss and yet at the same time, relief. It could have been disastrous, our living together here, trying to build a house with little money and no work. We would have been like so many English who come to Tuscany with dreams of restoring a wonderful ruin. Then they knock down a few walls and find a bottomless pit waiting to drain all their money away. "Does Richard intend living here full-time?" I ask.

"I've no idea what his plans are."

We've almost driven out of Trestina and through Ronti, when Julian swings the car right, up a familiar, long, twisting track, past a stack of logs and a broken chair, into an L-shaped driveway. Roger the agent's house where Richard and I had drunk wine and shared with him our exotic dreams of buying an old house, doing it up, and living in Italy. It seems everywhere I go, Richard's shadow waits, only biding its time before stepping out to confront me.

"Hi, Lorri."

Gerry waves from the garden. She looks different. Her hair is blonder, she wears shorts and a man's shirt, and the large even teeth, slotting perfectly into her gums, sparkle in the sunlight.

"You look marvelous," I say, and kiss her.

"It's all due to my wonderful Rob Roy here. He's taken control of my life." I look questioningly at Julian. I want to giggle. Is this really what he wants? We watch him slope away, pulling off his T-shirt as he enters the house. "He's such a moody devil, but I love it when he goes all mean and evil on me. Then I have to think of all the things I can do to win him round, to see that sexy smile of his. Julian, wait for me, I'm coming . . . I'm coming!"

I look on, lost for words as Gerry runs after him into the house. Am I supposed to follow or what? I can't help feeling it's all staged for my benefit.

I look round the garden. The old stone table, still under the chestnut tree, where we'd eaten lunch. It had been splattered with bird shit and Roger had thrown a cloth over it, apologising for the state of things. Then he'd served a delicious lunch of *mozzarella* and cherry tomatoes and *pecorino* and pears washed down with copious glasses of the local white wine. We'd been ready to buy anything after that.

Crossing over the grass, I sit on the wooden bench in front of the apricot rose bush. I'd sat by the same roses, on the same bench, on the same torn Laura Ashley cushion two years ago, less torn then perhaps, and talked of the dream house we'd hoped to find. It had to have a barn where Richard could make furniture. He's in his own world when he works, I'd told Roger; sawing, carving, whispering to the wood, as though drawing forth entities to form themselves into a cupboard or chair, and Richard had laughed and said the wine was affecting me.

I close my eyes and listen to the silence. That affects me. A loaded silence, as if the atoms of the trees, the land, the vineyards are all piling up on one another and vibrating with energy around me. I breathe it in; I need all the energy I can get to make a success of my life here. I open my eyes, feeling uneasy, as though I'm being watched. But the surrounding land stretching to the distant mountains seems uninhabited, forsaken even.

How long am I supposed to sit here waiting while Gerry does whatever she's doing to Julian? I wish I hadn't come. I'm having enough of being pulled back into nostalgic memories. And it's unlikely that I can teach drama to a lot of unsuspecting students with Gerry chasing half-naked Julian around the house. My hands are sweating; I wipe them on my skirt. Astonishing really, I wouldn't have thought Gerry was his type, new teeth or not.

I get up and make my way slowly toward the house, my gaze traveling up the mass of vibrant creeper that covers half the wall. But of course she's his type: she has a house for him to live in and bring the students to if necessary. I can't help smiling, however cynically; Julian will get on in the theater, no doubt about that.

The upstairs shutters swing open suddenly and make me start. Julian leans out of the window; he appears to be naked. "Just showering," he calls. "The kitchen's the first door on the right. Help yourself to wine, it's in the fridge."

I have the most peculiar sensation that something isn't quite right. There is somebody in the kitchen waiting to see me. My immediate instinct is to run for I sense intuitively who it is. But I also know I have to see it through. I enter the large, square room, which has a marble table in the center and a fireplace wide enough to accommodate four people sitting close. I catch my breath. There he is, just as I suspected, standing in the corner of the room near the window, his shoulders hunched with tension.

Then an extraordinary thing happens. A larger person within me thrusts the smaller person aside and sweeps forward and holds him close.

"Richard, I cannot tell you what a joy it is to see you." I feel him resist slightly and let him go.

"Well, I'm not sure I can say that exactly, but, yes, I'm glad to see you, too. Would you like a glass of wine?" He pours white wine into two long-stemmed glasses, but his hand is shaking and he spills some onto the marble table. We stare at each other in silence. He looks as though he's holding onto every last reserve he has.

I can't understand what's happening, I feel sympathy for him, and I feel happy to see him.

"It's been a long time," he says quietly. "How are you?"

I look at him, anxious brown eyes, vulnerable mouth partly concealed in his neatly trimmed beard and mustache, hair receding; slight grayness at the temples. It is the face I've known and loved and carried within me for so long, and from which I am released. "I'm fine," I say. "Just fine. I hear you're buying a house here. Congratulations." I sip wine.

"Yes, well – " He gives an apologetic shrug. "A tobacco tower that needs everything doing to it."

"But that's wonderful."

"I hope it will be. I'll own the forest; it's in as well."

"Even more wonderful!" I smile and sip more wine. I feel happy, genuinely happy for him. He laughs awkwardly at the sight of Julian appearing sheepishly in the kitchen doorway.

"Julian, come and join us," he calls.

It has been a set-up, I realize. Poor Richard. He seems embarrassed, trying to engage Julian in lighthearted conversation. Whatever did Julian have in mind? To bring us together again?

Then Gerry appears, smiling with the new teeth. I swallow the rest of my wine, sway slightly, and sit down. I want to laugh. The wine must be going to my head. I feel absurdly happy. I want to hug everyone, especially Richard, and share his excitement of buying a property in Italy. "And how is your Italian?" I ask. "I speak it enough to get by."

"I'm sure you speak it better than I speak German," he says. "A language I dislike intensely."

"And what about work?"

"I teach English in a school."

"No carpentry?"

He shrugs. "I do it when I can."

Julian fills our glasses. And then someone else enters the kitchen: a woman of medium height with short fair hair and brown eyes. She walks over to Richard and stands beside him. "This is – er, Heidi – " He is clearly embarrassed, poor man. "I'd like you to meet Lorri – "

I'm on my feet, shaking Heidi's hand warmly in both of mine. She's lovely, absolutely right for Richard. I even give her a kiss. Richard looks on, amazed.

"I have heard so much about you," she says.

"Oh, dear. All bad, was it?"

"No, not all so bad. Very good also."

We smile at each other with a kind of understanding.

Julian pours wine. But now is the time for me to leave. "Excuse me," I say. "I have to get back. Ronaldo is waiting for me." Richard's eyes flick away, he doesn't want to hear about Ronaldo.

I leave the house in a kind of euphoria. Everything is vibrating with energy, the trees, the grass, and the sky has a luminosity I've never noticed before. Lionello is right; it is the air, the wine and the light combined that creates hallucinations. I follow the rutted track leading down to the road; I run a little, sometimes stagger a little. Had Julian's motive been to let me see Richard was with someone else? He could never have guessed at the effect it's had on me. For I'm delighted and relieved to know he has found someone who seems so nice.

My heart beats fast as I walk, skidding on loose stones, scraping my shin on a rock. Perspiration is running down my face. I control my breathing, long breaths in - out, in - out. My feet press forward while I stare ahead into the luminous space. Where do I think I'm going, exactly? I can't walk all the way back to the hotel. I sit on the stone wall and a goat in the field stares at me.

I begin to laugh. Perhaps someone will come in search of me – perhaps not. It's all so wonderfully crazy. The unease I'd felt in the garden - Richard must have been watching me from the kitchen window, planning what to say. "Oh, Richard, dear Richard," I say aloud. "I'm so happy we met and parted well and I'm so happy to be emotionally free." And then I remember I never asked him about his jacket; why he threw it away in the garage. But it doesn't matter any more.

I reach the road and stop for breath. It's miles of walking back to the hotel, but I may get a lift. I must keep going, feet moving forward, carrying me away from the house and all the memories.

I hear the sound of a car behind me. Julian draws alongside me in the Saab. "Lorri, for Christ's sake! What the hell's the matter with you? What are you doing? Why are you running off? Richard's totally confused – we all are." He looks anxiously into my face. "I thought . . . we thought, oh hell, we both thought, *hoped* we could bring you two together, because . . . well, you love him – don't you? He loves you. He told us he did. Which is why he wanted to see you."

"Julian - " I gasp for breath. "I've just met his lady – and she's lovely, and I'm happy for all of us, especially for myself."

"But . . . " Julian is shaking his head. "You've got it all wrong. That's the German woman he's buying the house from. They're just good friends, that's all."

I stare at Julian, wide-eyed. Then I start laughing, I can't help it. "Well, they won't be just good friends for long, I promise you. And I'm glad of it. She's exactly what he needs, I can tell." Julian is still shaking his head as though he can't believe what I'm saying. "Because you feel love for someone, it doesn't mean you've got to hang on to them and stay together forever, does it?"

"But that's what normally happens, Lorri."

"But I'm not normal – not since coming to Italy. I've made a certain choice and there's no going back. I can't be the person I was. Once you start down diverging paths, it changes you in the process.

"But you still love him? That's all that matters."

"Yes, a part of me always will. And that's why I'm letting him go and walking away happy, knowing that he will end up with that nice lady and be happy too. I thought seeing him again would break me. Instead it's freed me – pushed me through a door into the world, where all possibilities await."

"But if you love someone, you want to be with them."

"Some of the time. Then we'll see where it takes us. I've changed. I can't go back to being the person I was. I have to move forward no matter how challenging the new life I've chosen for myself. And now please, I must get home to Ronaldo."

"I'll drive you to your car if that's really what you want."

"It is."

"I think you're making a mistake, Lorri. Ronaldo won't make you happy."

"We'll have to see."

* * * *

The sun is sinking as I wind my way back around the mountain in the Auto Bianchi. There always seems to be a wind up here. The ragged clouds have a purple tinge; they race across the setting sun as though on some urgent journey of their own. The sky will burst open later, drenching the baking earth, clearing the air, making it possible to breathe again. Tree branches sway as I pass under them, leaves scattering against the windscreen. After half an hour of cautious driving, I see the sign ahead for Cortona.

The moon has risen by the time I reach Sinalunga. The wind has dropped and the stars are crowding together in the universe, but their light is for each other, unconcerned with the little car chugging up the hill. Only the lights of the village beckon welcomingly.

When I get out of the car, opposite Martino's, I see him again, the same old phantom, his arms full of bedding as he climbs the street steps to the alleyway. I climb slowly after him.

These memories that were once painful are less so now. If I had taken Richard back into my life and the same thing had happened, him searching for work in another country then meeting someone else, it would be worse. I'd be older, more vulnerable and unable to cope in the way I know I now can. Our relationship would become a hollow farce and I don't want that, I want to remember the good times, even though I know they can't be again. It's only now that matters, I tell myself, turning into the alleyway. I must concentrate on the present then the memories will fade in their own good time.

On reaching my front door, I flick the wall switch for the outside light. Nothing. I look up into the little glass shade. Someone has stolen the wretched lightbulb again!

* * * *

"You must no to enter!"

A bag of cement is still jammed against the kitchen door. "You must to enter only when I say."

I sit wearily on the hall stairs. I could have done without this. To come in and sit down with a glass of wine would have been enough. The fireplace surely can't be that important. Minutes pass. I am on the point of getting up when I hear: "Now you come."

I walk hesitantly into the candlelit kitchen, wondering what I will find. Then stop dead. A black head and shoulders rises from the fireplace, its prodigious wings stretching across the chimney. Flanking it are my brass candlesticks cemented into plaster, two flickering candles casting shadows across the ebony face which looks down at me, one eyebrow raised, the mouth smiling derisively. If it laughs, God help us, it will shake the building!

I stand transfixed, as though before some outrageous altar. The fire burning in the grate below, the two delicately carved male heads, the Father and the Son, on either side. How beautiful it would have been if it had been left at that.

"I make your face and mine," Ronaldo is saying, excitedly.

Long wavy hair framing the oval face, full mouth and cleft chin - somehow, I'm going to have to deal with this.

"But I see you no like."

"I - er, no, I - well - it's – er - overwhelming me slightly, that's all."

"I make for you with my love. I work all the day and the night."

"But why is it black, Ronaldo? Why did you have to make it black angel?"

"I take the black cement from Vittorio, cost nothing. But now you paint white. Now is yours. The angel of the 'ouse, I present to you with my love."

I think rapidly. Yes, I could paint it white; it would blend more into the chimney. It was either that or taking an axe to it, which would be like taking an axe to him. "It's - er, rather large, Ronaldo, isn't it?" I say. "Don't you think it's a little large?"

"Because is the *arch*angel, Lorri. The more big angel of all."

* * * *

"It's priceless! It's the Laughing Cavalier. All it needs is a hat with a feather."

It is Tuesday, my afternoon off from the students. Lisa has come for tea. She steps back to see the angel better and begins laughing again.

"You laugh now," I say, "but you should have seen it before I painted it. It was jet black." Lisa gives another burst of laughter. "What do you think I ought to do?"

"Nothing, it's a work of art. It's that self-satisfied grin on its face that cracks me up. It's so wonderfully over the top and if you can't be over the top in Italy where can you be?" She pulls out a chair to sit at the table. "How are things going between you? Never a dull moment, I imagine."

I pour the tea. "The language is the main problem."

"Teach him English then you can speak in both languages."

"We do. His English is improving, whereas, my Italian's deteriorating."

"You've only been here for three months, give yourself a chance. I've been here for ten years and I'm still not fluent."

"But you understand, which is more important. I understand a little, some days better than others, but miss the bits I really want to hear. Like old women coming up to me in the street and telling me important things about Ronaldo's life as a child, which I can't quite follow, it's so frustrating. It's like trying to see through a fog, every now and then you see the shape of something emerging, and then it vanishes again."

"You should put that down in your journal. It's a good description of trying to understand a foreign language. I wish I could write, I'd have plenty to say."

"You can. Just pick up a pen."

"It's not as easy as that, otherwise everyone would be doing it."

"They are, that's the trouble."

"So, what do you intend doing about it?"

"What, Italian? Continue trying to learn it. But I'm convinced even if I spoke the language fluently I still couldn't communicate with Ronaldo. He's so wrapped up with whatever he's doing; nothing else seems to matter. I asked him if he'd taken the lightbulb out of the street lamp and he looked at me as though I was crazy. How could I talk about something so mundane when he'd just created an angel? No, sorry, an *arch*angel."

Lisa digs into her basket for her tobacco tin. "He's changed for the better since meeting you, I'll tell you that. In fact, you seem to have had a curious effect on everyone's life here. Silka's left Vittorio, poor Gretta's died of a heart attack, Giuseppina's pregnant and Rocco passed out on your bed with epilepsy. Do you have this effect on everyone wherever you go?"

"Giuseppina's *pregnant*? Did I hear right?"

"That's what her mother said. She came searching for Vittorio but found me instead. I've been looking after the dogs. She seems to think Sherif is the father."

"*What?*"

"Which is why Sherif disappeared."

"I don't believe it. She's making it up."

"Who knows? And what about Rocco, what's happened to him?"

"Safely at home with his housekeeper. But he might be the one pinching the lightbulbs."

"Which means he's back on the prowl?"

"I hope not."

"It could be anyone. Down these dark alleys at night you can't see who anyone is."

"Which is why I keep putting hundred-watt lightbulbs in the lamp, which are then stolen."

"Obviously someone needs a lightbulb. Or doesn't want to be seen." Lisa lights her roll-up. "I shouldn't worry. Whoever took it will replace it before long; it's just a matter of convenience. That's the way of things here. People don't consider it stealing, it's neighbors helping each other." She sucks in smoke. "I think you're a catalyst, Lorri; you cause things to happen. You came here to change your life and everyone else's life has changed as well.

* * * *

As Julian has fallen out with Tonino, the manager of the *Mecurio,* the hotel is no longer available. Earlier, the students and I read through the text at a back table in the *Bar Centrale,* getting under the words, discovering their true intent. Mary was leaning across a collection of dirty *cappuccino* cups, halfway through her love speech to Bottom, the weaver: *'The summer still doth tend upon my state . . . '* when she began to cry. Not with the passion of Shakespeare's words, but because she had nowhere to wash. And then the full story came out. Julian has moved the students out of the hotel and into cheap rented rooms because he can't pay the bill.

In a small, shabby condominium in the High Street, a flight of stone stairs lead to the boys' room with three narrow beds and a cupboard. Up a further flight are the girls' room and a bathroom with a basin and running cold water.

"If my mother knew I was living like this," sobs Mary, "I'd have to go home. But Julian's begged us not to say anything to our parents."

"He keeps telling us not to worry," Hamish puts in. "He says we're going to be discovered and find work on the TV. That it's important to overlook these setbacks."

"My dad thinks he's gay. I had a job persuading him to give Julian money and let me come out here." Eddie laughs. He seems to be finding the experience a hilarious adventure.

"Listen to me," I say, with more calm than I feel, "Julian has brought us together to do something worth doing, and that's what we're going to do. We'll get this show on, no matter what happens."

And this afternoon we invented the Forest of Arden in the girls' larger bedroom, pushing the beds to the walls; a chair becoming a tree stump, a suitcase, a stone in the forest.

"I give you my word, it's going to be all right," Julian assures me on the telephone. "You can rehearse here in the house and then I've got a wonderful deal with the *San Martino* hotel in Città di Castello. They can sleep there until the castle's ready."

"I'm tired of hearing about this fictitious castle."

"It's not fictitious. I'll take you there when it's in a fit state. But wait till you hear – I've booked the theater for Thursday and Friday, so you can rehearse there all day. What do you think of that?"

"Yes, Julian, but the students are crowded together, they have one small bathroom with cold water and can't have a shower. And I didn't know you've been taking money off their parents. Why didn't you tell me?"

"Their parents are people I know in Glasgow. They're very happy their kids are having such a wonderful chance. And don't believe everything they tell you. They are in the *Mercurio* every morning using the bathroom and toilets. There's plenty of hot water there. Don't worry. They're not; they're too excited to worry. And they're swept away with you, you know. They talk of nothing else. How you've come along like a shining angel into their lives to guide them in the dark."

I am speechless!

21
The Show Must Go On

The beautiful theater in Via Fucci, Città di Castello, dates back to 1600 and seats about two hundred people. From the moment we walked into the auditorium this morning, the place became a reality. We scrambled onto the stage and, with books in hand, everyone began moving around, claiming their space.

At the end of the second day and using the hot showers in the dressing rooms, everyone seems to have forgotten about the uncomfortable conditions in the condominium. The boys suggest moving into the theater with sleeping bags, the girls nodding approval, no one minds the cold – the heating has broken down – we are fired by enthusiasm. But sleeping here isn't possible as the theater has to be locked at the end of rehearsals and the keys returned to the office in Via di Luce, round the corner.

Ten days before the performance Eddie is off the book, and apart from a few Scouse words creeping occasionally into Shakespeare's text, he seems to have become the character of Puck, Oberon's mischievous messenger.

'The King doth keep his revels here tonight. Take heed the queen come not within his sight . . . '

He has found a curious, gruff kind of voice for the part and prances about on the toes of his dirty trainers, hands moving in a jerky manner. There are moments when I can't hear the words for his accent, but that can be worked on, but one thing is clear - he's going to be a memorable Puck.

"We're going to have to get rid of that wee 'high tea' voice," I said to Tina earlier. "No one will hear you, and apart from that, you'll have a sore throat. Think from the diaphragm," I said, in a deep and resonating voice. What, I thought, are they learning in their elocution classes in Glasgow?

"Get into your head," I now say to Malcolm, as he clumps across the stage, " that you're the mighty Oberon, the king of the fairies."

Shrieks of laughter.

"All right, let me put it another way: you're the Lord of the Forest, whom everybody fears and reveres. Now, enter from upstage, shoulders back, head high. Move!"

Malcolm slides one large foot forward and falls over. Everyone collapses, concentration destroyed.

"Try to recapture what you found in the garden," I say to them the next day while seated round a table in the *Bar Centrale;* Eddie sits apart, mumbling his lines and twitching his face; several people are watching him and keeping their distance. "Memory sense," I carry on. "Remember the smells, the touch, the light, then bring that to your performance."

On Friday afternoon Julian sits in on rehearsals. Everyone performs adequately, but they're still clutching books – all that is, except Eddie, who is clearly in a world of his own. And when he hesitates, I'm not sure if it's part of the performance or he's forgotten the words. On the night, I shall prompt. For now, I follow the text as best as I can from the stalls.

"It's a bit of a shambles," Julian says to me afterwards. "When are they going to learn the lines?"

"Give them a chance," I reply. "They've not had it easy. What with rehearsing in bars and around beds, it's amazing they know as much as they do."

"And what language is Eddie speaking? I couldn't understand a word he was saying."

"But what about their living arrangements? Never mind Eddie."

"I'm moving them into the *San Martino*, like I said."

"Yes, but when?"

"I'm just waiting for a wee bit more money to arrive from the parents."

"Do they know how they're living?"

"Well – no, not exactly."

"But Julian, they'll tell their parents."

"No, they've promised not to."

"You can't be serious."

"Oh I am. I've never been more so. We'll get through this setback, you see if we don't."

* * * *

The weather has changed. There's a chill wind from the mountains, not unusual in Umbria, I'm told. We still have access to the theater; Annamaria, the guardian of the key, doesn't mind our coming in so long as we leave it clean and tidy. But Tina is coughing; she has a cold from living in such a damp place, she says. And Malcolm complains of a sore throat. We're all feeling miserable and tired, bundled up in sweaters, and we still don't know when the performance is – last week in September, Julian said, but it's October in four days' time and he's not been seen or heard of for three days and I've received only half my money this week.

I decide to cancel rehearsals, even though we can ill afford to waste time; we will go in a body to Roger's house and consult Julian this afternoon and demand they be moved into the *San Martino* hotel this evening.

Gerry answers the telephone; she sounds fraught. "He's in Scotland," she says.

"What's he doing there? We need him here."

"He's raising money. But don't worry, the show must go on – the Central School of Speech and Drama have promised to come on 18 October."

When I suggest bringing the students to sleep in the house, she panics. "We've only got two bedrooms. How do you think I can accommodate six people?"

"They could sleep on the floor on cushions," I suggest. "It would be better than where they are now."

"Out of the question. Roger would never allow it. I'm sorry, Lorri, but er – well, speak to Julian when he returns at the weekend."

Feeling somewhat defeated, we traipse to the nearest bar to have a word rehearsal.

* * * *

On Friday morning we meet in the theater for a dress rehearsal. We have four days left before the upper echelons of English drama arrive to judge us. "You will be here, won't you, before we perform?" Mary asks, her small pinched face gazing up at me in the dressing room.

"Of course I will," I reassure her. "Barring accidents. I'll be with you all the way. And I'm in the wings, remember, with the book if you forget the words. Which you won't."

At the end of the afternoon, I turn the lights off in the auditorium and dressing rooms. Then fighting fatigue, I step out into puddles of water; it's been raining heavily and the streets are awash. The students run for the bus as I head for my car.

On Monday morning I gather the students together in the dressing room. "Julian has telephoned. The judges are definitely coming," I say. "He collected them from Pisa airport on Sunday. Now he's trying to get you all booked into the hotel."

The girls cling to me. Mary weeps and says she is almost fainting with fear. "There'll only be about three or four people out there at the most," I say. "There's nothing to get alarmed about."

"We're very grateful to you," Malcolm says, his body draped in his white bed sheet, attempting to look like a Grecian Lord of the forest. "I could never have done this if it hadn't been for you. I wouldn't have had the courage."

Everyone nods vigorously and Eddie gives me a little kiss and blushes.

It hasn't stopped raining here all day, yet Sinalunga was only cloudy when I left for Cortona this morning. The mountain road is treacherous, the air thick with leaves scattering in the wind. I have planned to sleep in a B&B in Città di Castello on the night of the show; the return journey late at night will be too dangerous. Ronaldo has insisted on coming with me. He will drive, he says. I'm not too happy about that, for he drives fast. Around these bends it would be suicidal. He's been very thoughtful recently, bringing me a tray of tea and biscuits in bed on Sunday morning. He'd buttered the biscuits and stuck sultanas on them. It's obviously what he thinks an English woman likes. "No think I do this always," he'd said, and I'd laughed. But the sight of those sultanas and the care he'd taken, made me feel foolishly happy.

I drive slowly, easing the little car round the narrow curving roads and across the stone bridges. The glistening mountainside is deserted, the bars are closed, I am alone up here with nothing between nature and me. The Auto Bianchi's windshield wipers click rapidly back and forth.

Then heading on into the downpour, one of the worst things that could happen, happens: the car battery dies on me. No amount of coaxing it, turning off the lights, the engine, then waiting and trying again, makes the slightest difference. I sit huddled in the car with no phone - I left it in Sinalunga - listening to the ominous rumble of thunder and crackling fingers of lightning and no sign whatsoever of another car. I could die up here, of hypothermia.

There's only one thing for it – walk. Except I may never make it, I'll be blown off the mountain before I get anywhere near habitation. The show must go on all right. But right now the only show going on is the show of my life!

I push open the car door and stumble out onto the slippery road. I look back at the little Auto Bianchi abandoned against the rocks. Don't get sentimental about inanimate objects, I tell myself, and push forward into the wind and the rain toward Cortona.

* * * *

I have bronchitis. I have also had frantic phone calls from Julian begging me to return, promising to double my money. But Ronaldo won't allow it. He stays guard in the kitchen, concocting tasty invalid meals. It's because of him that I'm here, ensconced in bed. He and his friend Fillipo came looking for me. I saw their headlights and waved frantically. They brought me home and the next day went to fetch the Auto Bianchi, re-charged the battery with jump leads and drove it back. It's now safely parked in its usual place next to Martino's shop.

"They can't do it without you," Julian shouts down the phone.

"Of course they can," I croak. "*You* must do it, Julian. Explain to them I've got bronchitis which could turn to pneumonia if I go out. You've sat in on rehearsals. You lead them through it. Take my name off the production and add yours. It's your moment, take it and make the most of it. The show must go on, as they say."

* * * *

A week later, I get a letter from Eddie:

It was all a disaster, everyone forgetting their lines and going on with books and reading the words. I got through my part and I think I've got an agent. Some of the drama schools came like Julian said. He told everyone you had walked out of the production and left us in the lurch. I knew you must have had good reasons to do what you did. We all waited for you till the last minute hoping you'd show up. And when you didn't we just had to go on and do our best.

I'll always believe in you for nobody's ever said the kinda things you said.

All the best,

Eddie.

Gerry Croft has telephoned. She's very upset. The students have been holed up in one bedroom in the *San Martino* with the management demanding money, and Julian was last seen running through Citta di Castello with the *carabineri* on his heels.

I pick up the pen to answer Eddie's letter. At least one person stands the chance of benefiting from all this.

22
La Fiera

Ronaldo has decided to try tea in the morning instead of coffee; it's fresher in the mouth, he says. And with plenty of sugar and crumbled biscuits stirred into it to disguise the taste of the tea, it sets him up well for work.

He had shaken his first cigarette from the packet at eight this morning and then pushed it back. He would not smoke until after lunch. I am right, he said, it is a disgusting habit, especially first thing in the morning.

I am an angel, according to him. The way I live: clean and tidy, plates washed, dried and put away. Fresh blue towels in the bathroom, even the soap blue – little touches and attention to detail he's never known a woman bother with before. And most remarkable of all, he said, I don't cry. All the women he's known have cried, screamed and torn their hair. But now he is in danger, for angels are unpredictable; they fill the heart with too much ecstasy.

He stands up and buttons his shirt. "I go."

"Will you come back?"

"Where else I go?"

I shake my head, uncertain.

He looks into my eyes. "We stay together now." He shrugs. "But if you no want . . . "

I hold him with a rush of feeling.

* * * *

Bargaining, haggling, negotiating; there's going to be plenty of that these next few days. For the famous October *Fiera* market has returned with its music, noise, and a myriad items waiting on every stall.

In the afternoon Ronaldo and I walk jauntily down the hill with Lionello. I eye the spot where I'd had the accident in the hire car three months ago. How much has passed since then! Lionello is telling us how *La Fiera* has its origins in the last century where the people came from miles around to buy and sell cattle, to sing, juggle and dance.

Apart from the cattle, it seems to me, not a lot has changed. The tango music will be loud enough to hold a dance on any *Sinalunghese* balcony or terrace this evening. Even the Tuesday morning market gives way the *La Fiera*, leaving the Piazza Garibaldi and the two bars with an air of desolation.

Ronaldo and Lionello are getting on. They're walking along in front of me, arm in arm, as if they have known each other for years. Neither of them has stopped talking since they met. And they both talk at the same time, which makes me laugh. I can't understand how one can hear the other. Yet they seem to – right now, they're laughing at something or other. Lionello has become like a kind uncle to me. I am happy to think Ronaldo will now be included in the family.

Down-town is where the action is: *porchetta* – the whole roasted pig lying on a tray, its head and crusty eyelashes intact – I'm going to become a vegetarian as from this minute. Lace tablecloths, boots, leather bags, juicy fruit and home-grown vegetables, we pass stall after stall, easing our way in and out of the jostling crowd, turning left beneath the underpass, trying not get pushed in another direction entirely, while heading for the bar *Devine Comedia*, an oasis in this melée, where cakes, iced tea, coffee and homemade ice creams await. We'll be lucky if we find a vacant chair, for even the garden is heaving with humanity and the music plays on and on . . .

Having purchased some fruit and slices of the dreaded *porchetta* for Ronaldo and Lionello, it's back up the hill to the *Centro Storico* on leaden legs. No space for cars here – only enough room for feet, if you don't mind them being trodden on. What a relief it is to reach the Via Ciro Pinsuti, escort Lionello to his house and then make our way up to the alleyway and our own peaceful house.

Peaceful, did I say? I've forgotten: the music will play on until midnight, singers belching out romantic songs through a microphone, disco beat, even African drum solos last night.

* * * *

One day in October:
The weather has become hot again; the days are long, the light intense; they are flashing past like film slides, bright images on a screen, one after the other, often bewildering and sometimes loney. I can't quite remember what has passed and can only guess at what might follow. But there's always the reassuring sense that I am in the right place. It is somehow meant to be, however difficult.

Ronaldo has left!
I believe he's gone for good. He's taken his clothes and nothing's been left behind the curtain this time. It was all over that wretched archangel. Vittorio

called round and stuck his hat on its ear and then sat at the table and sobbed into his wine, saying how sorry he felt for himself because Silka left him and took his daughters to Germany. I sympathized for a while and then I went out. I couldn't stand it, they were drinking heavily, the two of them, and the afternoon had turned into an embarrassing display of maudlin self-pity.

When I returned, they had gone. Then I saw that all my efforts of painting the angel white had been ruined. It was smeared with wine stains, under the eyes, hollows of the cheeks, the cleft in the chin. I felt so angry I slopped white paint over the whole thing. Then when Ronaldo returned, having drunk too much wine, and saw what I'd done he was furious and said I'd destroyed his artistic shading and that Vittorio was right, I understood nothing. Then I lost my temper; I threw the empty paint tin at him and it hit him on the nose.

I have waited all night, all this morning and afternoon and evening for him to return. But he hasn't come. I doubt if he ever will, he's too proud. Which is just as well, for he's done the work of saying goodbye for me; I would never have found the strength to do so.

There's only one thing for me to do now; I'm already doing it, I'm finding the tools to refurbish myself.

23
Flying in the Mind

"My dear young lady, he will return," Lionello says. "He has taken the key, you say? That is the proof."

"It's been three days."

"The right amount of time to think things through. And when he returns, it will be for always because then he will have decided to make the commitment."

"How can you be so sure?"

"Because I think I understand his mentality. He cannot allow himself to trust too much. He told me something of his life when we were walking down the hill together. He has been in the institution since he was three years old. Do you know that?"

I shake my head. "No. Not for that long, I didn't."

"The sisters – nuns, I believe you say – cared for him and many others like him. Then from the age of six the priests took over with the education. It has not been easy for him. He laughs and makes jokes with me. But I see he has much pain inside. I must say, I like him, I believe he has a very good heart and I also believe he loves you."

"Did he say so?"

"No, he did not need to. I felt it to be true."

I shake my head. I have no words.

"You look so sad. But it is *Giulietta e Romeo*; Shakespeare understood how to write the love story. It was not easy for them also."

"And it didn't end well."

"But your story will, I am convinced. And I have heard only good reports. The people approve that you have chosen to be with a good Italian man, especially one who has had such a bad start in life. No, I am mistaken, it is not Shakespeare, it is more like Cinderella, except he is Cinderella and you are the Princess Charming come to rescue him. Huh! I like it so much."

"I feel he rescued me."

"You have rescued each other. And now . . . " Lionello pours a good measure of Martino's special red wine into two crystal glasses. Then he hands one to me. "I hear the women saying they consider you to be a saint. I think it is more interesting to be a wicked woman. We must think of some way to start the letters flowing again."

"They never flowed exactly. There were only two."

"And you never discovered the culprit?"

"Never."

"The people here are like this. One day they are for you, the next against you. But I hear only good reports of you from Tonina. And, you see, all the fear you had of coming here alone was worth it."

"It was daunting at the time though."

"But why should it have been? It's not as if you had nowhere to go. And you knew some people, like myself, and that peculiar man, Vittorio, you told me about. And you spoke some Italian."

"Enough to order a meal."

"So you would not have starved. You were not going to your execution by coming here. What was there to be frightened of?"

"The unknown."

"But you've been here before."

"But not to live, and alone."

"Yet you went to Devon, you say, on your own when you separated from Richard."

"That was different. It was my country."

"How did you overcome this fear?"

"I found a counselor in Devon called Mike who taught me how to fly - in the mind, that is. I visualized wings, big gray feathery things growing out of my shoulder blades. Then I had to lift myself up and fly above my fear, look down at it from a great height and see it for the small thing it really was. But it was those hours at four in the morning when the fear was at its worse, all the doubts and anxiety, I felt responsible for my future and also the cats. And then one day I had a brainwave. I went to the chemist and bought a baby's dummy. I sucked the dummy like a baby and was able to sleep and think more rationally in the morning."

"You took no pills or sedatives?"

"No. The dummy was my sedative."

"And now? How will manage until your Ronaldo returns?"

"*If* he returns."

"Will you buy another dummy?"

Lionello is laughing, and so am I. "No more dummies," I say. "I'm over that stage. I'll manage better than before because I have myself to rely on and I'll try not to let myself down again."

"You have not let yourself down. You have come here for a purpose, to make a new life. And you know, this place has a way of looking after its people. It seems to understand who is right and who is not and it pushes the wrong ones away. I joke, of course. But, you know, there are things here that are not easy to explain with the logic."

"Like the apparition I saw in the church in Siena I told you about. A trick of light? It comforted me, nevertheless."

"Toscana plays tricks not only with the light but also with the mind. I believe it is healing you and your spirit has found the wings your counselor in Devon was speaking of. Perhaps I should have taken up that profession, it may have helped me to communicate with Tonina who insists that I should cover these wonderful old floor tiles with atrocious modern ones. She says they are uneven. That is their beauty, I tell her. But she says they are dangerous, that I will fall over and break my legs. What will she do, I wonder, when I tell her I am thinking of changing my life?"

I look at him.

"I have been inspired by you and I think I am in love."

"Who with?"

"A lady in Montepulciano, several years younger than me. Tonina will be outraged. Do you think I should buy her a dummy to keep her quiet?"

I let myself out through the front door and walk past the rockery at the end of the garden. I stop and stare at the tallest stone. Then I see it, quite clearly, the face, and the aquiline profile and the three-cornered hat. How come I never saw Napoleon before? And as I walk away, I turn and look again. I swear he winked at me. Or is it merely a trick of the Tuscan light?

* * * *

What is frightening for one is not for another. And as I stand at my bedroom window with a letter in my hand later today, I remember how I stood at this same window with Richard looking out at the village lights, and for one awful moment had imagined myself living here alone. I'd felt nearly overcome with panic.

I wonder if something was trying to tell me that it would be so. Like on the morning when we had nearly finished restoring the bathroom and were about to return to England. I was on my way down the street steps to the car when I remembered I'd forgotten something and ran back for whatever it was. I'd been on the point of closing the front door when I had the strangest sensation that the place was calling me back. I'd walked away with the insight that one day the little back alley apartment in Vicolo della Mura would be more important to me than I could ever guess.

I re-read the letter that arrived this morning:

I love . . . too much.

You are my lover, you are my sister, you are my mother, you are my family, you are more of all. Thank you for to exist.

Grazie di esistere.

Ronaldo.

24
Via Spadaforte

Sixteen years later:

I'm sitting on my roof terrace overlooking Vicolo della Mura, the alleyway where it all began. I feel as if I'm on top of the world, looking down on it all.

I have Lionello to thank for the house. He found it. "I believe I have discovered absolutely the right house for you," he said, one morning, as we walked up to the *piazza* together, along with Giulio, the estate agent. We turned right opposite the church, then along past the paper shop into Via Spadaforte and stopped outside number thirty-nine, a sad, derelict old village house.

My heart sank as Giulio Barbetti, whom I mistakenly called Barebotti, pushed open the warped front door and led the way into a narrow, gloomy damp hallway that smelled of cat pee. Things got worse as we climbed the steep stairs to what was supposed to be a downstairs apartment. But all I could see was a black hole consisting of two rooms and a small bathroom with a filthy sit-up bath. Upstairs was only marginally better, with two spacious sunny front bedrooms, but the bathroom was pokey with a cracked hand-basin and a shower full of rubble. There was no kitchen to speak of, only a stained sink in a dark room and a door hanging on a hinge that led into an even darker sitting room with a rickety steel ladder protruding through the ceiling.

Lionello stepped gamely up the ladder after the agent, while I remained below, watching his linen-clad legs disappear through the hole in the ceiling. And then I heard footsteps and a door opening. Unwillingly, I climbed the ladder. This was absurd. I couldn't live here. What on earth was Lionello thinking, bringing me to a dump like this? The price was right - about the only thing that was. Fifty -nine thousand euros, the agent said, reduced from eighty-five thousand. It had been on the market for a long time. Hardly surprising, I thought, climbing cautiously up the steel rungs. Who would want to live here? I couldn't wait to get out of the place.

Crawling through the hole above me, I found myself on the floor of a dusty room under the roof and as I stood up, eye-level to an enormous beam, I saw light streaming through a door, leading out onto a large terrace.

"This is like Hollywood," Lionello was saying. "No house in Sinalunga has a *terrazza* like this. You will be the queen of your castle up here looking down on us poor villagers below."

It was indeed a surprise: Montepulciana on my distant right, the mountains of Cetona beyond, Cortona on the far left with the mountains of Umbria undulating along the horizen. I looked up at moldy green corrugated plastic that served as a roof. That would have to come off, then we could enjoy the sun. But the space - it was worth the climb to see such a panorama.

We all descended the rickety ladder. "This will have to go," I said, "and proper stairs built." Lionello and I paused in the doorway before descending the rest of the stairs to the front door. "There's so much to be done," I said. "I'm not sure I can take it all on."

Lionello breathed in the moldy smell, almost as if he was smelling roses. "This place could be a breath of fresh air," he said. "And most important of all, think what Ronaldo can do."

I never stopped thinking of what Ronaldo could do. Making me happy one day and tormented another, I had accepted him back into my life and the time had finally come to find a more spacious home for the four of us. Billy and Gertie, acclimatized to rooftop existence, would enjoy sitting in the sun on the terrace as much as I would. Fortunately, I had most of the money needed to buy the house from the sale of Vicolo della Mura.

The first couple who answered my advertisement in the German newspaper bought the flat. "You won't sell it before we've seen it, will you?" they'd pleaded on the telephone from Hamburg. They paid me the asking price in spite of the fact that it had no central heating. Franz and Innes had fallen under the spell of 'La Casetta' in Vicolo della Mura, as I had done all those years ago with Richard. And so there I was, about to start building a house again with another man, a very different man - a temperamental, artistic and obstinate man. But one I couldn't live without.

* * * *

My dream had finally become a reality. I managed to get a small mortgage to pay for the rest of the house and Ronaldo and I, with several of his friends, got to work. We began with the roof and worked gradually and tortuously down to the second floor. It wasn't easy living on a building site for two years. Even though we fashioned a bedroom, bathroom and makeshift kitchen, everything was covered in dust no matter how hard I worked to clean our living area.

Around that time, Gertie, the black and white cat, became ill with kidney failure and died in my arms one morning amidst the rubble. We buried her in the overgrown garden of an abandoned chapel in Petroio, a hamlet twenty minutes drive away from Sinalunga. Billy howled for her every night for two weeks. We none of us got much sleep during that period.

Ronaldo was temperamental, his ideas changing with his moods. I never knew what I would find next: faces carved in the walls, a Roman arch leading to *la sala*, Doric columns in the bathroom. I remembered Vittorio's words, "he want to be like Michelangelo, he think he *is* Michelangelo come back from the dead."

We got there eventually, after nearly three years of struggle, juggling with banks and me meeting my tourist in the *piazza* covered in paint. "You'll have to accept me as I am," I used to say. "I'm renovating my house along with my life." Then I led them into one of the properties I was managing, weighted down with marmalade, porridge and marmite they had been kind enough to bring me from England.

And here I now am, sitting on my terrace, looking down at the little chapel, the three cypresses and listening to the bells still clanging in the *piazza*.

Not a lot has changed in all these years. The *carabinieri* have gone. They moved down the hill toward the station into a modern house, leaving another fine old building standing empty and derelict, waiting, perhaps, for another *straniera* to take risks, to lovingly restore it?

Sergio still plays his tango, the sound drifting out into the street, all the way down to Martino's shop. But I suspect he's too old for dancing round the furniture. The *carabinieri* bought him a small dog for company and it sits on the balcony, barking ferociously at everyone passing beneath. Martino is still selling his moldy fruit and Ornelia, Rosalba, Giovanni, are all still there. Only Tosca is missing; she has gone to live in a home near the priest's house behind the church.

And *'Lorri's Tuscan Houses'* are keeping me going. Italian owners have offered me their properties, ranging from cottages to villas, which I run with the help of Lisa, when I'm away teaching drama to students who, enticed by the sun and good food, come bringing their dreams of stardom.

Julian is still living with Gerry Croft and has now become a television star in a popular English soap. With the money he's made, he bought a derelict castle in Umbria, which Ronaldo restored and the students come out every year to study at *The Castle School of Drama*.

Richard still visits his forest house in Umbria with Heidi, the German lady who sold it to him and with whom he now lives - as I thought he would. *Far away enough not to disturb you,* he wrote. *But close enough if you ever have need of me.* The person inside me who took control of events on that fateful day, I hope she returns. Life is so much easier without the ego becoming hopelessly enmeshed.

Maudie, when she finally accepted that Sherif was not going to join her in England, packed up and went to Bristol. "I've decided that the only way to find enlightenment is through creative study," she wrote. She enrolled in a creative writing course at the university, since when nothing has been heard of her.

And Vittorio and Silka? She has married again and still lives in Italy. He lives with a Rumanian woman who cooks and serves the food in his bar. Michael Jackson wanted to buy the entire hillside once. Everyone wanted to sell for the huge price offered. But Vittorio, for the first time in his life, had found a certain peace up in the hills, "my corner of paradise," he called it, and there was no price that could take that from him. As everyone had to agree to sell their property, the deal fell through.

The Bar Silka became Bar Vittorio when Silka left. But nobody came. He changed the name to Bar *Paradiso*. But as there had been a *Bar Paradiso* on every street corner in Napoli where he grew up, he changed it again to *Bar Eremita*. (Hermit's Bar) Then the people came out of curiosity. Now they drink the *Rosso di Montalcino* all night with the gray-haired man who, some like to believe, is the aged Al Pacino himself, living incognito in the Tuscan hills.

Lionello died two years ago. I walked down the long Sinalunga hill with all the villagers behind the coffin, the church bell toning slowly, sadly - dang-dong-dang. The only bell that toned for Billy, the tabby cat, when he died last year was inside my head. I buried him next to Gertie under a pile of stones outside the abandoned chapel. He lived to be eighteen, a venerable old cat known as *Signor* Billi by the locals.

And finally, I am speaking Italian – well, sort of. With an English accent, I'm told, but at least I understand and can express myself. I also understand that taking the risk and coming here was the best thing I ever did, no matter how painful at first.

So, you are probably thinking, will I stay here forever?

Who knows?

I must consult this special person I have found inside myself. But now, it's time to eat. An irresistible smell of onions and garlic, tomatoes and red peppers is wafting up the stairs from the kitchen. For Ronaldo, not satisfied with restoring castles, is also a superb cook.

About the author

Laura Graham was born and brought up in a crofter's cottage on the Isle of Tiree in the Hebrides. No television, few children to play with, a multitude of sheep and cows, which swam in the sea, it's hardly surprising she grew up to have a vivid imagination.

Arriving in London at the age of seven was like landing on another planet. The Hebridean accent, the kilt and the sheep, were soon forgotten in the struggles of English schooling.

At seventeen Laura won a scholarship to LAMDA, then worked as an actress at The Young Vic theater, took the title role in Strindberg's Miss Julie, understudied Helen Mirren in Genet's The Balcony, played Helena in The Midsummer Night's Dream and had numerous television roles.

http://www.lauragraham.co.uk

Acknowledgments: And thank you to David and Chloè, Claire, Paul, Katie, and of course, Rosalbo, for your belief in me.

Printed in Great Britain
by Amazon.co.uk, Ltd.,
Marston Gate.